THE WOMAN NEXT DOOR

NATASHA BOYDELL

D1419701

30131 05764918 5

LONDON BOROUGH OF BARNET

Copyright © 2021 Natasha Boydell

The right of Natasha Boydell to be identified as the Author of the Work has been asserted by her in accordance with the Copyright, Designs and Patents Act 1988.
First published in 2021 by Bloodhound Books.
Apart from any use permitted under UK copyright law, this publication may only be reproduced, stored, or transmitted, in any form, or by any means, with prior permission in writing of the publisher or, in the case of reprographic production, in accordance with the terms of licences issued by the Copyright Licensing Agency.
All characters in this publication are fictitious and any resemblance to real persons, living or dead, is purely coincidental.

www.bloodhoundbooks.com

Print ISBN 978-1-914614-43-9

ALSO BY NATASHA BOYDELL

The Missing Husband

1

Sophie rested her head against the soft rim of the paddling pool and looked up at the cloudless sky. In the distance she could see the white undercarriage of an aeroplane as it flew over London. She imagined the passengers inside; snoozing, reading or watching a video, as they headed off on business trips or holidays to far-flung destinations. She started to move her arm out of the water so that she could trace the contrails with her finger but changed her mind. It was too much effort. Instead, she observed her hand on the surface of the water, sandwiched in between a fallen leaf and a dead, floating fly.

She was sweating. The once ice-cold hosepipe water in the paddling pool had been warmed up by the sun and beads of liquid trickled down her face. She reached for her cola on the grass beside her, pressing the chilled can to her forehead for a minute before opening it and drinking in great gulps. When she was satisfied, she put the can back down and watched her feet for a while. They were poking out of the water at the other end of the pool, the weeks-old coral-coloured nail varnish peeling off at the top of her toenails. She should remove it but she was just so... so what? Hot? Tired? Lazy? Lethargic, that's what she was. Lethargic.

The heatwave had begun in the middle of June and now, six weeks later, it was still going strong. The neat rows of semi-detached houses in Pemberton Road, the north London street, sweltered beneath the relentless daily bombardment of sun so that when she looked at them, they blurred at the edges. The lush green garden lawns had turned yellow and along the edges of the garden Sophie's plants had all wilted, a cruel reminder that she kept forgetting to water them. In the corner of the cracked patio, a pile of discarded children's toys lay in an unruly heap – footballs, tennis racquets, space-hoppers.

Sophie glanced at them and frowned. *I should tidy them up,* she thought, *and put them back in the shed where they belong.* Instead, she drained the dregs of her drink and closed her eyes. After a few minutes she opened them again and glanced down at her phone on the grass beside the pool. She had another two hours before she had to pick the children up from school. Should she go back inside and do some work? She'd done none whatsoever today and an all too familiar feeling of guilt was niggling at her. But there was absolutely no breeze and it would be claustrophobically hot in the house. Why were British homes so unprepared for summer? No, she was better off out here. She could bring her laptop outside though, sit under the umbrella and at least fire off a few emails. *Yes, in five minutes,* she decided.

The sound of a door opening nearby made her start. Sophie raised her head slightly and listened with curiosity as she heard flip-flops slapping across the patio of the house next door. She instinctively glanced at the garden fence, as if she might develop X-ray vision and see through to the other side. A few seconds later she heard the unmistakable pop of a bottle of something fizzy being opened and another set of footsteps joining the first.

'Christ on a bike, it's hot,' a male voice said.

'Tell me about it,' a woman replied. 'Who'd be so stupid as to move house in a heatwave?'

They both laughed. 'Well, we did it anyway. We're in.'

'Thank heavens,' the woman said. 'The journey over was hairy though. Remind me never to follow a removal van again. Every time it turned a corner, I imagined your great aunty Vera's china set being smashed to pieces. And I've got a headache. Where are the painkillers?'

The man snorted. 'They're packed away somewhere along with the Calpol and Strepsils in any one of boxes one to thirty-two if you want to look for them. Anyway, we'd better get started with the unpacking: we've got a lot to do before my parents bring the kids over tomorrow.'

'In a minute, Jack. Let's just stand out here with some bubbles and enjoy our new home.'

After that it was silent and Sophie suddenly felt conspicuous, like she was intruding on a private moment. But if she moved, they'd hear her and know that she'd been listening. She stayed as still as she could in the water, too afraid to move or even to breathe. Her skin was beginning to wrinkle, and she felt exposed in her faded, too small spotty bikini, even though she knew that the strangers couldn't see her. Every second that ticked by was like an hour as she closed her eyes and pretended that she was invisible. Eventually she heard the flip-flops slapping back towards the house and the back door closing, and she finally relaxed.

The interruption had given her a new burst of energy that just a few minutes before she couldn't imagine ever having again. With a fresh purpose, she heaved herself out of the paddling pool, grabbed one of the kids' frayed hooded towels and put it over her head so that the edge of the towel barely skimmed her backside. She hurried self-consciously into the house, wondering if anyone was watching her from a window next door. Once she was back in the sanctuary of the kitchen, she typed out a text message to Alan, her husband.

Breaking news! The new people have just moved in next door!

His reply came a few minutes later.

Go on then Detective Brennan. What have you found out?

She grinned and replied.

They've only been there a few minutes. Will investigate and report back.

He quickly responded.

Let's debrief over a curry tonight.

She smiled with anticipation, checked there was a bottle of white wine in the fridge for later and then padded upstairs to the bathroom for a shower. Fifteen minutes later she was washed, dressed and just as sweaty as she'd been before.

'Sod it,' she said to herself, looking in the mirror. There was no point attempting foundation in this heat. Instead, she dabbed on some tinted moisturiser, half-heartedly ran a mascara wand through her eyelashes and grabbed her phone. She still had ages to go before her two children, Tom and Katie, finished school but when the weather was nice some of the mums often gathered earlier in the park. She'd take her chances and hope there was someone there to chat to. Perhaps she'd get an iced coffee on the way. The prospect made her mouth water.

She glanced guiltily at her laptop on the way out but even that wasn't enough to dampen the Friday feeling that had overcome her. 'Sorry,' she said to it as she passed. 'I promise you'll get some action on Monday. But it's Friday afternoon and I've got places to go and people to see.'

She closed the front door behind her and made her way down the steps, glancing curiously at the house next door as she passed. There was a large SUV in the driveway and as she peered into it, she spotted some child car seats. She looked up and saw that all the windows of the house had been thrown open, presumably to get some air circulating. It had been empty for months after the previous owners, an elderly couple, had moved into sheltered accommodation. It had only been on the market for a few days before the sold sign went up outside. That was the way in this area now – fixer-uppers were like gold dust and were quickly snapped up, usually by families looking to upsize. She and Alan had been lucky to get theirs ten years ago before the area became so popular. There was no way they'd be able to afford a property here now.

As she walked past the house Sophie looked at the front door, silently willing it to open so that she could meet the new neighbours, but it remained resolutely shut. With a small wave of disappointment, she carried on walking down Pemberton Road towards the school. She'd stop at the supermarket and pick up a bottle of bubbles and a card, she decided. Then she could drop it round over the weekend. The children were going to be thrilled when she told them the news: they loved a bit of excitement, especially the prospect of making new friends. She'd probably have to prise them down from the top of the back-garden fence when they got home that afternoon, the nosy little sods.

She reached for her headphones, plugged them into her ears, turned on a pop playlist and made her leisurely way towards the park. As the music lifted her spirits, she smiled to herself. The sun was shining, the white wine was chilling, she had the whole weekend ahead of her and Alan was coming home early. So what if she hadn't done any actual work for longer than she cared to remember and she was feeling unmotivated? Life, she decided, could be worse.

~

Later that evening, after Tom and Katie had gone to bed, Sophie and Alan chewed over the prospect of the new neighbours as they chewed on their curry.

'They've definitely got young children,' Sophie confirmed. 'I saw child seats in the car.'

Alan swallowed his korma thoughtfully as he digested the new information. 'They've got a hell of a job ahead of them doing up that house if they're planning to live there at the same time. It looks like it hasn't been redecorated since the First World War.'

'Come on, Alan, that's an exaggeration, it's not that bad. Anyway, it's good for the area, this regeneration. It pushes up the property prices.'

'Tell me about it: it's keeping us in kormas.'

Alan ran a building company and his bread and butter were families buying run-down houses and paying him a fortune to do them up. And there were enough projects in Finchley alone to keep him busy for life. You couldn't walk down a single street without seeing skips and vans parked up, builders chatting on the pavement outside while having a break from doing rear extensions and loft conversions. But Alan had a strict three-mile no-work zone around the house. 'You've got to be able to leave your work behind when you come home,' he always said.

'I hope they're nice,' she said. 'It'll be lovely to have some friendly neighbours, and some pals for the kids to play with. I wonder if they'll go to the same school as Tom and Katie?'

Alan shrugged and reached for a second helping of naan bread. She could sense him losing interest already. It was different for him: he left the house early each morning and returned home in the evening, tired and ready to put his feet up and doze off in front of the TV. He enjoyed socialising but only when Sophie organised it. Alan was a family man but new people moving in next door were of little concern to him. For Sophie though, their home and neighbourhood were her whole life. It was where she lived, worked, made friends and raised a family all in one. And new people moving into the street was her equivalent of office gossip.

She had been a reporter in her twenties, covering stories for local, and later national, newspapers. But after they had children the long, unsociable hours and constant travelling went from being an adventure to a logistical, guilt-ridden nightmare. Eventually, she'd thrown in the towel and become a freelance writer. Now her old dressing table doubled as a desk and her kitchen was the staffroom for one. She enjoyed the flexibility, but she missed the colleagues terribly.

They mopped up their leftover curry sauce and cleared away the takeaway together in companiable silence, then relocated to the living room to watch TV. Alan turned on an old nineties comedy show and within minutes he was chortling away, glancing at Sophie occasionally to see if she was laughing too. But although she smiled back at him, she was distracted, hot and bothered. As she reached for her cold glass of wine, her mind wandered back to earlier that day and the new voices she'd heard from next door. The woman had sounded well-spoken and fairly local. The man definitely had a northern accent – Manchester, maybe, she thought.

Restless, she got up and walked over to the window to open it, desperate for even a puff of breeze. That curry had been a bad idea. As she returned to the sofa, she spied the card and Prosecco that she'd bought earlier, sitting on the dining room table ready to be delivered by hand in the morning. *Oh well, I'll meet them soon enough*, she thought, and with that she grabbed her wine and portable mini fan, curled up next to Alan and switched her attention to the TV.

2

Angie was rinsing coffee cups in the sink when the doorbell rang. She glanced at her watch. It was 9am. Jack thundered down the stairs and opened the front door before she'd even had a chance to dry her hands.

'Hi, we're the neighbours at number 47. We just wanted to come over and introduce ourselves,' a woman's voice said.

Christ, they're keen, Angie thought, before wiping her hands on her sundress, plastering on her best smile and heading out to greet them.

In the hallway stood a woman about her age, maybe few years younger, and two children. The boy seemed to be vibrating with excitement, like an overeager puppy, as his eyes searched the house. Angie suspected he was looking for signs of other boys his age. The girl hid behind her mother's leg, peering out shyly before quickly withdrawing when she caught Angie's eye. The woman was barefoot, apparently having crossed the driveway with no shoes on. She was dressed in a T-shirt and khaki shorts, her fair hair scraped back into a bun and a friendly, open, freckly kind of face that made Angie warm to her immediately.

'Sorry for the early intrusion,' she said, looking a little sheepish. 'The kids were just so excited to meet you, they'd have come round at 6am if they could. You'd have thought Father Christmas had moved in next door.'

Angie laughed and stretched out her hand, trying to relax and not think about the endless things she had to do that morning. 'No problem at all, we're thrilled to meet you. I'm Angie, and this is my husband, Jack.'

The woman shook it firmly, before handing over a bottle of fizz and a card. 'I'm Sophie and this is Tom and Katie.'

'Thank you so much,' Angie said effusively, giving the bottle a quick once over, mentally categorising it as cheap and cheerful, and sticking it under her arm as she opened the card.

'It's nothing really; we just wanted to welcome you to the neighbourhood.'

'It's very kind of you,' Angie said, and gestured for the neighbours to follow her into the house. 'Come into the kitchen and sit down. The place is a mess and there's boxes everywhere but at least we've got a table and some chairs. Tea? Coffee?'

Sophie hesitated, perhaps worried about intruding, but then she nodded. 'Coffee please,' she replied, following Angie and sinking down onto one of the chairs. Angie saw her glance around the room. The house was a typical four-bed semi-detached. When Angie and Jack had come to view it, along with several other houses in the area, they'd both tried to look past the dark green carpets, avocado bathroom suite and dilapidated kitchen and visualise the potential. It was a nice-looking house, they agreed. They'd have enough money to refurbish it to a high spec, it was close to good primary and secondary schools, and walking distance to Angie's mum's house.

'We'll do a loft conversion and rear extension,' Jack had said, already making mental notes and measurements. 'Then the kids can have a bedroom each. They'll want that soon.'

'It's a lot of work,' Angie had replied, wrinkling her nose when she spotted what looked suspiciously like damp in one corner of the living room. 'Can we manage it?'

Jack had wrapped his arms around her and given her a squeeze. 'We can manage anything, you and me.' They'd made an offer that day and four months later here they were.

'Obviously the house is a fixer-upper,' Angie said now, as she turned the coffee machine on and reached into the fridge for a couple of juice cartons for the children.

'Yes, the elderly couple you bought it from had lived here for forty-odd years and I doubt that they'd done anything to it for a long time,' Sophie confirmed. Her children sat obediently at the table opposite their mother, but Angie could see them fidgeting.

'There's a whole pile of children's toys in those boxes over there,' she told them. 'Why don't you go and get some out to play with?'

The boy, Tom, leapt up enthusiastically and ran over to the boxes. The girl, Katie, looked uncertain but after some gentle urging from her mother, she went over to join him. Angie caught Sophie's eye and they both smiled.

'How old are your children?' Sophie asked.

'We've got four – Benji is eleven, Indie is ten, Eloise is eight and Freddy is five.'

Sophie's eyes widened in amazement. 'Four kids? Wow!'

Angie was used to that reaction. 'I've always wanted a big family and so has Jack. He's one of five and I'm an only child so we both had our own reasons.'

'Do you work as well?' Sophie asked, spying her laptop, notebook and two mobile phones at the end of the table.

'Yes, I'm a solicitor.'

'Blimey, are you Superwoman too?'

Jack, who had just entered the room, laughed as he overheard Sophie's remark. He put his hand on Angie's shoulder and she smiled up at him. 'She claims not to be but we're pretty sure she is,' he said. 'We haven't discovered where she hides the outfit yet, but the kids are onto her.'

'Where are they now?' Sophie asked.

'With Jack's parents,' Angie explained. 'We thought it would be easier to have them out of the way while we moved and did the bulk of the unpacking. They're arriving later this morning.'

'You must pop over to ours this afternoon. Tom and Katie will be so excited to meet them.'

'How old are Tom and Katie?'

'Tom's seven and Katie's five. She's just finishing up her first year at school, actually. So where did you move from? Will the children be moving schools?'

Angie sipped her coffee and nodded. 'We lived in Greenwich. But we decided to move north to be nearer my mum. She's not in great health and it used to take me the best part of an hour and a half every time I wanted to pop in to see her. This way I'm just down the road. So yes, the children are moving school much to their disapproval.'

As Sophie chattered away about what the local schools were like, Angie glanced at her watch. Her new neighbour seemed perfectly pleasant but she was absolutely itching to carry on with unpacking before the children arrived. Sophie must have sensed her impatience because she quickly drained her coffee and stood up.

Angie felt bad. 'Please don't feel you have to rush,' she said.

'It's fine,' Sophie reassured her. 'You've got loads to do and I'm sure you just want to get cracking. I'd be the same in your shoes. Anyway, the kids have got homework to do. We'll leave you to it, but do pop round when you get the chance so we can meet the children.'

Angie smiled with relief as Sophie called out to Tom and

Katie, who reluctantly relinquished the toys, and all three headed towards the front door.

'Lovely to meet you,' she said, waving them off. She closed the door behind them and walked back into the kitchen, her mind already full of the many tasks that lay ahead. Jack, who had been out in the garden, stuck his head inside the back door. 'They seemed nice,' he said.

'Yes,' Angie replied dismissively. She reached for her phone to check her emails and then turned her attention to unpacking the tableware. There were four large boxes on the kitchen floor waiting to be sorted through. She started digging out plates and glasses, shoving them straight into the dishwasher and then paused as she unearthed a large crystal salad bowl from its layers of kitchen roll. Christ, she hadn't seen this bowl in years. It had been a wedding present from a distant relative – she couldn't even remember who now – and had been in the back of a kitchen cupboard gathering dust ever since. Looking at it now, she remembered her wedding day, nearly fourteen years ago. *How much has changed since then*, she thought. *How much we've changed.*

She stared at the bowl, trying to decide what to do with it. It was only a silly bowl but its future now seemed like the most important thing in the world. She didn't even like the damn thing but it was a symbol of her marriage, her intent. Did she bury it in a cupboard, never to be seen again or did she put it out on display, a proud emblem of their shared past, their union. She quickly hand-washed it and left it out to dry on the kitchen surface. She'd put fruit in it.

She was cleaning the downstairs loo when the children arrived just before lunchtime. They bustled into the house with barely a glance at their mother and raced up the stairs, jostling each other out of the way as they went, desperate to have first dibs at the best bedroom. Within less than a minute they were bickering and she marched up the stairs, put her hands on her hips and started dishing out instructions.

'Ellie and Indie, you're sharing the big bedroom at the front until the loft conversion's done. Me and Daddy are in the one next door. Benji and Freddy, you two are in the back bedrooms. We've already put your furniture and boxes in there so there's no room for negotiation.'

The boys raced towards their allocated bedrooms without further ado and Eloise, known to everyone as Ellie, wandered amiably into her shared room too. Indie, who had become a stereotypical tweenager the minute she reached double digits, observed her mother with a sulky expression as she twirled her hair angrily around a finger.

'Why do I have to share?' she demanded. 'Ellie is such a pain; she follows me everywhere and steals all my clothes. I *need* some privacy.'

Feeling ratty herself after a hectic morning, Angie tried to swallow the irritation that was rising up inside her, reminding herself that she had been a young girl once too, and replied: 'It's just until we do the loft conversion, darling, and then you'll have a whole room to yourself.'

'I still don't see why the boys can't share.'

'There's a much bigger age gap between the boys, Indie. It's hardly fair to ask an eleven-year-old to share with a five-year-old who goes to bed two hours earlier. We've been through this.'

Indie regarded her mother sullenly. Angie wondered, not for the first time, what had happened to her sweet, angelic little girl. But then she was looking at the past through rose-tinted glasses because Indie had never been particularly angelic. She'd been trouble from the moment she was born, with her scrunched-up eyes and scowling face, her tiny fists squeezed tightly in protest as Angie tried to bathe her or dress her. She'd been the fussiest baby of the four, the toddler with the most tantrums, a stubborn pre-schooler. But she was captivating, with her huge dark eyes, olive skin and determined pout that had broken her parents' hearts more than once over the years and was going to shatter many more when she was older. When she laughed, the whole world laughed with her, but when she was in a bad mood, they all ran for cover.

As a baby, Indie had almost put her off having more children but then Ellie came along – their kind, funny, down-to-earth Ellie – and she'd sighed with relief. A few years later Freddy had arrived, an amiable, sporty little thing compared to his more sensitive, theatrical older brother and Angie and Jack had finally declared their family complete.

As a mother of four and criminal law solicitor, it took a lot to intimidate Angie. She stared Indie down now until the girl finally relented and huffed off into her room, throwing herself dramatically onto the bed that Angie had already made up with her favourite bedding. Angie saw Ellie glance up at her sister and then back down again, wise enough to know not to bother trying to talk to her. Jack, who she suspected had been deliberately hiding while the bedroom politics were negotiated, crept up the stairs and peered into the various doorways.

'Just seeing my parents off,' he said. 'They're meeting my brother for lunch, but they'll pop by tomorrow on the way home to check out the house. All sorted?'

'I think so,' Angie replied. 'Although Indie threw her toys out of the pram and now she's sulking. Poor Ellie, having to share with her.'

'It's not for long. We've got builders coming round next week to give us some quotes. Hopefully we'll start work by the end of the year.'

'I'm dreading it,' Angie admitted. 'It all seemed like a thrilling idea at the time but now the prospect of living through months of building work is terrifying.'

'It'll be fine, Ange,' Jack said reassuringly. 'It'll be worth it in the end.'

Angie thought of their lovely little house in Greenwich, which was too small for the six of them but had hosted so many years of happy times and suddenly felt an overwhelming loss. Had it really been a good idea to uproot their family, take their children out of school and away from their friends, and move to a new area? Their whole life was in south London. They had a community there, a support network, a fantastic group of friends. They had been a popular family, always hosting parties, playdates and sleepovers. Would these friends, who had promised to visit regularly, be true to their word or would the prospect of driving through the congested streets of London every time they wanted to visit prove too much of a barrier? Would they be happy here? Had she completely misjudged things by insisting that they move?

'Mum, my new room is awesome,' Benji, her eldest, said as he emerged from his bedroom.

'Mine too,' Freddy exclaimed, appearing at her side clutching his favourite toy dinosaur. 'Thanks, Mummy and Daddy! T-rex loves it too!'

Angie looked at Jack who nodded at her. 'See, Ange, it's going to be okay.'

Looking around at the peeling wallpaper and piles of unpacked boxes, she couldn't imagine how it was ever going to be okay, but it was done now and she had to make the best of it. This was their home sweet home, for better or for worse. She took a deep breath and said, 'Now, I don't know about you reprobates but I'm absolutely famished. Who fancies walking to the high street and finding somewhere to get a spot of lunch?'

With a flurry of activity and a hunt for sun hats and sandals, Angie grabbed Freddy by the hand and followed the rest of the family out of the house, locking their new front door behind her and making her way down the road, under the relentless gaze of the midday sun.

Sophie was doing the ironing when she heard sounds coming from the street outside. She glanced out of the window and saw the new neighbours walking past. The younger two children were holding their mother's hands while the older girl was a short distance ahead, her headphones clamped over her ears. The older boy was in front, chatting to his dad. Crikey, there were a lot of kids. How anyone managed to raise four children and have a high-powered career was beyond her. As she watched them disappear, Sophie reflected on their meeting earlier that day.

Angie had seemed nice enough. She hadn't been up for much of a chat but then she had a lot of unpacking to do, so Sophie could hardly blame her. There was something about her though, something that Sophie couldn't quite put her finger on. She had come across as a bit reserved, not frosty but lukewarm perhaps. She was absolutely beautiful, though. How did she find the time to look like that with four kids and a job? And her husband looked like a cardboard cut-out of the perfect man.

The whole encounter had made Sophie feel a little intimidated and she had been struggling to shake off the feeling ever since she got home. She should make more of an effort to do some exercise, she thought to herself now, and stop stealing chocolate from the kids' treat jar. And from Monday, she was definitely going to get back to work. Although the children would be breaking up for the summer holidays in less than two weeks, so perhaps she should wait until September now. Yes, she felt better already.

Sophie still told anyone who asked that she was a writer, but the truth was that she hadn't had any work in months. When she first started out on her own, she pitched story ideas all the time and, because she knew lots of people in the industry, she quickly gathered a regular list of clients. *This is easy*, she thought. *Why didn't I do this sooner?* In her first year she had made good money and she'd been so proud of herself.

But then the economy had dipped into a recession and the newspaper and magazine industry, already in a downhill spiral, had started making even more journalists redundant and slashing its budgets for freelancers. It got harder and harder to get jobs and the ones she did get paid a lot less, sometimes half what she'd earned before. At the same time Alan's business was struggling as well because no one wanted loft conversions when they were worried about losing their own jobs, and he'd had to make some cuts.

'Why don't I come and work with you for a while?' she suggested to him one evening, while he was poring over the accounts with a grim look on his face. 'I can help you with admin, answering the phones, booking in jobs, invoicing, that sort of thing. I could even do a bit of publicity. It'll save you having to pay someone.'

Alan had looked up at her in surprise. 'Are you sure, love? I mean, I could really use the unpaid labour but what about your work?'

'Things are slow with work anyway. I can still pick up the odd job here and there and then when the business gets back on its feet, I'll build up my own clients again.'

He'd looked at her with such relief and she could see the emotion in his eyes. 'Thanks, Soph, you have no idea what this means to me.'

'We're a team,' she told him. 'Stronger together, remember?'

They'd always been a team, ever since they first got together twelve years ago. Before Alan, Sophie had been stuck in a pattern of dating commitment-phobic men and it always ended badly.

'It's because you've got horrendous taste in men,' her friends would tell her over tearful debriefs. 'You always go for the bad ones.'

Sophie knew they were right but she couldn't seem to break the pattern. Then one evening, on a night out for someone's twenty-fifth birthday, she bumped into Alan while queueing for drinks at a bar. He grinned at her and she looked away self-consciously before curiosity got the better of her and she met his eye again. He was fairly handsome in his own way. Tall and broad with sandy hair, a lived-in face and extensive laughter lines, he seemed relaxed in his own skin. They chatted briefly before she was dragged off by her friends to the next bar, but he asked for her number and the next day he called and invited her out for a drink.

It was that simple. She couldn't believe it. Where was the game-playing? The angst? The staring at her phone willing someone to text her? There was none of that with Alan. From the very beginning he was a true gentleman, and he made it crystal clear that he had no intention of messing a woman around and that he wanted to settle down and have a couple of children. He was such a contrast to the men she normally went out with that she nearly dumped him several times. It all just seemed a bit too easy and part of her still craved the fireworks. But as she got to know him, she fell in love with his warmth, honesty and kindness. He loved her and he would do absolutely anything for her, and in time, she realised that he was the one.

Ten years of marriage and two kids later, she hadn't regretted her decision once and if anything, she loved him even more now. And that's why she'd known that she had to do this thing for him. She had started working for him the next day and she stayed on for a year, by which time the economy had improved and business was coming in again.

'It's time for you to go,' he told her one day over dinner. 'You've been amazing, I can't thank you enough but let's face it, it's hardly your dream career. I'm making enough money to hire someone permanent now and I think you need to get back to your proper job.'

'So you're firing me?' she said, in mock outrage.

'Yep,' he replied, wagging at finger at her. 'Sophie Brennan, you're fired.'

She had laughed along with him but she also felt sad and realised how much she'd enjoyed working alongside Alan and being part of the family business. She also knew that he was right, it was time for her to go back to her day job.

But getting back on the horse after a year off wasn't easy. She'd lost touch and her motivation seemed to have fallen by the wayside. It didn't help that Katie had just started school and wasn't settling in well. She'd always been a sensitive child but it was still a shock after Tom had adapted to school life so easily. Peeling her weeping daughter off her each morning and watching her being dragged away by her teacher took its toll and the last thing Sophie felt like doing afterwards was getting rejected by editors.

At around the same time, she was asked to join the parents' committee at the children's school, a role she'd agreed to because she was terrible at saying no but found herself enjoying. She got increasingly involved, made some new friends and found that she didn't mind how much of her time it took up. It was the perfect excuse to avoid the inevitable fact that she'd lost her way in her career. She told herself she didn't mind – she had a wonderful husband, two amazing children and with Alan's business doing well again they had enough money to pay the bills. But occasionally she found herself feeling lost at sea, especially now the children were both settled at school and didn't need her in the way that they used to when they were tiny.

'Do whatever makes you happy,' Alan always told her whenever she tried to talk to him about it. 'If that's writing, then go for it. If you want to study and retrain, we'll make it work. If you want to take a break and focus on the children for a while, do it: you've earned it, love.'

She sometimes felt like she didn't deserve him.

'Mum, can we go to the park?' Tom's question brought her back to reality and she realised that she was still staring out of the window, long after the family next door had disappeared.

'It's scorching hot out there, Tom. Perhaps we should go later, when it's cooled down.'

'What can we do then? I'm bored.'

Alan came in then and took in his children's fed-up faces. 'Fancy going down to the lido for a dip?' he asked.

'Yessss!' Tom and Katie jumped up in unison. 'Can we, Mum, please?'

'It'll be rammed,' Sophie warned Alan. 'You'll probably have to queue to get in.'

He shrugged. 'We don't mind do we, kids? We're not in a rush. Why don't you stay here and chill out, Soph? I'll take Tom and Katie.'

She looked at Alan, and then at the children, and made her decision. 'Nah, I'm coming with you. It's got to be better than ironing. I'll close my eyes and pretend I'm in Mallorca!'

And she went off to dig out their swimming costumes.

3

Angie looked at her calendar. She had about half an hour before her next client meeting. Picking up the phone, she called Jack.

'What's up?' he answered.

'How did it go this morning?' she asked.

'Yeah fine, no dramas.'

Benji had started at secondary school a couple of days ago but it was the first day of primary school for the others. Jack had offered to take them as Angie had an early client meeting. There had been a few tantrums from the children that morning as they were packing their bags, which she knew was first day nerves, and she'd been eager to find out how it went.

'Thanks, Jack. I can pick them up from school later, I'll be done in time, but we do need to sort out breakfast and after-school club ASAP. Have the builders been round yet?'

'Yeah, they're here measuring now so I'd better go.'

They'd been living in Pemberton Road for two months, although sometimes it felt like they'd only moved in five minutes ago. They'd barely had time to unpack before they had left again for their summer holiday in Italy. After the disruption of moving, the break had been just what they all needed. She'd been glad of the time away from staring hopelessly at the peeling wallpaper and dusty carpets. They'd returned home after a blissful three weeks away, sun-kissed, refreshed and, she hoped, ready to embrace their new life.

The following weekend some of their Greenwich friends, Simon, Alex and their three children had come round for a barbecue. While the younger children had water fights in the garden and the older ones watched TV inside, Angie had showed Simon and Alex round the house. Alex had oohed and ahhed in the right places, making Angie feel a bit more positive.

'It's got so much potential, Angie,' Alex said enthusiastically. 'When you do the extension and the loft, it'll be amazing. And you and Jack have such good taste, I just know it'll look like something from *Grand Designs*. What's the area like?'

'It's nice,' Angie said. 'It's changed a lot since I was a child. There's a little strip of cafés and restaurants that look promising. And a decent park. But it's not Greenwich.'

'Do you miss it?'

'Terribly. I've been fretting about whether we made the right decision. But it's done now, so I have to crack on with it. I'm sure it'll be fine once the children are settled into school and the work is done on the house. But heavens knows when that will be and I forgot how much I hate living in chaos. I need order in my life.'

'What are the neighbours like?'

'One side is a family with two young children. They seem okay. The other side is a young couple; she's pregnant. We haven't seen much of them, to be honest.'

'Well, I think it's a real find. You'd never have been able to afford anything this size in Greenwich. And you're close to your mum now, which is what you wanted.'

Angie had nodded and looked away. She had told all of their

friends that was the reason why they had moved to Finchley but it was only one of the reasons. There was another one which no one but she and Jack knew about. A decision – more of a demand really – she had made and Jack had had no choice but to agree to. At the time it had seemed like the perfect idea, an opportunity to put the past behind them and start afresh but now, in the cold, harsh reality of it all, she wasn't so sure. Recently she had been wondering if she had overreacted. She had made a rash decision which was not appropriate to the situation and now she was paying the price.

When Alex and Simon left to go home later that day, promising to visit again soon, she had almost pleaded with them to let her come too, away from this crumbling, old, smelly house and back to her previous life. She felt abandoned, like a child whose parents were going off somewhere exciting without her. Jack and the children had waved them off and headed straight back inside without a second thought but she'd lingered on the doorstep, watching the empty street long after they had gone. She looked up and down Pemberton Road and wondered if it would ever feel like home and then scolded herself for being so negative. *I'm just tired after a long week*, she told herself. *I need a good night's sleep and it will all seem so much better in the morning.*

Since then she had been determined to be more positive, especially now that she knew the children had gone off happily to their new school. She turned to her computer and tried to concentrate on preparing for her next meeting but her mind kept drifting. She thought about Jack at home, chatting away to the builders like they were old friends, making them a cup of tea, probably dishing out the expensive biscuits she'd bought from Harrods for her mother, and felt a familiar pull in her heart. She loved that man, sometimes so much that it frightened her.

They had met at university in Durham. He was captain of

the football team, the one who all the girls swooned after and then wept over when he lost interest. The sort of boy you'd heard of before you'd even met him. They were on the same law course and after sitting next to her in a lecture one day, he seemed to take a shine to her. Not in a romantic sense back then, more in a kindred spirit kind of way. Jack was intelligent but everyone assumed that he was a bit of a jock and he didn't do himself any favours by acting like one. But with Angie, he told her over coffee a few months after they met, he felt different. He liked talking with her about the meaty stuff, as he called it – politics, history and religion. He seemed to seek her out, appearing alongside her as she walked to lectures or sitting next to her when she was studying in the library.

After a while they got into a habit of having lunch together every Thursday in between classes. It became her favourite part of the week. Soon she was looking for him every day, breathing a subconscious sigh of relief when she spotted him coming towards her through the crowds or making a beeline for her in the lecture theatre. In the evenings, whenever they saw each other out in a student bar or club, he always gave her a nod or a wave – he was never rude to her – but they rarely spoke. They had two completely separate lives, sets of friends and university experiences, that only converged at certain times of the week.

She'd be lying if she said she wasn't attracted to Jack from the start. Everyone was attracted to Jack and they definitely sparked off each other. So perhaps she had a tiny crush on him. But Angie knew that she wasn't Jack's type. This became more obvious with each new girl she saw him with, and there was no point in fantasising that she was. Pining after him would only cause her a heartbreak that she didn't need in her life. She was at university for one reason only, and that was to gain a first-class degree and get a job in a top law firm.

She was driven even at eighteen, after years of her mother

drilling it into her that women had to work harder than men to be a success. Patricia had raised Angie on her own and had worked hard to make sure that Angie had all the opportunities in life that she hadn't, and Angie didn't take that for granted. She didn't want the distraction of a stomped-on heart or the awkwardness of her friendship with Jack being ruined over a drunken fumble on a night out. So, she made the decision to enjoy their friendship for what it was and stop daydreaming about anything more. After a while she started going out with another, more straightforward boy, and her coffees and lunches with Jack eventually petered out. When they graduated, they lost touch completely.

She assumed that she would never see Jack again and had almost forgotten all about him when she bumped into him by chance, several years later. She was working as a trainee solicitor at a firm in central London. One morning she was ordering her usual black coffee on the way into the office, her mind preoccupied with the many things she had to do, when she heard a familiar voice.

'Is that you, Ange?'

Her stomach lurched. She turned around and there he was, Jack the jock, as she used to call him teasingly, looking every inch as devastatingly handsome as he had always done.

'Christ, do you not age at all?' she replied in delight, hugging him warmly before moving aside to let the other people in the queue get to the counter. She waited while Jack ordered his own coffee and then he stepped aside too and observed her with a look of relief.

'I can't tell you how happy I am to see a familiar face, Ange. I've only just moved to London and I've got to say, I'm not sure how I feel about it yet.'

Jack was originally from Manchester and as they waited for their drinks, he explained that he'd moved back in with his parents after university, given up on law, and got a job as a runner for a TV production company. He had quickly worked his way up the ladder and into a city centre flat with a friend, before being offered a new job in London.

'It was too good an opportunity to turn down but apart from a handful of people from university who I haven't spoken to in ages, I don't really know anyone in London,' he said.

Angie doubted it would take Jack very long to make new friends but she could imagine how overwhelming it must feel to move to a new place. And as a loyal Londoner born and bred, she had wanted to make him fall in love with her city. If he happened to fall in love with her too, she had reflected later, perhaps that wouldn't be a terrible thing. But she convinced herself that she was only joking because she had always assumed that Jack the jock wasn't hers for the taking.

'I'll take you out,' she had informed him as she collected her coffee. 'Show you all the places to be, introduce you to some of my friends. How about this weekend?'

'Perfect,' Jack said, reaching for his phone so that he could take her number. 'I'm looking forward to it already.'

Then his coffee arrived and they parted ways. As she dashed to the office, clutching her hot drink, she could feel herself grinning from ear to ear.

They arranged to meet at a bar in Islington the following Saturday. He turned up twenty minutes late and scanned the crowded room with an easy confidence before spotting her sitting in a booth with her friends. As he waved and headed towards them, her friend Carly hissed into her ear, 'Blimey, Angie, you didn't tell me your old mate was *hot*. What's his story?'

'I don't know,' Angie hissed back. 'I haven't seen him for years.'

'Well, I get first dibs if he's single and straight,' Carly replied, smoothing her hair with both hands and sitting up in her seat as she beamed at the incoming Jack.

After introductions and a trip to the bar, Jack squeezed himself in between Angie and Carly, who tried valiantly to monopolise his attention. But when it was established that Jack had a girlfriend back in Manchester, Carly rapidly lost interest and turned away, leaving Angie and Jack free to catch up on old times.

'I'm not surprised you got a contract at such a prestigious law firm,' he told her. 'You were always top of the class. Everyone wanted to sit next to you so they could steal your notes.'

'Oh, so that's why you hung around me like a little puppy!' Angie said, laughing in mock outrage. 'Well you could have just said, it would have saved you a lot of coffee money.'

'I know but I'm a gentleman. You've got to put the effort in if you want to take someone else's hard work and claim it as your own. Otherwise it's just rude.'

They talked all evening, long after her friends left to go on to a club. It wasn't until the bell rang for last orders that they realised it was time to go home. As they left, he asked her if she was free for lunch the next day.

They met in a pub for a Sunday roast and then went back to his shared house for a cup of tea. The house was a typical bachelor pad, with a huge widescreen TV and rows of empty beer and wine bottles lining a shelf in the kitchen. She had a vision of him and his all-male housemates holding raucous house parties and bringing girls back after nights out. *He'll have forgotten all about me in a few weeks*, she thought.

But, if anything, the opposite happened. They started meeting up more and more. He texted her most days, even though she knew he was making new friends and building a social life of his own in London. Each time she heard her phone beep with a message, she would grab it hungrily, feeling a thrill if she saw his name on the screen. Deep down she knew that she was heading down a slippery slope but she still refused to acknowledge her feelings to anyone, even herself.

'Oh we're just friends,' she would say, whenever any of her pals made a comment about how much time she was spending with him. 'Anyway, he's got a girlfriend in Manchester.'

But that didn't stop her from enjoying his company or fretting when she hadn't heard from him in a few days. It didn't stop her wondering what he was doing. Was his girlfriend visiting for the weekend? Or was he out with his housemates at some club or bar, doing shots? Was he thinking about her too? It was sometimes like torture, not knowing what he really thought of her, if he just saw her as a friend or something more. He had changed since university though, that much was clear. Not in any profound way, he'd just matured a bit, settled down, although he still had an element of Jack the jock about him, that hint of cockiness that was simply a part of who he was and probably always would be.

One Friday evening he invited her out for a drink with some of his colleagues. She had been looking forward to it all day and had rushed to the bathroom as soon as she finished work to reapply her make-up and fix her hair. But the minute she arrived she could tell that he was in a bad mood. She sat beside him, trying to catch his eye and draw him into conversation, but he barely acknowledged her. Feeling hurt and disappointed by his behaviour, she turned away from him and started talking to one of his workmates instead, a slightly older guy called Harry who seemed lovely. The more she chatted with him, the more she could see Jack scowling and downing beer. Finally, she'd had enough of his cold shoulder and she dragged him off to the bar on the pretext of helping her get a round in so that she could confront him.

'What's going on Jack? Why are you being so rude?'

He pulled her aside, out of sight from the rest of the group and leaned into her. She could smell the alcohol on his breath and realised that he was even drunker than she'd thought.

'Harry fancies you,' he said.

'Okay,' she replied. She wasn't sure if it was a statement or an accusation.

'Do you fancy him?'

She was confused and irritated by the confrontational tone in his voice.

'What does it matter to you if I do?' She wondered if he was upset that she'd been flirting with his work colleagues. Perhaps he was worried about his reputation.

'It just matters to me,' he replied, looking intensely at her with those ridiculous piercing eyes that had ripped many a young woman's soul into tiny little pieces over the years.

'Why?'

'Because I love you.'

'Oh, come off it, Jack, you're drunk,' she said, a lot more dismissively than she felt. Inside she was erupting with shock, joy and disbelief. Could he really mean it?

'I'm not that drunk, Angie, I know how I feel. You're the most beautiful, intelligent, ambitious and all together amazing woman I have ever met in my life.'

He tried to kiss her then, but she put her hand on his chest to stop him. 'Jack, I don't want you to do anything that you might regret. Sleep on it, okay, and we'll talk tomorrow.'

She kissed him on the cheek, grabbed her bag, said goodbye to his friends and left the bar. Outside she leaned up against a wall to catch her breath. Had that really just happened? She loved him, of course she did, but was it really possible that he felt the same way or was it just the beer and a touch of the green-eyed monster talking? As she walked to the tube station, she felt like she had somehow entered a parallel universe, one where being with Jack was a possibility rather than a fantasy, and she wanted to grasp it with both hands. But she was terrified in case it was all a mistake and life returned to its normal state tomorrow.

It took her hours to fall asleep. She lay in bed, wondering how she had ended up falling so madly in love with this boy. She had always been so pragmatic, so able to keep people at arm's length, but now she was completely helpless. The next morning she woke up with the sensation that something monumental had happened and felt a rush of joy when she remembered what it was, followed by a sinking feeling that it was still a dream that wouldn't come true.

Two hours later, as she was staring at her phone, he turned up at her flat looking sheepish, handed her a bunch of flowers and asked her to go for a walk with him.

'I was actually just about to go shopping,' she told him and immediately kicked herself for being churlish. But the truth was that she didn't want to go for a walk with him. She was too afraid of what he had to say, having already guessed that the flowers were an apology. He was going to tell her that he was a drunk idiot who was talking rubbish and didn't mean a word he said.

'Where?' he asked.

'What do you mean where?'

'Tesco? Sainsbury's? Asda?'

'Does it matter?'

'Well, yeah.'

'Morrisons?'

'I love that place. Let's go.'

Bemused, she nodded and went to get her bag. They made their way down the stairs and out onto the street together. *This is weird*, she thought. *What's going on here? Is this just an opportunity for Jack to stock up on milk and bread or is he trying to prove that we can still be friends?* For the entire ten-minute walk to the supermarket she waited for him to say something but he didn't. With each step they took, her nerves multiplied. Finally they got there and she grabbed a basket, marching over to the toiletries aisle to get some tampons and feeling mortified when he followed her.

'I was drunk, Ange, you're right,' he said as she reached self-consciously for some Tampax. He didn't bat an eyelid. 'But the reason I got so drunk was because I hated the idea of you and Harry getting together. As soon as you walked in, he asked if you were single, so I knew he was keen, and it made me realise that I was being stupid for hiding how I feel about you. I meant what I said and I mean it now too. I'd rather put myself out there than risk losing you again.'

'But you have a girlfriend,' Angie reminded him, still clutching the tampons.

'Not anymore. I broke up with her this morning.'

Angie stared at him in wonder. 'Is this really happening, Jack?'

'Only if you want it too.'

She took in his beautiful, sincere face and right there, surrounded by sanitary towels and pantyliners, she reached up and kissed him for the first time. 'I do.'

They finally broke away, grinning at each other, after someone shouted at them to get a room. She was flushed with pleasure. 'Shall we get out of here?' she asked.

'Actually, I really need some fish fingers,' Jack began, before seeing Angie's face. He gently took her basket from her and put it down on the floor.

'Come on,' he said. 'The fish fingers can wait.'

They were married three years later. It was quite an affair – all their old university mates used it as an excuse for a reunion and the party went on until six in the morning. Angie had never smiled so much in her life. She looked around the room at their friends, old and new, her mother's proud face barely visible from under the huge hat she'd bought especially for the occasion, and Jack's large, jovial family who had welcomed her with such warmth, and she felt that she would never, ever be this happy again. *Dreams really do come true*, she thought.

When the party finally ended, they made their way up the stairs, hand in hand, to their hotel room and crawled into bed together. Angie, drunk on champagne and love for Jack, turned to him in the darkness. She was finally ready to share the thing that she'd kept a secret for so many years, even from herself. She stroked his arm lightly and whispered, 'I've loved you from the very minute I met you, Jack, back when we were eighteen years old. I've always loved you.'

She waited in anticipation for his response, his surprise when he realised how long ago he'd won her heart, his realisation that she'd been his for so many years, but there was nothing but his steady breathing. He was fast asleep.

4

Sophie, Alan, Tom and Katie stood huddled together in the garden, their backs turned against the bitterly cold wind, and observed the carnage.

'Wow,' Tom said.

'Wow indeed,' Alan agreed.

A storm had wreaked havoc across the country. Trees had been ripped down, roof tiles hurled to the ground and garden trampolines thrown onto railway tracks. Reports of power cuts and floods dominated the news headlines. Overnight, the storm had destroyed part of the battered fence in their back garden, taking down three panels and leaving a gaping hole, where they could now clearly see into the neighbours' garden.

'I told you that fence was an accident waiting to happen,' Alan said. 'It's been looking like the Leaning Tower of Pisa for years.'

'Whose is it though?' Sophie asked, wrapping her coat tightly around herself and folding her arms across it. 'Ours or theirs?'

'I'll have to double-check the deeds but I'm pretty sure it's theirs.'

As they stood, pondering the broken fence, Sophie saw two curious little faces appear from the other side. The younger two Taylor children. She gave them a little wave and shortly afterwards Jack and Angie arrived, wearing their dressing gowns.

'Hi, neighbours,' Sophie shouted at them over the wind. 'We may have a problem.'

The Taylor family had been living next door to them for about nine months, although Sophie barely saw them except for the odd hello when they were putting the bins out. The only reason she even knew their surname was because she occasionally took a parcel for them. She had tried to start a conversation with Angie a couple of times but she was always in a rush. She wasn't exactly what Sophie would call the chatty type. The children went to breakfast and after-school clubs every day, so Sophie never bumped into them on the school run either.

But it didn't stop her forming opinions about them. Angie was obviously one of those high-flying women who probably looked down her nose at people like Sophie, with her oversized jumpers and lack of career. She always looked so groomed and polished whenever Sophie saw her. She was perfectly polite but Sophie found her a bit unapproachable, superior even.

Jack was a bit friendlier. He always gave her a wide smile and a wave whenever he saw her and he'd brought round a bottle of wine to apologise for the noise during their building works. She suspected that he was one of those men who survived on his good looks and charm alone. She doubted there was much substance underneath.

She had no idea about the children. She had asked Tom and Katie once if they played with them at school, but they were in different classes and they had barely known who they were.

Now the children gazed at each other from across the garden, caught up in the excitement of the early morning drama but not sure yet whether it meant anything interesting for them or not.

'Is it ours or yours?' Angie asked, looking at the fence.

'We don't know for sure,' Sophie replied. 'We think it's yours, but we need to check.'

Jack and Alan started lifting the panels and debris together and stacking them to one side. Meanwhile the older two Taylor children had emerged to see what all the fuss was about.

'We'll get it fixed ASAP if it's ours,' Angie said. 'Although we can't be the only people this has happened to after the storm, so it might take a while to get someone to come out.'

'There's no rush, don't worry,' Sophie said as she looked behind her and noticed that Tom and Katie had disappeared.

'Where are the kids?' she asked Alan, assuming that they had got bored, or cold, and gone back inside to have breakfast.

'They're over here,' Angie replied, gesturing behind her. Sophie took a couple of steps forward so that she could see into next door's garden and spotted her children playing on the neighbour's climbing frame as if it was a public playground.

'Oh gosh, I'm sorry, I was so busy gawping at the fence I didn't even see them sneak off,' Sophie exclaimed. 'Tom! Katie! Come back here!'

'Don't worry about it,' Angie said. 'It's fine.'

Sophie watched anxiously as Ellie and Freddy joined Tom and Katie on the climbing frame. She was embarrassed by her children's boldness although Angie didn't seem perturbed.

'We'd better get the kids inside, Soph,' Alan called out to her, his voice competing against the residual wind. 'It's freezing out here and they're still in their pyjamas.'

'I'll round them up,' Sophie agreed, calling out to them. They reluctantly returned to their own garden and with a final wave to Angie, they all raced back inside.

'That was fun,' Tom said as he tucked into his cereal. 'Their climbing frame is really cool.'

'I'm sure it is but you can't go wandering into their garden any time you like, okay?' Sophie told him sternly. 'Just because the fence is down doesn't mean you have the right.'

Tom and Katie nodded solemnly. But later that day after school, they both ran through the house and disappeared out of the back door the minute they got home, leaving a trail of discarded bags and lunchboxes in their wake. The wind had died down but it was still cold and Sophie watched them from the kitchen window and shivered. Children never seemed to feel the cold in the way that adults did. She moved away to put the kettle on and when she turned back to the window, a few seconds later, they had both disappeared.

'Dammit,' she exclaimed crossly, reaching for her coat and trainers and yanking them on. She trudged huffily up the garden and looked through the gap in the fence until she saw her children, as pleased as punch, sitting in her neighbour's treehouse. She frowned at Tom, who had obviously been the instigator. Katie would never do anything so rebellious without her brother.

'Guys, this is not okay. You can't just go next door and start playing whenever you feel like it,' Sophie told them sternly. 'This isn't our garden.'

'It's okay,' she heard a small voice say. It was Ellie who was marching up the garden in her raincoat and wellies, flanked by Freddy. 'We want to play with them.'

Sophie watched as Ellie climbed up into the treehouse, followed by Freddy. She stood there for a minute, at a loss as to what to do. While it was rather heart-warming to see them making friends, she didn't feel that she knew Angie and Jack well enough to let her kids play in their garden without their permission. She felt horribly conspicuous herself, hovering on the divide between the two gardens, and wondered if Angie was watching from the window, maybe tutting her disapproval at their audacity. Should she make them come back inside? And how safe was that rickety treehouse anyway, especially after the storm? The last thing she needed was a trip to A&E. Before she had a chance to decide, Angie emerged from the house.

'I'm really sorry,' Sophie called out to her. 'They just disappeared through the fence before I had a chance to stop them. I'm fetching them back now.'

'It's fine,' Angie said. 'Let them play. Ellie and Freddy were terribly excited when they saw them from the house. They couldn't get their wellies on quick enough.'

'As long as you're sure,' Sophie said. The two women stood side by side watching the children huddled together in the treehouse, chatting away as if they'd been friends for years rather than just a few minutes. *If only it was so easy for grown-ups*, Sophie thought, feeling awkward. She was relieved when Angie broke the silence.

'I was just going to make a cup of tea; would you like to join me?'

'Okay, thanks,' Sophie replied.

'Come inside where it's nice and warm. The kids are fine out here.'

With a final, nervous glance at the treehouse, Sophie followed Angie into the house. She felt a rush of warmth as she stepped over the threshold and then gasped as she looked around her. The house had been completely transformed. They'd been having work done to it for forever and she knew from the absence of builders' vans and drilling that they were finally finished but she couldn't believe how incredible it looked. The old, dated kitchen and dining room had been combined and extended to create one immense family room with a huge kitchen, furnished with pale granite worktops and a central island, with a neat row of stools next to it. Above it, three pendant lights hung from the ceiling.

On one side of the room the entire wall was lined with a floor to ceiling bookcase, stacked with neat rows of books. There was a huge grey corner sofa with a big fluffy rug in the corner and on the other side a long, elegant dining table with wooden benches. In the centre of the room, tucked into a column, was a wood-burning stove, its flames flickering. The whole thing looked like something from an interior design magazine When she took her trainers off, Sophie felt the warmth of the smooth tiles on her socks. *Underfloor heating*, she realised blissfully.

'This place looks unbelievable,' she told Angie.

'Thanks,' Angie replied, switching on the kettle and fetching mugs. 'It was one of the most stressful things we've ever done but now it's finished, I feel like we've reached the light at the end of the tunnel. I hope the refurbishment work wasn't too noisy for you?'

The constant drilling had been horrific but Sophie shook her head politely. 'Not at all, it was absolutely fine,' she lied.

'They've just finished the loft too, so we've finally moved upstairs into our new bedroom. Indie is ecstatic to have a room all to herself. Would you like a little tour?'

'Yes please,' Sophie said enthusiastically, relishing the chance to have a nose around. Angie led her from room to room, each one looking as beautiful as the next, and Sophie felt a pang of envy. She loved their family home, it was a happy, lived-in space, but it was cluttered and starting to look a little worn out too. In contrast, Angie and Jack had created something that looked like an Instagram show home. Sophie knew that even if they had the money to spend on that quality of furniture, fixtures and fittings, she simply didn't have the eye for it and there was no way she'd be able to make it look as stylish as this. Even the children's toys had been arranged perfectly into some sort of Scandi-style storage that definitely didn't come from Ikea, stacked away into neat cubby holes along one length of the front room, which Angie referred to as the den.

'This is the children's space,' she explained. 'They can hang out here with their friends, play, watch TV, paint, whatever they like. Then when they've gone to bed, I can close the door and shut away the mess.'

Lucky kids, Sophie thought, as she considered the mess that permeated every room of her own house. The loft room was equally impressive, with a modern four poster bed and even a small dressing room with racks for Angie's endless collection of shoes and boots. In a little nook to the side of the bedroom was a desk with a computer on it.

'Our study for when we work from home,' Angie explained.

'It's absolutely amazing, the whole house,' Sophie told her. 'You must be so pleased.'

'I'm getting there,' Angie said. 'The whole thing was incredibly difficult – the noise, the chaos, the dust. We escaped as often as we could and tried to spend as much time out of the house as possible. Tempers got rather frayed and by the end of it, I think we were all pretty sick of it, and each other. But now it's done, I can see that it's been worth the effort.'

They headed back downstairs and Angie finished making the tea while Sophie checked on the children, who were still up in the treehouse.

'They have a secret stash of snacks up there, so we probably won't see them for a while,' Angie said when she came back. It was all so perfect – the beautiful home, the treehouse, the outdoorsy, independent children. Sophie wondered again how Angie had time to do it all and look so well turned out at the same time. Glancing down at her jeans and faded jumper, she couldn't help but feel out of place in this pristine house.

We live in different worlds, she thought. As if reading her mind, Angie put the tea down on the table in front of her and said in a confiding tone, 'I nearly lost it on several occasions. In the half term I had to ask Jack's parents to look after the children so I could have a break. You're seeing the finished product here but the journey to get there was extremely messy on all levels.'

That made Sophie feel a bit better. 'How are you all settling into the area?' she asked.

'Fine,' Angie replied, sitting down. 'The younger ones have settled into school very well. Benji seems to be plodding along in secondary school although I don't think he's made as many friends as we'd hoped. He definitely misses his old gang. Indie has surprised us; she was the fiercest opponent to us moving but actually she's happier than ever. She's slotted right in with a group of girls in her class and they're as thick as thieves.'

'How about you and Jack?'

'Oh Jack's absolutely fine. He's immune to stress so the refurbishment didn't bother him in the slightest and he's found a local café that gets his coffee snob seal of approval. He's got an easier commute to work and he's started coaching a local junior football team.'

'And you?'

Angie looked thoughtful before replying, 'I'm happy to be closer to my mum but I do miss my old life in Greenwich. We lived there for so long and it was just easy. I'm still in touch with most of our friends but we can't just pop round like we used to.'

'Have you made friends in the area yet?'

'I'm trying to but with work being so busy it's challenging. I don't do the school runs.'

Sophie nodded sympathetically, seeing Angie in a new light.

It was hard, she thought, constantly juggling responsibilities, not being able to drop any balls.

'Anyway, how are you?' Angie asked. Sophie sensed that she was keen to change the subject.

'Oh fine, you know, same old,' Sophie said dismissively, realising with embarrassment that she had nothing interesting to say to Angie, unless you counted the fact that she went to the supermarket this morning and bought an absolute steal of a coat.

'How's work going?'

Sophie was about to reel out her standard response of, 'Oh yes, all fine, thanks,' but instead she found herself being honest. 'A bit rubbish.'

'How come?'

She wasn't sure if it was the warm, welcoming house, Angie's attentiveness or just a need have something to talk about, but Sophie found herself telling Angie about how she'd gone to work with Alan and had been struggling to get back into her old job ever since.

'I just feel a bit old,' she admitted. 'I know that's silly because these days being in your thirties is considered young and I've got another thirty years of working age ahead of me at least. But I've just lost my energy and drive for it and I can't seem to get it back. And I think I probably have a touch of imposter syndrome too, since having the children and my career break.'

Angie nodded. 'Oh yes, I know all about that.'

'You do?'

Angie laughed at Sophie's obvious surprise. 'Of course. I see these young hotshot solicitors joining the firm, willing to work every hour God sends and absolutely determined to be made partner, already planning to run before they can walk. And I just think, *Christ, all I want to do is go home and have a glass of wine in the bath*.'

Sophie grinned as she took a gulp of tea. 'I can relate. I get these email alerts where editors tell writers what topics they're looking to cover and it's all vaginal steaming and breadcrumbing. I honestly thought that was something to do with baking at first. These twenty-somethings think all you need is a laptop and a blog to be a writer. And I want to judge them but they have, like, a hundred thousand Instagram followers and I have twenty-three. So, who has the power really, them or me? I feel like my trade is dying – or at least my career is – and I'm not sure I even care anymore.'

Angie looked like she was about to say something but before she got a chance, the bifold patio doors opened and four children piled in.

'Mum, we're going to hang out in the den,' Ellie said. 'Can Tom and Katie stay for dinner?'

Sophie was about to protest but Angie nodded and replied, 'Sure.' She looked at Sophie. 'It'll just be fish fingers and potato waffles but they're welcome to stay.'

Sophie looked at her children's expectant faces. She was worried about overstaying their welcome or putting Angie out, but she'd actually been having a surprisingly good time chatting with her and it seemed no one was ready to go home just yet.

'Go on then,' she replied. 'As long as it's okay with Angie.' The children whooped and ran off to the den and Sophie smiled at Angie. 'Thank you, it's really kind of you.'

'It's nice to have a playdate actually,' Angie said. 'Normally I'm working so the children go to after-school clubs. But I was in court this morning and didn't have much on this afternoon, so I picked them up early. I'm sure one of those young trainees is already eyeing up my desk.'

'We're often around after school so any time you find yourself at home early again do pop over,' Sophie said. Then she added, 'Actually we're having an Easter party at ours on Saturday. Nothing fancy, just an egg hunt for the children and a couple of beers for the parents. Would you like to come? It'll be a chance to meet some of the other parents from school.'

'We'd love to,' Angie replied with what seemed like genuine enthusiasm. 'Thank you.'

～

Alan was already back from work by the time they got home. Tom and Katie, who were still overexcited, jumped on him and started regaling him with stories about their new best friends.

'We had waffles for dinner and we ate them in front of the telly!' Tom said triumphantly. 'And Ellie and Freddy said that we can come and play any time!'

'Lucky you,' said Alan. He turned to Sophie. 'And did Angie say that you could come and play any time too?'

Sophie gave him a withering look and then said, 'She's actually really nice though.'

'You seem surprised.'

'I am a bit. It's not that I didn't like her, it's just that she's never seemed particularly interested in making friends before. But she couldn't have been more lovely this afternoon. Still though, Al, you should see their place, it's incredible. And she was telling me about her job, she represents some really high-profile clients. I couldn't help but feel a bit plain Jane.'

'You, my love, are anything but plain.'

'Aw, thanks. Anyway, I'm not saying we're going to become bosom buddies or anything, but I definitely think neighbourly relations have warmed up a notch. And she's feeling a bit lonely, so I've invited them all over for the Easter party.'

'Good for you.'

'What do you think of Jack?'

'Hardly know the guy.'

Alan was the least satisfying person to gossip with she'd ever known.

'Well, let's see if they turn up anyway,' Sophie said, as she opened the fridge and started rooting around for vegetables to prepare their dinner. 'At least I've done my bit.'

5

Sophie was yanking a dozen anaemic cupcakes out of the oven and fervently wishing that she'd just bought some from the supermarket like she normally did, when the doorbell rang. 'Can you get that, Alan?' she called, but there was no response. Cursing, she dashed to the door, brushing flour off her clothes, and found Angie, Jack, Ellie and Freddy on the doorstep.

'Hi, come in!' she said with false bravado.

'Are you okay? Sorry we're a bit early,' Angie said, frowning as she took in Sophie's flustered expression and dishevelled appearance.

'No, no, you're fine, I'm just in baking hell,' Sophie admitted as she ushered them in. 'The kids are upstairs playing computer games,' she told Ellie and Freddy, who immediately started to make their way up the stairs. Angie and Jack followed her into the kitchen.

'Alan's somewhere but I have no idea where – probably playing games with the children,' Sophie explained. 'He always makes a hasty exit when I attempt to bake.'

Angie examined the carnage, observing the production line

of cupcakes in various states of disarray and rolled up her sleeves. 'Jack, you get the beers, Sophie, you get the icing.'

Sophie imagined this was exactly how Angie dealt with her wayward clients, but she obediently opened the cupboard to look for icing. Jack grabbed four beers, left two on the kitchen surface for Angie and Sophie and headed off in the same direction as the children.

'Sorry we're early,' Angie said again, as she started decorating a batch of cupcakes. 'I know it's annoying when people turn up before they're expected, but we'd just got back from dropping Indie and Benji off at their friends' houses and we thought we might as well come straight over. Ellie and Freddy were so excited about the party, they were driving us potty.'

'It's fine,' Sophie said. 'To be honest I'm glad of the help. Thank you. I don't know why I decided to go all Nigella. I really don't have what it takes.'

'They look great,' Angie said, finishing her dozen cupcakes in frustratingly quick time. 'Now while we wait for the last batch to cool down, what else needs doing?'

With Angie's help, the house was party ready by the time everyone arrived. Alan and Jack had hidden eggs all around the garden and the children grabbed buckets and dashed off to look for them, while Sophie introduced Angie to some guests. As she was heating up some soup and bread in the kitchen, one of her school mum friends, Eve, sidled up to her.

'He's a bit of a dish, that Jack,' she said.

Sophie slapped her playfully with a wooden spoon. 'He's also married to my very nice neighbour,' she reminded Eve.

'Never hurts to look,' Eve said shamelessly. 'I don't suppose he does naked yoga in the garden, does he? Because if so, I'm coming round for breakfast.'

Sophie laughed in wicked delight. 'He's all right but he's not my cup of tea.'

'What, tall, dark and handsome isn't your cup of tea?'

'He's too... I don't know... perfect looking. He looks like a cardboard cut-out. I prefer my men more real and rugged. Like my Alan.'

'Well good job you're married to him then,' Eve said, sticking her finger in the soup.

'Oi, get away with you.' Sophie laughed, batting her away. Eve winked and wandered off to introduce herself to Angie. Sophie observed the two women talking easily together and enjoyed a moment of satisfaction. She loved it when a good party came together. Smiling to herself, she put the soup and bread on the table and went outside to watch the egg hunt.

'How's it going?' she asked Alan.

'Yeah fine, they're all losing their tiny little minds.'

'Perfect.' She stood next to him and watched the children running around frantically in different directions. 'They'll be as high as kites when they've scoffed all of those eggs. We'd better make sure all the guests leave before the sugar rush wears off.'

'Yeah, we don't want a repeat of last year.'

'What happened last year?'

'One kid vomited all over the kitchen floor and another one beheaded all of Katie's Barbies and she cried for three hours straight.'

'Oh *God*! How have I forgotten that?'

'I wish I had.'

Two hours and three meltdowns later, everyone had left apart from Angie, Jack and the kids.

'Can we stay a bit longer, please?' Ellie begged.

'Five minutes,' Angie agreed, as Alan opened a bottle of wine. They all sat down, glad to finally be able to relax, and Sophie started absent-mindedly picking at the leftover party food.

'That was a great party,' Angie said, raising her glass to Sophie and Alan.

'It really was,' Alan agreed. 'I thought we were in for it when you said you were baking.'

'Sod off,' Sophie said, throwing a cheese puff at him. She turned to Angie. 'Thanks so much for your help, I couldn't have done it without you.'

'It was nothing,' Angie said. Sophie imagined her hosting a party. She pictured everything prepared to perfection, Jack dishing out glasses of Chablis while their guests discussed very important matters, instead of which child at school had head lice. She wondered what Angie thought of her house. Compared to her immaculate home it probably looked like a pigsty. But she seemed comfortable enough relaxing on one of Sophie's kitchen chairs, glass of wine in hand. *Perhaps we're not that different after all*, she thought.

As the four of them chatted easily about house extensions, children and TV shows that Jack had worked on, the promised five minutes of extra playtime turned into an hour. By the time the Taylors finally went home Sophie couldn't even be bothered to tidy up.

'Leave it all, Alan, we'll do it in the morning,' she said as she followed the kids upstairs to start their bath. 'What do you make of them?' she asked him, curious to hear his opinion.

'Yeah, they're all right,' he said. Coming from Alan, that was high praise indeed.

6

Angie lingered in the back doorway, observing her husband. Jack was out in the garden, looking at the barbecue with the primal sense of achievement that men get when they successfully make fire. He was wearing shorts, a T-shirt and a novelty apron that the children had given him a couple of Christmases ago, which declared *All This And I Can Cook!* His eyes were hidden behind a pair of aviator shades. Even after all these years, he still gave her butterflies.

She peered up into the treehouse and could just make out four sets of legs. In the three months since the storm, Tom and Katie had become regular visitors to their garden, and often their house too. At first Sophie had been apologetic about her children's uninvited appearances, but Angie had reassured her that they were welcome. They were nice kids and Ellie and Freddy were delighted with their new playmates. They hardly ever mentioned their friends in Greenwich these days, it was all about Tom and Katie.

Once the initial awkward politeness had passed, they had settled into a rather pleasant routine of sorts. Sophie had started popping by for a cup of tea and a chat when she came to fetch the children. Angie now found herself glancing at the gap in the fence whenever she was in the kitchen, instinctively looking in anticipation for her neighbour. No one had mentioned that the fence probably should have been fixed by now. Or that they both had perfectly good front doors they could use.

Sophie had surprised her. In Angie's line of work, you often *could* judge a book by its cover. When she had first met Sophie, she had categorised her as one of those mumsy-types who was so obsessed with her children that she didn't talk about anything else. But she was wrong. Sophie was funny, sharp as a tack and interesting. She had googled her name once after learning that she was a writer and had become absorbed in her articles. She clearly had talent and Angie couldn't for the life of her understand why Sophie had given it all up. Still, she seemed happy enough and who was she to judge. Besides, Angie was just pleased to have made a new friend.

Although she still kept in touch with their Greenwich set, they didn't meet up that often anymore. Her fears that they would drift apart once they'd moved out of the area had come true. It just wasn't easy or convenient to meet up anymore, it took more of an effort to plan. And with busy lives and young children, that often fell by the wayside. She didn't blame them. In any case, the children had made new friends nearby and wanted to play with them at weekends now.

Watching Ellie and Freddy with the kids next door was like a tonic to her lonely memories of being an only child with no one her age to play with. She remembered Jack saying to her once, years ago, 'I can't wait for you to see what it's like to be part of a large family.' Now she knew.

They had been living in Pemberton Road for over a year but to Angie it was only just starting to feel like home. She knew that a big part of that was their new friendship with the Brennan family. She hadn't confided in anyone but she had found the past few months a challenge. While the others seemed to have adapted to their new lives, she was in limbo, stuck between her old existence and her new one and not entirely sure where it left her. She had been the one who insisted they move but ever since they had, she'd yearned for their old life back in Greenwich, before it had all gone wrong. When they'd been happy.

Things between her and Jack were good at the moment, though. He'd made a real effort over the past year to prove that he'd changed for good. For her part she was trying harder to be more considerate and less critical. On the surface everything was great, so why did she still have this niggling, unshakeable feeling that something wasn't quite right?

When she and Jack had got married, she'd felt like she was living in a fairy tale. They were still in their twenties then, working long hours and socialising with friends during the week but at the weekend they preferred to hole up in their new flat in Clapham and play house. It was the novelty of it all back then. They turned down invitations to parties and dinners, cooking a Sunday roast for two instead and going for long, lazy walks together. Saturday nights went from dancing until the early hours in some dingy club to curling up on the sofa with a film. At the same time, she was climbing the ranks in the law firm where she worked and earning a reputation as one to watch. During those blissful first few months of marriage, she had everything that she had ever wanted and she couldn't imagine ever feeling unhappy again.

She could pinpoint the exact moment when her bubble finally burst. It was a Friday evening and they had planned to go home after work and get a takeaway. She'd had to work a little later than expected and she had rushed home eager to get back to Jack. As she raced up the stairs, she imagined him waiting for her, with a cold beer. But when she entered the flat, it was dark.

'Jack?' she called out, although she already knew that he wasn't home.

Rummaging in the bottom of her bag for her phone, she checked it to see if he'd called or texted but there were no notifications. She typed out a quick text to him and went into the bedroom to get changed into something more comfortable. Four hours and several unanswered calls later, Jack still wasn't home and Angie had worked herself up into a frenzy. She messaged a couple of his friends to ask if he was with them, thinking that perhaps he went out for a quick drink after work and had one too many, but no one had seen him. Finally, she crawled into bed at midnight and waited, wide awake, for him to come home.

He eventually did, at 6am. Angie had barely slept a wink and was on the verge of calling the police and reporting him as a missing person when he walked into their bedroom looking dishevelled, disorientated and smelling like a brewery.

'Jack, what the hell?' Angie said, sitting up. 'I've been out of my mind with worry!'

'Sorry, I'm sorry,' Jack said, sinking down onto the bed and peeling off his shoes and socks.

'Where have you been?'

'I went out with a client for a drink after work and it all got out of hand. I tried to text you but I left my phone at work.' He leaned back against the pillow and closed his eyes, as if to him, the conversation was over.

'Jack, this is not okay,' Angie persisted. 'You were supposed to be coming home last night. I had no idea where you were and I've barely slept a wink. You know I don't care if you go out with friends, but you need to tell me. You can't just not show up.'

'I know, I'm sorry, Ange,' he said, groaning as he shifted position. 'It won't happen again.'

Except that it did happen again. And again. It was as if Jack had grown tired of playing house and had decided to return to his old, single lifestyle. Angie was furious and terrified. Her deepest, darkest fear was that she loved Jack more than he loved her, and his behaviour was adding fuel to the monster of anxiety inside her. In all other areas of her life, she had always been cool, calm and in control, but Jack was her weakness.

The problem was that every time she confronted him, he looked at her like she was overreacting, throwing his hands up in protest. 'Angie, I love you. It's not like I'm cheating on you. I would never do that. I'm just blowing off a little steam, okay? We're still young, let's act like it.'

It went on for months, until Angie lost complete confidence in her own feelings. On one hand she was well within her rights to tell Jack his behaviour was not appropriate, that they were married and he had to act like it. But on the other hand, she wondered if Jack was right. They were young, independent people. They didn't own each other, they didn't have children, they could do what they liked. And after all, he was only going out to have a bit of fun with the boys, she told herself, he wasn't having an affair. As time went on, she learned to turn a blind eye, convincing herself that he wasn't doing anything wrong at all.

Then one Sunday afternoon, they were taking a walk across Clapham Common when Jack announced, 'I think we should start trying for a baby.'

Angie was caught completely off guard. They'd talked about having children, and agreed that they both wanted them, but she had assumed they were a long way off yet. She was only twenty-eight and making great strides in her career. Plus she loved the freedom that they had to go out whenever they wanted and book holidays at the drop of a hat. She'd always imagined she'd be well into her thirties before they started trying for a family. Surely they weren't ready yet?

She turned to him in surprise. 'Where has this come from, Jack?'

'I've just been thinking about it a lot lately,' Jack replied with a shrug. 'We're married, we love each other, what's stopping us?'

'Our lifestyle? My career?'

'You'll still have a career, Ange. I'm not asking you to become a Stepford wife. Many women build successful careers around their families, you know.'

'What about our lifestyle, then? You won't be able to go out till six in the morning and rock up pissed as a fart anymore, Jack.'

'Ouch,' he said, flinching away from her sheepishly. Then his expression became serious. 'I'm done with it, Angie. I've had enough. I know I've been behaving like a total idiot over the last few months. I think I just needed to get it out of my system, and now I have.'

'What's brought on this sudden change of opinion?' Angie asked.

'I think I finally realised what a dick I was being on Friday night. I was sitting in a bar at 3am, staring at my beer, and I thought, *What the hell am I doing here? I have a beautiful wife waiting for me in my bed at home. That's where I want to be, not here in this dive.*'

'I'm thrilled that you've had such a life-changing revelation, Jack, I really am. But you're not the one who has to carry the baby, go through the horror of labour and put her career on hold to care for a newborn. It's my life that will change the most, not yours, and I'm not saying I don't want children – because you know that I do. I just don't know if I want them right now.'

'Just think about it, Angie, that's all I'm saying. Think about it.'

'I will,' she agreed, with no intention of actually doing so, and changed the subject.

Three months later she was pregnant.

Jack looked up from the barbecue now and saw her watching him. He gave her a thumbs up. 'I think we're about ready for those burgers, Ange,' he called out to her, and she nodded and went back inside to fetch them. By the time she returned to the garden, Sophie and Alan had appeared through the gap in the fence.

'I brought dessert,' Sophie said, proffering a cheesecake and some ice cream.

'Lovely, thanks,' Angie replied, taking them off Sophie and heading back into the kitchen to put the ice cream in the freezer.

'How's it going?' Sophie asked, following her in. 'What's happening with that court case?'

Angie had been working on a highly publicised case for the last week. 'The last prosecution witness should finish on Monday, then it's our turn,' she told her.

'It's all very exciting,' Sophie said.

'If it goes in our favour, perhaps I can put you in touch with my client as long as she agrees?' Angie offered. 'I think she's fairly keen to do some publicity.'

Sophie's eyes lit up. 'That would be great!'

'Leave it with me.'

'Thanks, Angie, I really appreciate that.'

'On another note,' Angie said, 'I think Ellie has a little crush on Tom. I found this picture in her room the other day.'

She reached into her pocket and pulled out a folded drawing that Ellie had made of her and Tom together, surrounded by hearts.

'Oh my goodness, that's the cutest thing I've ever seen,' Sophie gushed. 'Do you remember your first crush?'

'Vaguely,' Angie said, scrunching up her eyes as she tried to remember. 'I went to a girls' school so it was slim pickings but there was a boy at my Saturday morning drama club and I just adored him. Then one day another girl told me he'd left a note in her bag asking her to be his girlfriend and I went home and cried all day and then refused to go back to the club.'

'Oh dear,' Sophie said. 'Mine was one of my brother's friends. I remember that I used to put my mother's make-up and heels on whenever he came over to play. He never even noticed me.'

'What a tool,' Alan said, ambling into the kitchen.

Sophie grinned at him and Angie watched them, thinking how easy their relationship was, like two pieces of a puzzle that fit naturally together. They were always laughing or joking with each other and she'd never seen a cross word pass between them.

'Are you all right, Angie?' Sophie asked. 'You look a million miles away.'

'Oh sorry, I was just daydreaming,' she replied. 'Can you help me get these salads outside?'

By the time they had set the table, Jack was shovelling burgers onto plates and Angie went to round up the children. They all crowded round, jostling each other to get to the food first, and then dispersed as quickly as they had arrived.

'Don't you want to eat with us?' Angie called out to them.

'Nah, we're eating in the treehouse,' Tom replied, as the four youngest children headed up the garden, each balancing their precariously full plates with two hands. Indie took her plate inside, texting a friend with one hand as she walked, and Benji had already disappeared.

'Charming,' Angie said.

'Ah, enjoy it,' Jack said, taking off his apron and sitting down at the table. 'They'll all be pestering you soon enough.' He held up his beer glass. 'Cheers, Brennans.'

They were still sitting outside as the sun set later that day, savouring the warmth of the summer evening. Jack had been filling them in on the football squad he coached and Alan had been regaling them with stories of some of his clients' most unusual requests. 'They wanted his and hers toilet thrones in the bathroom!' he told them as they all laughed uproariously.

Angie and Sophie went to check on the four younger children who had all fallen asleep top to tail in the den. They tiptoed around the room covering them with duvets and blankets before closing the door quietly behind them.

'Alan and I can carry them home,' Sophie whispered.

'Leave them here,' Angie replied. 'They look so comfortable. Come and get them in the morning.'

'Okay,' Sophie agreed. 'Thanks for a lovely afternoon, I've had such a great time.'

'Me too. Let's hope it's the first of many barbecues.'

They smiled at each other, both basking in the pleasure of an unexpected friendship, and returned to the garden to find Alan and Jack finishing off their beers.

'Well I'm three sheets to the wind, so I think it's time to go home,' Alan said.

Jack said goodbye and started checking the football scores on his phone but Angie watched Sophie and Alan disappear through the fence, laughing at a joke she hadn't heard. At the last moment, Sophie looked back and waved at Angie. She smiled and waved back and then, with a glance at Jack, she started collecting the empty glasses and made her way back inside.

7

'Mu-um, where's my schoolbag?'

Sophie sighed impatiently, counted to ten and shouted back, 'By the front door, where I told you it was thirty seconds ago!'

The first day back at school was always a shock after a long, lazy summer. They'd gone on holiday to Spain, spent a long weekend with Sophie's parents in Devon and the rest of the time they'd stayed at home, chilling out, going to the park and seeing friends. As soon as school finished the Taylor family had gone on their usual three-week summer jaunt and then the children had been at holiday clubs for a fortnight, leaving Tom and Katie pining for them like little lost puppies. They had taken to sitting in the treehouse for hours, waiting for their friends to get home from football camp, or drama camp, or wherever it was they were that day.

Finally, in the last week of the holidays, the children had been at home and Sophie had barely seen Tom and Katie. She'd taken advantage of the uninterrupted time to send a few emails to her old contacts asking if they needed any freelance writers, but all she'd received was a plethora of out of office replies. Everyone, it seemed, was still on their summer holidays.

She finished making the children's sandwiches and looked out of the window at the back garden, which was its usual chaotic mess. Grass and dead insects were floating in the half deflated paddling pool and the lawn was littered with toys. Her eyes fell to the gap in the fence, and she thought about what a glorious summer it had turned out to be.

Once Angie and Jack got back from holiday, they'd got into an unspoken habit of meeting up in the garden at weekends. Someone would inevitably light a barbecue or bring out some snacks. While the children played the adults sat around chatting, often for entire afternoons. She and Angie would stay out long after Alan and Jack had drifted back inside.

The previous weekend they'd ended up chatting in the garden until midnight. They had sat side by side in reclining chairs, a bottle of wine between them and the scent of jasmine lingering in the air. Angie was great fun although she was still a closed book when it came to talking about herself. She never gave anything personal away but she was surprisingly easy to talk to.

They discussed Sophie's career, or lack of it, and Angie was the only person other than Alan who knew the full extent of her never-ending writer's block. It had been a relief to finally be honest with someone. They talked about parenting too, its challenges, its rewards. As mothers they couldn't be more different. Sophie knew she hovered around Tom and Katie like a hummingbird whereas Angie was more hands off, telling her that she and Jack believed in giving their children the freedom to make mistakes and be who they wanted to be.

There was no doubt that the Taylor children were confident and felt free to follow their own paths. She'd noticed it particularly with Benji, the eldest. He hated studying, loathed sport and was only happy when he was at drama class or rehearsing for a play. She thought that someone as successful and motivated as Angie would be pushing him to do well academically. Or perhaps Jack would be disappointed that his oldest son didn't like football. But they didn't seem to care.

'He's only got to scrape through his GCSEs and then he can go to drama school,' Jack had said one evening, when they were having dinner together.

'You don't mind if he doesn't do his A-levels?' Sophie had asked, intrigued.

'Christ no, Benji would hate that. The quicker we get him out of that place and into a performing arts school the better.'

Sophie had turned to Angie, curious to see her response, but she had nodded in agreement. She was too embarrassed to confess that she had already started contacting tutors for Tom, in the hope that he might get through the eleven-plus exams and secure a place at a grammar school. As a teenager herself, she had loved drama but her parents had refused to let her go to performing arts school. She had diligently stayed on for her A-levels and then gone to journalism college, putting all thoughts of Broadway behind her. She thought now how lucky Benji was to have such supportive parents, who made it so easy for him to pursue his dream.

In contrast, she found herself worrying about how much she hovered around Tom and Katie, fretting about whether they were fitting in at school, what marks they got in their spelling tests, whether they'd do well in their SATs, whose sleepover they hadn't been invited to. When she had voiced her fears to Angie, though, she had dismissed them as though they were nothing.

'You love them, they're happy, they're safe, don't worry about it,' she said.

'Yes, but I'm like a mother hen, clucking around them all the time,' Sophie persisted.

'That's because you care and that's the most important thing. I've seen a lot of unhappy, unloved children in my career, Sophie, and I can tell you that you have absolutely nothing to worry about. Stop beating yourself up; you're an excellent mother.'

And with that the conversation was over as far as Angie was concerned. Sophie sometimes wished she had her confidence, her certainty. Despite their growing friendship she was still a little intimidated by Angie and how she managed to juggle her life so effortlessly. It wasn't just her career but her family life too. She sometimes stole glances at Angie and Jack, observing how Angie looked at him so adoringly, how tactile he was with her. *They are so in love*, she thought, *even after all these years of marriage and four children*. While she adored Alan with every bone in her body, it was a very different kind of relationship.

It wasn't that they had lost the passion because they never really had it in the first place. And it had never bothered Sophie because they were happy and they loved each other. As her mother always said: 'The most important four words for a successful marriage are "I'll do the dishes".'

But occasionally she would glance over at Angie and Jack, dancing to a song or feeding each other olives, and she would feel a short, sharp pang of envy. It was as if they were living in a movie.

Whereas her life, she thought as she finished off the packed lunches, was definitely not a Hollywood blockbuster.

'We're leaving in T-minus three minutes,' she called out to the children who were slung across the sofa like sloths, watching cartoons. 'Shoes and coats, *now*.'

She herded a reluctant Tom and Katie out of the house and spotted Jack locking up next door, with Freddy and Ellie in tow. She waved and waited for him to catch up.

'I don't normally see you at this time,' she said. 'Are the kids not at breakfast club today?'

'No,' Jack replied. 'I've decided to reduce my hours for a couple of months. We thought it would be good for Indie to have someone at home more until she's settled into secondary school. She's been feeling very anxious. So I'm on school run duty.'

'Poor Indie,' Sophie said. 'I remember my first few days of big school well and they were terrifying. Is today her first day?'

'Yes. Of course she insisted on making her own way there and Benji had to stay at least six feet away from her at all times.'

'Wow, she's so grown up!' The thought of her children walking to school on their own filled Sophie with terror. She was going to be a nervous wreck when they were older.

She got the distinct impression that Indie was pretty sassy, though. Of all Angie's children, she was the one that Sophie knew the least. She seemed to spend most of her time at friends' houses or glued to her phone. God help her parents when she was a proper teenager, Sophie thought, she was going to give them a hard time. In contrast, Ellie was the sweetest, most easy-going child that she had ever met. Even now, she gave Sophie a beaming smile and a quick cuddle before dashing off to catch up with the others, who had scooted ahead.

'Are you looking forward to holding the fort?' Sophie asked Jack as they made their way down the road together.

'I can't wait,' Jack said. 'I love being with the children, even though they walk all over me when Angie's not around. Angie says it's because I'm basically a kid myself. I'm glad for a bit of time off work too: this year's been intense. I feel like me, Angie and the kids have all been ships that pass in the night to be honest, so it'll be nice to have some time at home.'

Sophie nodded, as if she knew what he meant, but it had been a long time since she'd experienced the work intensity he was talking about. She remembered the old newspaper days, when she was on a deadline and the adrenaline was coursing through her body as she typed furiously, trying to write a story in time. But she didn't miss it, she thought now, not anymore.

'Well done on that piece in the press by the way, it was great,' Jack said.

True to her word, Angie had put Sophie in touch with her client after the court case and she'd ended up getting an exclusive interview. She had sold it for an eye-watering fee to a national newspaper. It had felt good to be earning money again, but she still hadn't experienced the rush of pleasure of seeing her words in print like she used to. It was probably time to accept that her heart simply wasn't in it anymore. But she had no idea what else she could do instead.

'Thanks,' she said to Jack. 'It was Angie who made it all happen.'

'She's great like that.'

Sophie nodded. 'I still don't know how she finds the time to do everything.'

'I know, she's amazing. A real role model to the children, too.'

A role model? That made Sophie think. Was she a good role model to her children? Yes, she was there to cuddle them and wipe away tears when they fell or had rows with friends, to help them with their homework and prepare them a home-cooked meal. Was that enough anymore or did she need to juggle a successful career to be considered a good mother these days too? Had parenting always been this complex and confusing, a constant battle of comparing yourself to others and worrying about whether you were doing it right?

'How did you two meet?' she asked Jack, changing the subject.

'We were at uni together, we both studied law although I realised two weeks in that I'd made a mistake and never got round to switching courses. Angie of course graduated top of the class. Back then we were just friends, but we bumped into each other years later and got together.'

'Did you fancy her at uni?' Sophie asked playfully.

'I think most people fancied Angie but we were all a bit terrified of her. She was always so intelligent, so driven, as if the pettiness of student life was beneath her, if that makes sense.'

Even after knowing Angie for a short time it made complete sense to Sophie.

'The lads used to call her the ice princess,' he said, chuckling, before quickly adding, 'I've never told her that, mind.'

'So, what was different when you met up again?' she asked him.

'We'd just grown up a bit, I think. As soon as I saw her, I remembered how amazing she was and I thought, *don't be a douchebag and let this one go*. So I gave it to her straight and luckily, she felt the same. And here we are fifteen years later, married with four kids. How about you and Alan?'

'Oh, nothing romantic. He chatted me up in a bar, asked me for my number and took me out. Here we are ten years later, married with two kids.'

Jack laughed and then rushed on ahead when Freddy took a tumble from his scooter. Sophie watched him as he picked the boy up and sent him on his way again before he even had a chance to consider crying. *He is a natural with children*, she thought.

'Where are you off to now?' she asked him after they dropped the kids off in the playground.

'Back home to do some work. How about you?'

'Coffee with the mums from the PTA. It's only September but we're already starting to think about the Christmas fair.'

Jack winced. 'Sounds like my idea of hell,' he said.

Sophie laughed. 'It's not that bad. They're a good bunch.'

'Still, rather you than me,' Jack replied. He said goodbye and headed off in the direction of home. Just as she was turning to leave, Sophie spotted Clara, one of the other mums on the PTA, striding towards her.

'Who's that?' she asked, looking at Jack's retreating back.

'Jack Taylor, Ellie and Freddy's dad. He lives next door,' Sophie replied.

Clara nodded absent-mindedly, already having lost interest. 'So, are you ready to plan the greatest Christmas fair this school has ever seen?'

'Not until I've had a coffee.'

'We'd better get going then.'

They walked together towards their regular coffee shop, briefing each other on their summer holiday adventures. It was quite nice to be back in the old routine after all, Sophie thought, already abandoning her plans to go on a post-holiday diet and thinking of the insanely good chocolate croissants they did at the café.

When they opened the door, she saw three of the other mums already sitting down at their usual table, chatting among themselves. One of them was feeding her baby while also trying to stop her busy toddler from running off. Sophie was about to step in when two of the others distracted the boy, seating him between them and offering him snacks to give his mum a bit of peace and quiet. They were a tribe, she thought fondly, they looked out for each other.

Andy, the café owner, waved when he saw her. 'The usual?'

'Yes, please. And a chocolate croissant.'

'I'll bring it over, darling.'

She went to sit down with the others, ready to get down to the important business of school event planning.

Children deposited safely at school. Back home now xx

Angie read the message from Jack as she dashed out of her office towards the court. She quickly typed out *Thanks* in response and pocketed her phone. Looking at her watch she cursed and picked up the pace. There'd be no time to get a coffee on the way this morning.

She'd been up late last night preparing for today's court hearing and she was tired and ratty. Most of the time she didn't mind the demands of her job, in fact she thrived on it, but occasionally it all felt a bit too much and today was one of those days. Freddy had wet the bed and she'd been up at 4am changing the sheets and then Indie had given her a hard time at breakfast about not being there to take her to school, despite the fact that she'd already declared she would be walking on her own.

'You're always working, Mum,' her eldest daughter had said, scowling at her over her half-eaten toast. 'You're never there when I need you.'

She'd heard it all before and she normally brushed it aside fairly easily, confident in the knowledge that she was a good mother. But for some reason it had stuck this time and a sort of melancholy had settled over her all morning. She thought back to the conversation she'd had with Jack on holiday, when he had suggested reducing his hours so that he could be around more for the children, and the relief she'd felt that he'd offered to be the one to do it.

She was the breadwinner so it made sense that Jack took on the role. But, still, he enjoyed his job and the social aspect of working as part of a team and she had been surprised that he was so eager to do it. It was another example of Jack 2.0, the new man, the changed man.

When Angie had discovered she was pregnant with Benji,

Jack had been thrilled. She was too, although a little shell-shocked by how fast it had happened. In the days and weeks that had followed their baby talk on Clapham Common, Jack had been true to his word. He'd stopped disappearing on late nights out, texted her when he was leaving the office and often came home with flowers or a lovely bottle of wine for them to share. She began to relax for the first time in months and enjoy married life again. It was over, she thought, she had her husband back.

So when Jack had brought up babies again a few weeks later, she had tried to be open-minded about it. But she still wasn't sure that the timing was right.

'Why don't you just come off the pill?' Jack suggested. 'And we'll see what happens. That way we're not actively trying for a baby. It won't be all ovulation sticks and period cycles. We'll just live our life as normal and see what happens.'

Basking in the glow of her once again blissfully happy marriage, and keen to please Jack, Angie had agreed. She'd read that it could take months for her reproductive system to kick back into gear after a long period on the pill and in those days that felt like forever. So, she'd dutifully ditched the little packets of contraceptives that had been part of her life for ten years and forgot all about it, until she missed her period a couple of months later.

She hadn't told Jack at first. Part of the reason was that she didn't want to get his hopes up if it was a false alarm, but the other part was that if she was pregnant, she wanted some time to process it before she shared the information. To her, pregnancy symbolised the end of their current way of life and she wasn't sure that she was ready for that yet. But as she sat on the tube on the way into work and contemplated the possibility, she felt something else too – anticipation. The feeling hit her out of the blue and grew in strength until by the time she got off the train in the city, she was desperate for the test to come back positive.

It was an instinctive feeling, one that overrode any other thoughts, almost visceral. She picked up a couple of tests from the chemist at the train station and locked herself into a toilet cubicle at work, peeing on the first stick and settling in for the ten-minute agonising wait for the result. But within a minute or so she saw the telltale second blue line starting to appear, faintly at first and then growing stronger. She stared at it, feeling something that she hadn't been expecting, a maternal instinct. *Is this what it feels like to be a mother*, she thought? *This overpowering feeling that I will do whatever it takes to protect this tiny being from harm?*

For the rest of the day everything else seemed pointless. The work, the office politics, her friend's row with her boyfriend that she regaled Angie with over a sandwich at lunch. She felt like she was floating on a cloud, way above the minutiae of everyday life, so that she could see what was happening around her, but she couldn't feel it anymore. She cherished having that small slice of time to herself for a few hours, when no one else knew their secret but her and the baby. They were in it together, just the two of them, and it was liberating.

But as soon as she left work, her bubble burst and she couldn't wait to get back home and break the news to Jack, to see the look on his face when he realised that he was going to be a father. The minute she got back to the flat, she presented him with the other, unopened pregnancy test and suggested that they find out together. It was misleading, but she didn't want him to know that she'd been harbouring this secret all day without him.

His face lit up at once and he grabbed her hand and pulled her towards the bathroom, insisting on keeping her company while she peed, even when she told him that he was giving her stage fright. After finally agreeing to leave the room, he returned as soon as he heard the flush of the toilet and they sat on the edge of the bath, side by side, staring at the test. The two lines were unmissable, and Jack punched the air before kissing Angie in delight.

'I am so, so, so happy and I am going to be the *best* dad to that kid,' he declared before rushing to the fridge to get some orange juice for a toast.

'You can have a beer, Jack,' Angie told him.

'No way,' he replied. 'We're in this together, Ange. If you can't drink, I can't drink.'

He poured two glasses of juice and they clinked glasses. He could barely sit still; he was as excited as a little boy on Christmas Day. 'How are you feeling?' he asked.

'Shocked, scared, terrified, happy, wonderful.'

'We're going to be amazing parents, Angie, you'll see. And I'm going to be a hands-on dad, I promise you. You don't have to worry about a thing.'

He abandoned the no alcohol promise after less than two days, but she didn't mind. She enjoyed her pregnancy more than she thought she would, and she realised with surprise that she was one of those women who thrived on being pregnant, who actually did glow with it. She didn't mind going out with friends and sipping a sparkling water, or simply being at home with the growing baby for company, curled up on the sofa and having a little chat with her bump. She even encouraged Jack to go out with his friends when he could.

'When the baby comes, you won't have the opportunity,' she reminded him. 'Go out now, have fun, enjoy yourself.'

He did, but he didn't go back to his old ways. And when Benji arrived, after a labour so quick it had shocked everyone, he was there holding her hand. He was her cheerleader, her biggest fan. What came as even more of a shock to Angie was how much she loved being a mother. She always said she wanted children but in reality, she had no idea if she'd be any good at it. She'd had no siblings to look after, and though Angie loved her mother, she hadn't found her particularly nurturing. So Angie had never considered herself maternal.

But from the moment Benji was born, she was smitten. Every bone in her body was exhausted from the labour but she was awash with new mum hormones, filling her with such joy that when they left her again a few days later, all she could think about was when she could have them back. And they were a team – Angie, Jack and Benji. True to his word, Jack was a hands-on dad from the very beginning, changing nappies, burping him when he was windy and helping her in the middle of the night as she got to grips with feeding.

He was so confident with Benji, easing him into a routine and reassuring Angie whenever she fretted that she was getting it all wrong. He was her rock in those early days and even when he went back to work at the end of his paternity leave, he texted her constantly and rushed home at the end of the day to be with her. She realised that one of the reasons why she loved being a mother so much was because Jack loved being a father and had made it easy for her.

Her plan had been to take nine months' maternity leave and then return to work but she never got round to going back on the pill, and just a few months after Benji was born she was pushing the pram around the park when she realised that her periods still hadn't returned even though she was no longer breastfeeding. She took a swift detour to the supermarket and bought a pregnancy test, telling herself that it was a false alarm and that she had nothing to worry about.

This time the two blue lines brought an avalanche of emotions. Benji was still only a small baby; how on earth would they cope with another newborn so soon? And there'd be no point going back to her job until after baby number two would there? Would her work even want her back after all that time? She knew that she was protected by maternity law but she also knew that what was written on paper wasn't always reflected in reality. Was this the final death knell on her career? She sat on the sofa and cried, scared, overwhelmed and exhausted. And that's where Jack found her when he returned home after receiving her SOS call.

In typical Jack style, he overlooked the negatives and extolled the positives. 'This is great, Angie; we know we want more children so what's the point in waiting? They'll be so close in age; they'll be best friends. Don't worry about your work; they love you; they'll be fine.'

Angie tried to reassure herself that Jack was right. She called her work and, as Jack had predicted, they were great about it. In the end she didn't see much point in going back for a few months so instead she decided to switch off her work brain, enjoy her second pregnancy and immerse herself in the pleasure of full-time motherhood for a bit longer. As her due date drew nearer, she was apprehensive about how she'd cope with having two under two but Jack's confidence and excitement was infectious, overriding her fears and anxieties.

Everything was different from the start with Indie. She had a difficult labour which ended up in an emergency caesarean. After such a straightforward experience with Benji, it had knocked Angie for six because she hadn't been expecting it, assuming her second labour would mirror her first. And Indie's dramatic entrance into the world set the scene for her childhood.

She was difficult from the start. She'd cry all night every night, turning tomato-coloured with indignant rage for reasons only she knew. She screamed if anyone held her apart from Angie, even Jack, who was not used to being rejected and was visibly hurt. They were still living in the Clapham flat at the time and the neighbours had started to complain about the noise. And on top of all of that, she also had a one-year-old who had recently learned to walk and was like a bull in a china shop. Life was chaotic and she felt out of control.

It was no wonder that Jack needed a break. It couldn't have been pleasant for him to come home to their tiny flat, once their haven but now no longer fit for purpose, to be greeted by a screaming toddler, a wailing baby and a stressed-out wife. When he had started finding excuses to go out again after work – a client to entertain, a colleague's birthday – she tried to be understanding but she was disgruntled, stuck in the poky flat caring for two tiny people while he was out having a good time. She couldn't go anywhere on her own, even to meet a friend for lunch, because Indie refused to drink from a bottle, breastfed every hour and loathed Jack.

As her resentment grew, so did his late nights and before she knew it, he was back to rocking up in the early hours of the morning, often just as she'd finally managed to rock Indie back to sleep, and the sound of him coming in would wake her up again. She would turn to him, incandescent with rage but unable to pass him the baby because he was so drunk, and he would simply collapse onto the bed and pass out as if he'd barely even noticed that they were there.

He was always sorry in the morning. It wasn't like the old days when he tried to justify his behaviour. This time he knew he was doing wrong but he couldn't seem to help himself. And she was just too tired and too irritable to deal with it sensibly, so instead she gave him the cold shoulder. It was a difficult few months for them all. In the end she decided to go back to work when Indie was six months old. She knew it was the right thing for her mental health.

On her first day back at work she handed a wailing Indie and clingy Benji over to the new nanny and walked to the train station, crying the whole way. She wasn't sure that she had ever felt so wretched in her entire life. But within a few weeks they had settled into a routine, Indie and Benji had decided the nanny was acceptable and Angie started to feel like herself again. Now that she was finally able to see things clearly, she confronted Jack.

'I turned a blind eye when we were first married but things are different now,' she told him. 'You can't carry on like this. You have a family now, you have responsibilities. We're supposed to be a team and we don't feel like one anymore.'

'I know,' he said, not even trying to defend himself. 'I've been immature and selfish. I was just finding it all so hard and going out and letting off some steam was my way of coping with it. But I've not been fair to you and I know that. It's going to stop, Angie, I promise.'

Throughout his episodes, as she started calling them, she had never thought about leaving him, not seriously anyway. If he was cheating on her then she was sure she would have felt differently but she trusted that he wasn't. This going out with the lads and having a few too many was simply his release, his way of getting away from it all.

They moved out of the flat and bought the house in Greenwich. Finally, they had some more space and it felt like freedom. Indie decided that Jack was her hero, not her enemy. True to his word, Jack stopped behaving unpredictably and pulling all-nighters. And Angie was back in control of her life. She got stuck into work and started seeing her friends. With a new balance she found that she was enjoying motherhood again and after a while it was easy to forget those difficult months and crave pregnancy and newborns. But this time Angie was not going to be caught off guard, she was the one in control.

Ellie and Freddy were planned with military precision and

born by elective caesarean. After each birth she returned to work within six months and when she kissed little Freddy good-bye, handed him over to the nanny and departed for the office, she told Jack, 'I'm done.'

He probably would have been happy to keep going until they'd birthed an entire football team but he knew better than to push her. They had four children, the big family that they wanted, and it was time to close the baby chapter of their life and move forward to the next stage. She was really looking forward to it, too. Now she could focus on her career, knowing that there were no more extended breaks ahead of her, and enjoy watching her four amazing, unique children grow up at the same time. For a while, everything went according to plan – the children bloomed, she got a new job with a bigger firm and life was good. Until it wasn't.

8

'Ah, it's good to be home,' Alan said, as he sank down into his favourite armchair and put a hand over his bloated belly. They had just got back from their Christmas road trip, visiting both sets of parents before returning home to bring in the New Year. As Sophie busied herself with unpacking, putting the washing on and finding innovative ways to store the children's new toys, she glanced at her husband who had dozed off in the chair, sleeping off the enormous amounts of food they had consumed over the previous few days.

It had been a great Christmas, as it always was, full of family time, playing games with the kids and generally chilling out. She was looking forward to a few more days of laziness before Alan returned to work, Tom and Katie returned to school and life went back to its normal pace again. She thought about her New Year's resolutions, which she made every year out of habit but rarely kept to beyond the first couple of weeks. This year they consisted of the usual: lose a stone, drink less and work out what to do about her career.

December was one of Sophie's favourite times of the year, bringing back fond memories from her own childhood. She always went over the top with the decorations and festivities in the house and garden, which thankfully the children were still young enough to love. Helping to organise the school's winter fair had got her into even more of a Christmas spirit this year. She had put her name down for manning the tombola stall and had been in the very thick of it when Jack appeared through the throng and made a beeline for her.

'Christ on a bike, this is hell!' he declared cheerily as he kissed her on the cheek.

'Is this your first Christmas fair?' Sophie shouted at him over the noise and chaos reverberating around the walls of the school hall.

'I braved a few at the kids' previous school but it was nothing like this. This is next level.'

'We do go a bit all out at this school,' Sophie admitted. 'Do you want to play the tombola?'

'Sure, why not.' Jack reached into his pockets and pulled out some change and Sophie handed him the bucket of raffle tickets. As he read the ticket numbers aloud, she handed him his prizes – a bottle of cordial, bubble bath and a soap.

'Congratulations,' she said, giving him a thumbs up.

He replied with a withering look. 'What a haul. I'd better go round up the kids: they've scattered like sheep without a shepherd. See you later?'

She nodded and got on with serving the next tombola hopeful. As she glanced up, she saw Jack being swallowed up by the crowds again. He had been doing the school runs for three months now and they'd fallen into a pattern of walking together most days. He didn't seem to be showing any signs of returning to work full-time and she suspected he was enjoying himself.

She had grown fond of him and now she looked forward to seeing him every day, feeling disappointed if she missed him. The children had grown accustomed to it too and now they automatically paused outside the neighbours' house and waited for them to emerge. The friendship between Tom, Katie, Ellie and Freddy seemed stronger than ever.

Despite her initial reservations about Jack, she had discovered that he was easy to talk to, funny and refreshingly self-deprecating. She could understand why Angie joked that she had five children, not four. She sensed that he had been acting the fool for so long that he didn't know any different but underneath it all he was actually incredibly thoughtful. They talked about all sorts of things on their walks to school. Sometimes they were so engrossed that they kept going, even after they'd dropped the kids off. They would pick up a coffee and head for the nearest park, doing a couple of circuits until Jack had to go and do some work. Most of their subjects were light but as the weeks went by and the trust between them grew, they became more involved. Recently they'd shared what it felt like to be married to the breadwinner and Jack had made a joke of it, but she suspected that it affected him more than he let on.

'I'm lucky,' he told her, 'I get to stay in a job I love without worrying about earning more money or climbing the career ladder. And I've had the opportunity to work reduced hours so that I can be around more for my family. How many men get to say that?'

'That's true,' she agreed.

'I'm lucky,' he said again, and she wondered whether it was for her sake or his. It wasn't that he resented having more parental responsibility because she could tell that he loved it, but she sensed that Angie's career had always been more successful and that as much as he tried not to let it bother him, it affected his self-worth.

It wasn't just Sophie who was enjoying Jack either. The other mums had got used to seeing him at the gates now and he always seemed to gather a flock of women around him whenever he was waiting to pick up Ellie and Freddy after school. On their walk back home together he would regale her with stories he'd heard in the playground.

'Apparently Frankie's mum has hired an amazing private tutor but won't give anyone else his number because she wants to keep him all to herself,' he told her gleefully.

'You're more of a gossip than me,' she said, one eyebrow raised.

'I love a bit of school gate drama,' he confessed. 'It's more exciting than EastEnders.'

Sophie wondered whether Jack would ever want to go back to his old working pattern and how much Angie must be earning that they could afford it. She suspected it was well into six figures and tried not to wince when she looked at her own accounts spreadsheet and saw that she'd made £2,610 in the last financial year.

But despite her growing friendship with Jack, it was still Angie who she looked forward to seeing at the weekend. Seven months after the storm, she had finally come round to tell her that they had chosen a contractor who was repairing the fence the following week.

'Tom and Katie will be gutted,' Sophie said ruefully.

'Ellie and Freddy too. But it can't stay like that forever.' Angie paused. 'Perhaps we could consider getting a gate put in? No pressure at all, I don't want to invade your privacy.'

Sophie loved it. 'It's a brilliant idea!' she declared. 'Let's do it!'

When she excitedly told Alan about their newly hatched plan, he rolled his eyes but said nothing. A week later the gate was installed, much to the children's delight. They used the gate most days now. And it wasn't just for their benefit either – a couple of Saturdays before Christmas, Angie had snuck round after the children had gone to bed, appearing at the back door with a mischievous look on her face. Sophie had suspected she was up to no good.

'What is it?' she asked, opening the door for Angie, who grinned and fished around in her pocket, pulling out a spliff.

'Angie! I didn't know you were into wacky-baccy!'

'I don't think they call it that anymore, darling,' Angie replied. 'Anyway, it's not mine, well not really anyway. Someone gave it to me and I thought it would be a shame to waste it.'

Sophie was dubious. 'I haven't smoked since I was a teenager.'

'Come on, just this once, it'll be fun.'

'It's bloody freezing outside, Ange.'

'Oh, come *on*! Live a little!'

Sophie looked at Angie's face, daring her to be a bit naughty, and she sighed and grabbed her coat. Outside they huddled together, taking it in turns to share the spliff.

'Didn't Jack fancy it?' Sophie asked, taking a puff and trying not to cough.

'Oh God no, Jack doesn't touch anything he can't drink.'

'Did you dabble when you were younger?'

Angie looked thoughtful. 'Not as a teenager, or at university actually. To be honest, I was a bit of a square. But just before I met Jack, I went out with someone for a few months who liked a smoke after work so I tried it a few times then. I didn't like it much – or him.'

'Why not?'

'Well, the guy was boring. And the weed made me feel out of control, which I hated, but I'm in the mood to give it another go this evening, seeing as I'm in much better company.'

The high from the drugs hit Sophie and she had to sit down on one of the freezing cold patio chairs. Angie perched delicately on the chair next to her.

'So where did it come from anyway?'

'A rather high-profile client who was being prosecuted for an excessive speeding offence found it in his pocket before his hearing and gave it to me to get rid of for him. I completely forgot and it was only when I was looking for something earlier that I discovered it.'

'Ooooh, who's the client?'

'I can't tell you that.'

'Oh go on! Go on, go on, go on!'

'No!' Angie said, laughing.

'Is he an actor?'

'No.'

'Musician?'

'No!'

'Footballer?'

'Stop it, Sophie!'

'He is!' Sophie said triumphantly. 'He's a footballer.'

'I'm not telling you anything.'

'Fine,' Sophie said, starting to feel giggly. 'You're a bit of a rebel though, Angie Taylor.'

'Not normally,' she replied. 'Maybe I'm having a midlife crisis.'

'You're not going to buy a Porsche, are you?'

'Can you imagine,' Angie said, her voice rising a few notches, 'trying to cram four children into a Porsche?'

'Benji and Indie would have to sit on the roof,' Sophie said, feeling the hysteria rising inside her at the image.

'Freddy could go in the boot!' Angie said and they dissolved into uncontrollable giggles. Soon they were both bent double, tears rolling down their faces.

'Bloody hell, the state of you,' Alan said, standing over them with an amused look on his face. They'd been laughing so hard that they hadn't even heard him coming outside.

'Al, come and join us!' Sophie said, recovering for a brief moment before she started laughing again.

'You're all right, Soph love, I think I'll leave you to it,' he said and handed them a packet of crisps and some chocolate. 'Thought you might want these for the munchies.'

'Oh, Alan, you're a hero,' Angie said, grabbing the crisps and opening them while Sophie took the chocolate.

'Enjoy, ladies,' Alan said, rubbing his hands together in the cold, 'I'm going back inside.'

After he'd shut the door, Angie turned to Sophie, stuffing crisps into her mouth. Sophie wasn't sure she'd ever seen her eat junk food before. 'He's a keeper, that Alan,' she said.

'He really is,' Sophie replied, smiling wistfully. Then she added, 'So's Jack.'

She saw Angie's face cloud over before she shrugged and ate another handful of crisps.

'Everything okay, Ange?' she asked.

'Yes, yes, yes,' Angie said. 'Now pass me that spliff.'

They stayed outside for forty-five minutes, until they could no longer feel their hands or feet. Eventually, they reluctantly called it a night. As they stood up to go in, rocking a little unsteadily, Sophie reached over and gave Angie a hug.

'Night, Ange,' she said.

'Night, darling,' Angie replied.

It was amazing, Sophie thought afterwards, how you could go for years without knowing somebody and then they came into your life and you wondered how you survived without them for so long. She remembered how quickly she had dismissed the Taylors as 'not our type of people' but now, just a few months later, life didn't feel right if she didn't see them most days.

They were having a New Year's Eve party together that evening and she was looking forward to letting her hair down. Tom and Katie were fizzing with excitement and had dashed off to select which of their new toys to show Ellie and Freddy. Sophie left Alan to doze a little longer while she went upstairs to get ready. After a quick shower, she stood in front of her wardrobe in her towel and considered her options. Her usual going out clothes, which were normally perfectly adequate, suddenly looked frumpy and boring. She suspected that Angie would be looking even more glamorous than usual this evening, given the occasion.

As she observed her clothes with a new-found distaste, she remembered the parcel that Angie had given her on Christmas Eve, before she had left to visit Jack's family.

'It's for New Year's Eve,' Angie had said, giving her a hug and rushing off to supervise the children's packing.

Sophie ran downstairs and found the present, alone under the tree where it had been abandoned in her own dash to get ready for their trip. Glancing at Alan, who was now snoring, she picked it up and took it back upstairs with her. Sitting on the bed, she ripped open the perfectly wrapped gift and gasped when she saw what was inside.

It was a beautiful silk gathered dress, with tones of black and bright blue running through it. She slipped it on and looked at herself in the mirror, running her hands down the dress and feeling the smoothness of it against her skin. It fit perfectly. She thought of the candle and chocolates she had given Angie for Christmas and felt horribly embarrassed, but it didn't last. How could she feel bad when she had a beautiful dress like this? She blow-dried her hair and did her make-up while the children, who had drifted into the bedroom, lay on her bed waiting for her. When she was ready the three of them made their way downstairs to wake up Alan.

'What the...?' Alan spluttered as Tom and Katie launched themselves at him full pelt. Then he spotted Sophie and let out a low whistle.

'Wow, looking good there, Mrs B,' he said. She grinned and spun around in a little circle.

'Stunning,' he said, looking at her in admiration. 'Right, I'd better up my game.'

He stood up and climbed the stairs, emerging twenty minutes later wearing his best shirt and a smart pair of jeans. She could smell the aftershave on him. This was a big effort for Alan and she wolf-whistled at him. 'Looking mighty fine there, Al.'

'I can't let the side down, not with you looking like that,' he told Sophie, and then glanced at his watch. 'Right, we'd better be off.'

They let themselves out of the back door and through the gate into Angie and Jack's garden. Tom and Katie ran on ahead, desperate to go inside and see their friends after a forced separation over Christmas, but Alan paused and turned to Sophie.

'I love you, Soph, you're something special.'

She gave him a quick kiss. 'You're not too bad yourself.'

Inside the party was already in full flow. Ellie had got a karaoke machine for Christmas and Jack was singing 'Living on a Prayer' at the top of his voice.

'Brennans!' he shouted with delight when he saw them, coming over to shake Alan's hand effusively and give Sophie a hug. 'Happy Christmas and all that.'

'Where's Angie?' Sophie asked.

'Upstairs getting ready, she'll be down in a minute. Alan mate, what's your tune?'

Jack and Alan commandeered the karaoke machine again and Sophie went upstairs to find Angie. As she knocked softly on the bedroom door it opened slightly and she saw Angie inside, looking ridiculously beautiful in a long red dress, her dark hair loose around her.

She turned and clasped her hands together in delight when she saw Sophie. 'You look incredible, I knew that dress would suit you,' she said.

'I'm mortified,' Sophie told her. 'It must have cost a fortune. My present to you was rubbish in comparison.'

'Nonsense,' Angie insisted, 'I love that candle.'

'I brought you some champagne,' Sophie said, handing a glass over to Angie, who took it gratefully and clinked glasses with Sophie.

'To a new year,' she said.

'To friendships,' Sophie replied and they both took a sip.

'How was your Christmas?' Angie asked.

'Lovely. The usual eating too much chocolate, playing board games and watching the Strictly Christmas Special. How about you?'

'Fabulous. It's always a hoot when we spend Christmas with Jack's family. They managed to get four of the five siblings together – one's in Australia – and there were twelve children all together. Jack's mum put on this vast spread. I don't know how she did it. The children were in heaven: they love their older cousins. I don't think they wanted to come home.'

'Muuuuuum, I need a lift to Amber's house! Now!' came a shout from downstairs.

Angie sighed. 'Indie's having a sleepover at her friend's,' she explained.

'How's she getting on at school?'

'Oh fine, she's got a good group of girlfriends and there's some boy she's being all coy about. I'm not sure how much she's actually learning, but she's having fun.'

'Jack certainly seems to be enjoying the school runs.'

'I know. I must say, if you'd told me at the beginning of the year that Jack would be a virtual house husband, I'd have told you to stop being so ridiculous. Life is unpredictable, isn't it?'

For a moment Angie looked lost, completely absorbed in her own thoughts.

'Are you okay, Ange?' Sophie asked, waving a hand in front of her.

Angie recovered and smiled at Sophie. 'Oh yes, I'm absolutely fine. Now let's get Indie off to her friend's house so we can all relax and get the party started. We can't spend all evening hiding away in the bedroom with dresses this fabulous on.'

Sophie raised her glass again. 'Amen to that.'

As they walked down the stairs, listening to the deafening sounds of Jack and Alan belting out 'Get The Party Started', she turned to Angie and said, 'I think they already have.'

9

Angie sat on the cold, hard garden bench, shivering. Despite the cold February weather, she wasn't wearing a coat and she pulled the top of her turtleneck jumper up over her mouth and hid her hands in the long sleeves. She stared at the closed gate and wished that she was in a children's book and could walk through it into a secret garden, another world where life was much simpler. Real life seemed to have become horribly tangled. She started when the gate flew open and Sophie marched through it, clutching a soft toy.

'Bloody hell, Angie, you scared the life out of me,' she said, putting a hand to her heart. 'I was just coming round to drop off Freddy's dinosaur, he left it at ours. What are you doing out here?'

Angie barely acknowledged her.

'What's the matter?' Sophie asked, walking over to the bench and sitting down beside her.

'I'm late,' she said.

'Late for what?' Sophie was confused.

'*Late*, late,' she said, looking pointedly at Sophie and waiting for the penny to drop.

'Oh,' Sophie said, cuddling the dinosaur close to her for warmth.

'Oh indeed.'

'I take it this is not good news?' Sophie asked tentatively.

'Definitely not good news,' Angie confirmed.

'Okay, so have you done a test?'

'No,' Angie replied.

Sophie regarded her. 'Isn't that something that you should do?' she asked carefully.

'Yes.'

'I've got one in the bathroom,' Sophie said, jumping up, 'I'll go and get it now.'

'Why've you got a pregnancy test in the bathroom?'

Sophie looked down. 'Me and Alan, we've been trying for a third but it's not happening.'

'Oh, Sophie.' Angie felt even more awful. 'I'm sorry. Forget I said anything.'

'Nonsense,' Sophie said, looking up again and plastering a bright smile on her face. 'Your issue is my issue and we'll face it together. Now get yourself back inside and warmed up and I'll be over in a jiffy. Where are the brood?'

'Jack, Ellie and the boys are at football and Indie's in her room, not to be disturbed.'

'Right you are, now's our chance.'

Sophie stood up and marched back through the gate while Angie headed inside, wondering how she had ended up here. She'd been walking home from the tube station on Friday evening and had popped into the newsagents to buy a bottle of red wine when she saw some tampons on the shelf. She stared at them. Hadn't her period been due on Monday? She quickly grabbed her diary from her bag and opened it up. There it was: a little 'p' marked in pencil which denoted the start date of her period each month. Angie didn't like being unprepared.

How on earth had she missed this? She'd been so busy at work and there had been some trouble at school, with Freddy getting whacked by a ball and having to go to A&E and Indie giving a teacher some lip, and she'd forgotten all about her menstrual cycle. Angie's periods were like clockwork and she fell pregnant easily, so the odds were not in her favour. She did not want another baby. She was forty-two years old and had her hands plenty full enough with four children and a demanding job. There was no way she wanted to go back to sleepless nights and nappies. These were all very valid reasons, she told herself. But the real issue was that her marriage was still in recovery mode and this would destroy it for good.

Jack's last episode had come completely out of the blue. She had searched over and over again for a reason, something to explain why he did it, but the only one she came back to each time was that he was bored of playing husband and father and he needed a thrill, a break from the monotony. But this time was different because he went a step further.

They were still living in Greenwich at the time. She had been doing the laundry one Saturday morning, turning his jeans inside out before putting them in the machine, when she saw something pink poking out of one of the pockets. She hooked her finger through it and pulled it out, dropping it in horror when she realised what it was. The offending item, a hot pink thong, fell to the floor. She stared at it in disbelief. What did this mean? Had he been to a strip club? Was he sleeping with someone else? The walls were closing in around her as the realisation sunk in that, regardless of the answer, this was not okay. And then she felt something else – fury. Pushing the thong into her own jeans pocket with disgust, she strode into the living room where Jack was watching TV with the children.

'Jack, a word,' she said, beckoning him to follow her upstairs. When they got to their bedroom, she closed the door and turned to face him, pulling the thong from her pocket and waving it at him.

His face paled. 'Angie, I can explain.'

'Please do.' She could almost see the cogs turning in his head as he tried to work out what to say, how much to confess. He was so easy to read. 'You need to tell me the truth, Jack, because you know I'm going to find out anyway.'

He sank down onto the bed, his head in his hands.

'The *truth*, Jack,' she said again.

'Nothing happened,' he began. Her heart soared with relief for a moment before she realised that there was still no real happy ending to this situation.

'*Something* clearly happened,' she said.

'It was when I went out for work drinks on Thursday. A few of the boys went on to a late bar afterwards and we got talking to these girls. They invited us back to one of their flats for a nightcap and I was drunk and stupid, so I went along with the rest of them.'

Jack paused, looking at Angie pleadingly. 'We carried on drinking and then this girl started making passes at me. She kissed me and I sobered up pretty quickly, made my excuses and left. As I was leaving, she gave me her number and I threw it into a bin on the way home. I didn't even realise she'd put that in my pocket. We were both pretty wasted.'

Angie studied her husband carefully. Jack could be a juvenile prick but she didn't think he was capable of lying to her. She had the truth. But what did she do with it now?

'Why is it so hard?' she asked him. 'Being married to me? Being a father to our children? Why isn't that enough for you? You chose this life; we didn't force it on you.'

'It is enough, Angie,' he insisted, 'it *is* enough. I love you all so much. I don't know what's wrong with me, I don't. I'll get some help, I promise.'

'I've been patient over the years, Jack. I've forgiven you when you've gone out and pretended you didn't have a wife and children waiting for you at home. When you haven't even bothered to tell me if or when you were coming back. I've resented it, but I've done it.'

'I know, Angie, I'm sorry. I don't know what to say.'

She hated him at that moment, with his ridiculous little hangdog eyes. Why had she thought she was any different to the other girls whose hearts he had broken? Why had she thought she was better than them? In the end, she was the fool. She should never have married him; she'd been right about him from the start. Once Jack the jock, always Jack the jock.

'You need to leave,' she told him, glaring at him. 'I don't want you in this house.'

'Please, Angie...'

'You need to leave.'

'But nothing happened,' Jack insisted. 'I would never cheat on you.'

'But you nearly did. And it's only a matter of time before you do.'

'No!' Jack said, standing up and moving towards her. 'No, you've got it wrong.'

Angie held up her hands to warn him from coming any closer. 'You need to leave.'

He nodded, his face weary with resignation, knowing that there was no point in arguing with Angie when she had made her mind up. 'I'll go to Sam's,' he said. Sam was his brother and he owned a flat in east London. 'What will you tell the kids?'

'I'll work something out. I want you gone by the end of the day.'

She turned and left, forcing herself to summon a smile and making her way downstairs to check on the children, who were still watching TV, oblivious to the fact that their parents' marriage had been unravelling a few metres above their heads. An hour later Jack was gone.

She didn't tell a soul what had happened, not her mother, not her closest friends. She had never been one to air dirty laundry in public but the truth was that she was humiliated. The thought of people knowing that her husband had gone off to some poky flat to flirt with a cheap bimbo instead of coming home to his family mortified her. As the days passed, she kept it to herself, acting as though everything was perfectly fine while inside, she was breaking apart.

But, as angry as she was with Jack for making a fool of her, she still couldn't let him go. Yet again, she began to rationalise his behaviour and blame herself for overreacting.

After four days, the children were constantly asking where he was, and while it was easy enough to fool the younger two, Indie and Benji weren't stupid.

'What's going on, Mum?' Indie asked.

'Nothing for you to worry about,' she replied, putting an arm around her daughter.

'Are you and Dad getting divorced?'

'No, no, nothing like that, please don't think that. He's just helping Uncle Sam with something.'

'Has Dad done something wrong?' Benji asked.

'No, Benji, Dad's done nothing wrong.'

Angie couldn't bear it any longer. That night she called Jack and told him to come home. He turned up on the doorstep so quickly she almost suspected him of being outside the whole time. She opened the door and let him back into the house.

'I'm not sure what our future holds yet but we owe it to the children to try to work through this,' she said firmly, in a tone that brooked no argument. 'If it happens again, I'm leaving you.' He nodded his agreement, not even trying to mitigate his behaviour.

After that he did everything he could to make things right, knowing that this time he had almost lost her for good. For her part, she acted normally in front of the children and other people, putting on an almost Oscar winning performance of the happy wife. But behind closed doors she wasn't ready to forgive him and she was unable to muster any warmth towards him, often giving him the cold shoulder. He didn't complain once.

They shared a bed but they didn't touch or even say goodnight to each other. For weeks they lived like cellmates in that bedroom, trapped in the prison of their unhappy marriage, but as time went on it became too exhausting to lead two separate lives and gradually, they began to blur into one. She softened a bit at the edges, then a bit more, as the familiarity and easiness to their relationship start to return bit by bit. He said something funny and she instinctively laughed before she remembered that she was angry with him. He put a hand on the small of her back and she didn't immediately flinch. One night he curled up behind her in bed and put his arm around her, and she relaxed into him. A week after that, they had sex for the first time in months.

Eventually she considered that his punishment had been served and knew that the only way they were going to move forward was if she truly forgave him. But she couldn't forget.

'Every time I go into that laundry room I see those disgusting pink knickers on the floor,' she told him one evening.

'What can I do, Angie? How can I make this better?'

'I think we need to move house. And not just house, we need a fresh start, a clean break. I think we should move somewhere completely new. We've been talking about how we need more space and now's our opportunity.'

'Okay. Anywhere in mind?'

'How about Finchley? Near my mum.'

'Yes.'

It was that simple, no debate, no arguments. He was so eager to please her that he probably would have agreed to move to Antarctica. She had no doubt that he loved her, that he needed her and the children. But it was like he had two different identities – the adoring husband and father who lived for his family and the thoughtless lad wishing he was still captain of the football team, chatting up girls in the nightclub and getting a kebab on the way home. She had married one but the other had snuck into the bargain.

They put the house on the market two weeks later. Their friends were shocked by the suddenness, but Angie had her solid explanation ready and everyone accepted it without suspicion. Freddy and Ellie saw it as a great adventure but Benji was distraught and Indie was furious. However, Angie stood by her decision and Jack backed her up, championing the move and reasoning with Benji and Indie, encouraging them to consider the positives.

When they moved, it was Jack who had kept them going with his enthusiasm, who made them all laugh and held them together during the stressful months of the refurbishment. And slowly, at their own paces, they had all begun to embrace their new life.

Benji and Indie had settled in at school and made new friends, Ellie and Freddy bonded with Tom and Katie, Jack got involved in the local community, and Angie found Sophie, who was now striding back down the garden.

'Got the test,' she mouthed as she came in through the back door, patting her pocket and looking around her furtively in case anyone was watching.

'I'm not sure I want to know,' Angie replied.

'Come on, Angie, this isn't like you. The sooner you know, the sooner you can deal with it.'

'Can we at least have a cup of tea first?'

'Okay,' Sophie agreed, switching on the kettle and moving around Angie's kitchen with a familiar ease. She made them both a drink and sat down next to Angie.

'Do you want to talk about it?' she asked.

'No,' Angie replied. Then she added, 'Yes.'

'How are you feeling about it all?'

'I feel really bad talking to you about this, Sophie. I had no idea that you were trying.'

'Forget about that,' Sophie waved Angie's concern away. 'This is about you.'

Angie looked at Sophie's friendly, open face and desperately wanted to confide in her. But just as she was on the cusp of blurting it all out, she stopped herself. She just couldn't do it.

'I love my children but I don't want another one,' she said simply instead. 'Four is plenty, five is too many. And I feel too old to go back to babies.'

'What do you think Jack would say?'

'Oh, he'd be delighted. Which is why he mustn't know about this until we know what's what.'

'Of course,' Sophie agreed. She stood up and held out her hand. 'Let's get this done.'

Angie took it. Sophie was right, she had to find out one way or another, even if she didn't want to know. Together they made their way quietly up to the loft room and Sophie waited for her on the bed while she went into the en suite. She came back clutching the test, sat next to Sophie and waited. After a few minutes, the result was pretty clear to them both. It was negative.

Sophie let herself back into the house and made herself a cup of tea. It was unusually quiet because Alan had taken Tom and

Katie to the park and she had the place to herself for a little while longer. She sank down onto the sofa and took a small sip of her scalding tea, craving the comfort that it usually brought her. She was feeling a little flat.

When Angie had told her that she might be pregnant, her first reaction had been jealousy. Sophie and Alan had decided to try for another baby last year but after months of 'planned fun' as Alan liked to call it, nothing was happening and she was starting to think that it probably wouldn't.

Yet here Angie was, not even trying for another baby – not even *wanting* one – having a pregnancy scare. But when she'd seen the distraught look on Angie's face, her initial envy had vanished and she had felt sorry for her. She knew how hectic Angie's life was already and could see how throwing a new baby into the mix might be the thing that tipped them over the edge.

Still, it had been a shock to see Angie so vulnerable, so unsure of herself. It was a side of her that Sophie hadn't seen before and she had immediately gone into mother-hen mode, taking control of the situation and clucking over her like she did with her own children. Under normal circumstances, Angie probably would have got irritated with her but she'd actually seemed relieved that Sophie was ordering her about. It had all been quite strange.

And after all the drama, the test had been negative anyway. Sophie was relieved for Angie but the whole experience had left her feeling low. Her own period had arrived that day with a vengeance, bringing with it the monthly wave of disappoint- ment and feelings of failure. She wanted to curl up on the sofa and feel sorry for herself. What was she any good at, really, she wondered. She had no career to speak of; she couldn't make babies. Was she even a good mother? Tom and Katie were happy children, she knew that, but she looked at Angie's big, bustling, unique family and felt that there was something wonderfully special about them.

Perhaps that was why she'd got a bee in her bonnet about having a third child. When she had first broached the idea with Alan, he'd looked at her in surprise.

'Another Brennan baby, huh? What's brought this on?'

'I don't know. The kids are growing up so fast, both of them are at school now, they don't need me in the way they used to. Maybe it's empty nest syndrome but I'm feeling broody.'

'Another baby is a big thing though, Soph. We've finally said goodbye to years of sleepless nights, nappies, toddler tantrums. Do we really want to go back to the beginning and start all over again? And we're no spring chickens anymore either. I'm not saying no, I'm just saying let's not rush into anything, we should think about it for a while.'

She agreed but the idea had lingered, a feeling of need – or at least want – that she couldn't shake off and a few weeks later she brought it up again.

'I know it might not happen for us, Alan. It wasn't plain sailing getting pregnant with Tom and Katie, but can we give it a go? Just let fate take its course?'

Alan had agreed, as she knew he would, but fate seemed to have decided that another baby wasn't in their future after all. And with two happy, healthy children she wasn't prepared to put them through the emotional and financial turmoil of fertility treatment. She simply had to accept that it wasn't meant to be, that she had so much in her life already to be thankful for, and most of the time she was okay with that. But today had hit her hard.

It's just a blip, she told herself, *a perfectly natural reaction to Angie's situation, and I'll get over it soon enough.* Alan would be back with the kids any minute now and perhaps they could all go out for lunch together, or maybe get last-minute tickets to the cinema. There was a new Disney film out that Katie had been wanting to see. Once she was distracted, she'd be absolutely fine again. But just for a little while longer, she sat alone on the sofa, drinking her tea, and allowed herself to imagine what could have been.

10

Alan zipped up his holdall and looked at Sophie, who was sitting on the bed watching him.

'I'll only be gone a few days,' he said.

'Take as much time as you need.'

Alan's mum had fallen and broken her hip, and because his dad wasn't in good health either, Alan had decided to go and stay with them for a few nights to help out.

'Sorry to abandon my cowgirl,' he said ruefully.

Sophie snorted. The children's school was holding a barn dance fundraiser for parents that evening and they'd booked a babysitter weeks ago so that they could enjoy a rare night out together. They'd even ordered cowboy boots and hats online and had been having a hoot putting them on and gleefully 'yee-hawing' around the house, much to the embarrassment of the kids.

'I'm sure I'll find me a lonesome cowboy to dance with,' she told him.

'As long as he doesn't sweep you off your feet.'

'As if! Unless he's Brad Pitt circa *Legends of the Fall*, in which case I need to tell you that I will be running off to Montana with him to live in a tipi.'

'Fair play to you, love. Even I wouldn't turn down Brad Pitt.'

They headed downstairs so that Alan could say goodbye to Tom and Katie, who had been making 'get well soon' cards for their granny. The kitchen table was covered in a sheen of glitter and torn up bits of paper and the children proudly handed their offerings to Alan. He hugged them both and they followed him outside and watched as he climbed into his van and, with a toot of his horn, disappeared down the road. Sophie couldn't remember the last time she'd spent a night without Alan and felt strangely bereft. At least she had the barn dance to look forward to.

'Tom, Katie, I'm going upstairs to get ready for this evening,' she told them. 'Do you want to come up and keep me company?'

The children grabbed their iPads and followed her upstairs and into the bedroom, where they flung themselves onto the bed to play games while Sophie hunted around for the hair straighteners. Thirty minutes later she was ready to go.

'You look cool, Mum,' Tom said, looking up and observing her plaid shirt, jeans, hat and cowboy boots ensemble. She gave him a thumbs up, sprayed herself liberally with perfume and headed downstairs to let the babysitter in. Once she had briefed the sitter and said goodbye to the children, she let herself out of the back door and through the gate into Angie and Jack's garden so that they could walk to the dance together.

'Howdy, pardner!' she called to Jack as she entered the kitchen and saw him leaning up against a kitchen cupboard drinking a beer. He tipped his hat when he saw her and gave her a wink. Her stomach gave an involuntary little flip. He may not be her cup of tea, as she kept telling everyone, but he was a bloody good-looking man and he looked particularly sexy in his cowboy get-up. She looked away quickly and said loudly, 'Angie getting ready?'

'Afraid not. Angie's not feeling very well so she's gone to bed and sends her apologies. It's just a cold but she's run-down which has made it worse. Where's Alan?'

'Gone up to his parents for a few days: his mum had a fall. She's fine but he wants to help.'

'I guess it's just you and me then, pardner.'

'I guess it is.'

Jack drained his beer. 'Let's go,' he said. Hollering goodbye to Angie and the children, they let themselves out of the front door and headed down the road. It was a brisk evening and she shivered a little bit.

'Do you want my scarf?' Jack offered, glancing at her.

'No, you're all right,' she said.

'Honestly, it's fine.' He unravelled his scarf and turned to her, wrapping it carefully around her neck. She smelt his aftershave on it and started to feel giddy. What on earth was wrong with her this evening? Perhaps it was just the anticipation of a night out.

When they arrived at the school, she gave a little gasp of pleasure. The hall had been decked out wonderfully. There was bunting and lights hanging from the ceiling and a band was setting up on the stage, which was furnished with hay and a wagon wheel. In one corner a makeshift bar had been set up and Jack went off to get them a couple of beers, while Sophie looked around, marvelling at how they had managed to make the boring old school hall look so atmospheric.

Being on the PTA committee, she knew a lot of people and it was impossible to go from one side of the hall to the other without bumping into someone who wanted to chat. It was a good forty-five minutes before she managed to break away and her eyes searched the hall, looking for Jack to make sure that he was okay. She spotted him in the corner, surrounded by a group of Year Three mums who looked like they were rounding in on him. She caught his eye, and he mouthed 'help me' at her.

Chuckling to herself, she made her way over to him. 'Sorry, ladies, but this cowboy promised me a dance,' she said, whisking him off to the dance floor.

'Thanks, Sophie, I didn't think I'd ever get away,' he said. 'Nice bunch of ladies but pretty intense. One actually asked me whether me and my wife practised swinging and I'm not entirely sure if it was a joke or not.'

Sophie roared with delight, and then switched her focus to the instructions being barked out by the line dance teacher. They were both terrible dancers and they giggled at each other as they attempted to follow the instructions and failed miserably.

'Another beer?' Jack suggested, when the song finally finished.

'I definitely need one after that ordeal,' Sophie agreed. As he disappeared through the crowds towards the bar, Sophie spotted Eve walking towards her and gave her a grin.

'Having fun?' she asked.

'Yes, but more to the point, are *you* having fun?' Eve replied, looking at her pointedly.

'What are you on about?'

'Just saying that Jack's looking *Brokeback Mountain* hot tonight.'

'Don't be daft, we're neighbours. His wife is a good friend of mine if you remember?'

'Oh, calm down, I'm only messing,' Eve said, giving her a nudge. 'I'm just saying, he's not looking too shabby, is he? Lucky Angie.'

Sophie had to agree, although she couldn't imagine ever being married to someone as good-looking and charming as

Jack. After he returned with their beers, Eve whisked him off for a dance and she stood by the side and watched them. Eve was much better at dancing than Sophie and did a good job of following the dance moves and helping Jack to keep up too.

As she sipped her beer, Sophie thought about Alan. How long had it been since they had been out together, just the two of them, without the kids? She couldn't even remember. Most evenings they just watched TV and went to bed. Perhaps she should suggest a night out. It was just what they needed after the last few months, a bit of fun. She knew that she'd become a bit fixated on having another baby even after she promised Alan that she wouldn't. And they were in danger of turning into a boring old married couple, if they hadn't done already. She'd book something as soon as he got back from his parents, she decided. Stifling a yawn, she looked at her empty beer bottle and decided to call it a night. She grabbed her coat and bag and went to tell Jack she was leaving.

'Wait, I'll come with you,' he said.

'No, you stay a little longer, have fun,' she urged him.

'Will you be okay, walking home on your own?'

'I'll be fine, Jack, honestly.'

He doffed his hat at her and then turned away to continue dancing with one of the Year Three mums who had commandeered him. With a final glance at the dance floor, Sophie put her coat on and made her way out of the school hall into the cold night air.

Angie sat in bed, playing absent-mindedly with her phone before throwing it onto the duvet with a sigh. She thought of Jack at the barn dance and felt guilty that she'd feigned illness to get out of going with him, but the truth was that she just wasn't in the mood. She couldn't be bothered to make polite conversation with people she didn't know or care about, or to pretend that she and Jack were the perfect couple. Recently she had found that she had little energy for anything anymore and she wondered what had happened to her.

Angie had never wallowed in bed in her life. She was a fighter – she got up, put her warpaint on and took on the world. But at the moment all she wanted to do was crawl under the duvet and hide away. Which was tricky when there was a six-year-old trying to sail a remote-control boat in the bath and a nine-year-old arguing with her sister over a hairband. Angie tried to block out the noise. She blinked a few times, willing tears to come so that they might provide her with some emotional release. But, unfortunately, Angie didn't cry either.

Was this some sort of PTSD? Was it a delayed reaction to years of Jack making her feel insecure? Was it guilt that she was somehow to blame? Or was it just the sheer relentlessness of life, of juggling a career with four children and feeling like the wheels might fall off at any moment? She had powered through for so long, telling herself and anyone who would listen that she was fine, because fine was all she knew how to be. But what if she wasn't fine after all?

It was the pregnancy scare that had been her final undoing. The horror at the prospect of being pregnant, the knowledge that her marriage probably wouldn't survive it had made her realise how precarious this life she had built was. It could collapse at any moment and she'd be powerless to stop it. And underneath it all was the niggling fear that it was her fault. If she had been a better wife to Jack, if she was more doting, if she hadn't put her career first, perhaps things would have been different for them.

She had thrown herself into work because it gave her back her identity. But she'd been hiding behind it for too long, letting it mask the cracks that were appearing at home. She needed to find a way to recalibrate, to get the balance right between work, family and marriage. If one pillar toppled, the whole tower came tumbling down.

As the screaming between her two daughters escalated on the other side of the door, she threw the covers aside in frustration.

'Indie! Ellie! Stop that right now,' she yelled, yanking open the bedroom door and squaring off with the girls who were standing in the hallway. Indie was clutching a piece of Ellie's hair in her tightly shut fist. The girls stopped what they were doing and looked at her in surprise. She rarely shouted at the children.

Indie took in her dishevelled hair and dressing gown. 'What's up, Mum? Is it your period?'

'No it's not my period, it's you two screaming at each other outside my bedroom door.'

'Sorry, Mum.' Ellie looked sheepish.

'Give me that hairband,' Angie said, yanking it from Indie's hand. The children followed her, glancing at each other, as she marched down the stairs and threw it into the kitchen bin.

'Why'd you do that?' Indie demanded, looking horrified.

'Because I'm fed up of hearing you two bickering over things. So the new rule is, if you can't share it, I'm throwing it away.'

'Oh great, Mum, brilliant parenting technique,' Indie said, her temper flaring to match her mother's.

Angie was in the mood for a full-on barney and was about to fire back when Ellie, ever the peacemaker, said: 'Come on, Indie, let's put a film on before bed.'

With a final, resentful glare at her mother, Indie relented and followed her little sister to the den. Angie poured herself a glass of red wine and collapsed onto a kitchen chair. This was the problem, she thought, she simply didn't have time to think any more; she was constantly firefighting. And now she had an actual moment of peace to herself she felt restless, like she'd completely forgotten how to relax. She automatically reached for her laptop, opened up her work emails and started making her way through them. She was still there at 11pm when Jack got home, and he started when he saw her.

'Christ, Ange, you scared me, I thought you'd be in bed. How are you feeling?'

'Much better,' Angie lied. 'How was your evening?'

'Quite fun in the end,' Jack said, pouring a glass of water and coming to sit next to her. 'I was hopeless at the dancing but we all had a laugh.'

'Did you walk back with Sophie?'

'No she left early; she had to get back for the babysitter.'

Angie had a brief moment of panic at the thought of Jack alone with a bunch of women and no close allies to report back on his behaviour but she quickly put the thought out of her mind. She had to trust him, she just had to, because if she didn't then their marriage really was over and she simply couldn't accept that. Not after everything they'd been through.

'You coming to bed?' Jack asked.

'In a minute,' she replied, glancing back down at her laptop. She heard him go up the stairs and tried to concentrate on what she'd been doing but her focus had completely gone. After a few minutes she gave up and closed the laptop, turning off the kitchen light and making her own way up the stairs. By the time she got into bed he was snoring. She lay next to him and watched him sleep for a while. Then she reached over to her bedside table for her sleep spray, squirted it liberally all over her pillow, put on her lavender eye mask and tried to summon some sleep.

11

'Look! Shop-bought cupcakes! Live it, learn it.' Sophie waved the box of cupcakes at Angie. It was the morning of their annual Easter party and Angie had come over to help her prepare. However, unlike last time when the Taylors had turned up at the front door unannounced, Angie had come via the gate and let herself in through the back door, as comfortable in Sophie's home now as she was in her own.

'They look beautiful, but I was rather fond of your home-made ones,' Angie replied as she washed her hands in the kitchen sink and turned to Sophie. 'Where shall we start?'

'You can start by telling me what's going on.'

'What do you mean?'

'Something's on your mind and I think it's time you talked about it.'

Sophie had sensed that something was up with Angie for a few weeks now but had been reluctant to probe her because she knew Angie valued her privacy. She didn't like to 'bang on about her feelings' as she said. However, she had become increasingly subdued and Sophie was beginning to worry about her. Angie had been relieved when the pregnancy test came back negative so her withdrawn behaviour now didn't make sense. She'd even quizzed Jack about it on the way to school a few days ago but had drawn a blank.

'Everything okay with Angie?' she'd asked, trying to sound light.

'Yep, why?'

'I don't know, I just thought she seemed a bit out of sorts, that's all.'

'She's still getting over that cold and she's been really busy at work. Plus Ellie and Indie are in some sort of ongoing feud which is tedious. But other than that, she's fine.'

Sophie wasn't convinced and she had even started to worry that perhaps Angie was upset with her for some reason. Had someone said something to her about Sophie dancing with Jack at the barn dance? Nothing remotely untoward had happened yet she couldn't help feeling paranoid because Angie had been acting strangely ever since that night. Perhaps she'd been annoyed that Sophie had left without him but that seemed ridiculous too, Jack was a grown man who was perfectly capable of making his own way home. She couldn't put her finger on it but something wasn't right, of that she was sure.

When she had woken up the morning after the barn dance, she remembered her promise to herself that she and Alan should make more time for each other. As she was making coffee, she called him at his parents, eager to hear his voice after spending a night in bed without him.

'Hey, love,' he said when he answered, sounding tired.

'How's it going?'

'Fine, although I'll need to stick around for a few more days. Mum is still in hospital so I have to ferry Dad to and fro. And I've been up half the night helping him to the loo so I'm a bit knackered. Are you okay?'

'Of course,' Sophie reassured him. 'I miss you though.'

'I miss you too, Soph.'

'Shall we come up too, Al? We could help you out around the house.'

'No it's not necessary, love, and two kids running around probably won't help matters. You stay put and I'll be home when I can.'

Later that morning she had popped next door to see if Angie was feeling better but Indie, without even glancing up from her phone, had informed her that her mother had gone to the gym. Next, she called Clara to see if she fancied a playdate but her kids had back-to-back birthday parties. Finally she tried Eve, who didn't even answer her phone. Feeling a bit discombobulated, she decided to take the children to visit her parents for the night. The next time she saw Jack was on Monday morning and he had been his usual, chirpy self. But ever since that weekend Angie had been acting strangely and she'd resolved to get to the bottom of it once and for all.

Angie stood in Sophie's kitchen, dumbfounded. How had Sophie known that something was up? No one else had said anything and she'd assumed that she was doing an admirable job of hiding her feelings, so Sophie's perceptiveness had caught her off guard. Her brain kicked into gear as she tried to think of the best way to respond to get Sophie off her case. This thing, or whatever it was she was feeling, was something she had to deal with – and get over – by herself.

'It's nothing serious, Sophie,' she said finally. 'My mum's not doing very well and I think she needs to move into sheltered accommodation. And I've been having a bit of a panic over my work-life balance. I feel like I'm missing out on a lot of things at home but it's incredibly difficult to cut down my hours at work because of the nature of the job.'

Sophie nodded in sympathy. 'I'm sorry to hear that; it must be hard. Is there anything that can be done? Perhaps you just need to take some time off? Or a sabbatical even?'

'What I need,' Angie said, 'is a good holiday.'

Sophie nodded. 'Me too! The weather's been appalling, hasn't it? I don't know what's happened to spring but I feel like we've been in the depths of winter for decades.'

'Have you booked anything for the summer yet?'

'Not yet, I'm usually more organised but time has got away with me a bit this year.' Sophie looked at her and said tentatively, 'Would you fancy doing something together maybe? We could get a big villa or a couple of apartments next to each other?'

Angie considered the prospect. They often went away with Simon and Alex in the summer holidays but she hadn't spoken to Alex in weeks and she had a feeling that she was being phased out. She couldn't blame her; she had made little effort with their friendship this year. What with everything else, she just hadn't had the bandwidth and a couple of Alex's messages had gone unanswered. She thought of her old Greenwich gang, of their weekend barbecues, park playdates and mum nights out. It all seemed like a distant memory now. She looked at Sophie and smiled.

'That would be wonderful!' she said. 'Perhaps we could do some research after the party? I'm thinking Greece, I'm thinking tavernas, I'm thinking beaches.'

'I'm thinking yes.'

As Angie started getting plates and cutlery out of Sophie's kitchen cupboards, she realised that she was feeling better already. Perhaps that was all she needed after all, something to look forward to after a long winter. A change of scene, a few weeks off work, good company and a chance to recharge the batteries. She'd been overthinking things and her brain just needed a break. Yes, she thought in anticipation, the winter months were always a slog but with the prospect of summer, she was feeling optimistic again.

'Indie's bringing her boyfriend to the party today by the way,' she told Sophie conspiratorially as she wrapped knives and forks in napkins.

'Oooh, what's he like?'

'Sullen and evidently incapable of conversation. But she seems to adore him.'

'I can't believe she has a boyfriend. When Katie gets her first boyfriend Alan is going to lose the plot. How's Jack about it?'

'Oh he's fine, he's pretty laid-back about things like that.'

'Do you remember your first boyfriend?'

Angie thought back and smiled wistfully at the memory. 'His name was Peter Banks and he went to the boys' school down the road. We went out for two weeks, after which time I left him for an older man. And by older man, I mean the school year above me, which was incredibly exotic. I must have been thirteen or fourteen. How about you?'

'I was seventeen – a bit of a late bloomer really. His name was Callum Brody and I'd known him since primary school. It's funny how you always remember the full names of people from your childhood, isn't it? Anyway, we went out for two years and then I moved away to go to journalism college and we drifted apart. I'm still friends with him on Facebook, though.'

'Do you ever think he's the one that got away?' Angie asked teasingly.

'Erm, no. Let's just say time hasn't been kind to him from the looks of his profile picture.'

Angie, absorbed in the conversation, admitted: 'I thought Jack was the one that got away.'

'How do you mean?'

'Well, I was mad about him from the minute I met him, back when we were students, but I refused to admit it to him or to myself. I thought that it would be unrequited love. And in any case, he was what can only be described as a Lothario back then. So I started going out with a different boy instead and tried to forget all about him. After we graduated, I thought about him from time to time and wondered if things would have been different if I'd told him how I felt.'

'Wow! Do you think it was fate that brought you together then, all those years later?'

'I don't really believe in fate. Just sheer bloody coincidence I'd say.'

'And look at you now! Happily married with four amazing children. I'd call that fate.'

Angie smiled, enjoying seeing her marriage through the eyes of her neighbour. 'Yes,' she agreed. 'Maybe you're right. Anyway, enough talk about boys, we've got an Easter party to get ready. Where's that cake stand?'

12

———

Sophie stretched back on the sun lounger and sighed happily. She was in heaven. Why hadn't they gone on holiday with friends before? The children were having so much fun together that she'd actually had time to read an entire book and sunbathe without constant interruptions: declarations of boredom, tiredness or hunger. It was bliss. She looked up as Jack emerged from the villa, carrying a bottle of beer in each hand. The glass was so cold that she could see the condensation running down it and her mouth watered in anticipation of the first taste.

Behind the protection of her sunglasses, she took the opportunity to have a sneaky glance at Jack. It was of little surprise that he looked ridiculously attractive in swimming trunks, paired with designer aviator shades, and she relished the view for a moment.

'Beer?' he asked, offering one to her.

'Yes please,' she said, sitting up to take the bottle from him and feeling immediately self-conscious in her swimming costume in such proximity to Jack. She knew she didn't have a bad figure but compared to Angie she still felt like a frump.

'Where are Angie and Alan?' she asked.

'They've gone to the supermarket to stock up on beer and snacks.'

'And the kids?'

'Playing cards inside.'

Jack got on the sun lounger next to her and they lay in companionable silence. They were staying in a villa on Kefalonia that Angie had found. Trust Angie to discover something a bit special, off the beaten track. Sophie would have just booked something through a big tour operator and be done with it, but Angie had spent hours poring over the internet and making enquiries. And the result was pretty spectacular.

The six-bedroom property, with its blue shutters and white-washed walls, was plenty big enough for them all, with the four younger children sharing two rooms and Indie and Benji having their own. The villa was nestled on the side of a hill overlooking the sea, three miles away from civilisation. From the beautifully manicured garden, with its own private pool, you could see for miles. In the heat of the midday sun, a pergola covered in vine leaves offered the perfect shade to sit outside and eat lunch with a cold glass of wine. Most of the time everyone had been content to spend the day at the villa. They'd taken a couple of trips to the nearest town to go to the beach, have a meal, browse the little shops and buy an ice cream. Sophie had never seen Alan looking so relaxed and couldn't remember ever having had a better holiday herself either.

But they only had one night left in paradise before they had to fly back home to rainy London. The Taylors, however, were hopping onto a ferry to spend ten days on another Greek island and Sophie was yearning to go with them. But Alan needed to get back to work and there was no way they'd be able to afford it. The villa had been eye-wateringly expensive, and Sophie had baulked at the price when Angie had first told her. Perhaps sensing her shock, Angie had immediately offered to pay extra.

'We've got four children, you've only got two,' she said. 'We'll be taking up more of the bedrooms and eating far more of the food. Let us chip in a little extra.'

Sophie had been too embarrassed to accept but Alan had no such qualms. 'She's right, though, isn't she,' he said. 'There's more of them. Anyway, they can afford it.'

But Sophie, feeling too proud, had stood firm and in the end they'd split the cost, with the agreement that Jack and Angie would put more into the food, drink and taxi kitty. She suspected that they kept sneaking extra cash into the kitty when she wasn't looking but she was far too relaxed to care anymore. Now she had one glorious day left to enjoy before they had to pack up and return to reality and she was going to enjoy every last second of it.

'Fancy a dip?' Jack asked.

'Sure.' She started to peel herself off the sunbed. 'Last one in's making dinner!'

She dived into the pool and as her body hit the ice-cold water she felt a glorious rush of adrenaline. She swam the length of the pool, enjoying the sensation of being underwater, until her throat started burning and she returned to the surface. When she looked up, Jack was also in the water, watching her.

'You're a good swimmer,' he commented.

'Under-sixteens county champion,' she announced proudly.

'Well, you've still got it, Brennan.'

'Why thank you,' she replied with a grin. He swam towards her and she splashed him playfully.

'Oi.' He laughed, splashing her back. Soon they were splashing each other furiously, giggling like children. He grabbed her leg and pulled her underwater with him and as they floated underneath the surface, she saw him move towards her, as if he was about to reach for her, and she panicked and launched herself up to the surface. She quickly swam to the side of the pool, pulled herself out and towelled herself dry before putting her sundress back on.

'I'd better go and check on the kids,' she said.

'Okay doke,' Jack replied, as he climbed onto a pink lilo that was drifting past him and started to float along on his back. 'Bring us another beer on your way back out, will you?'

It was as if nothing had happened. But, *had* anything happened? She was so confused. For a moment she had thought that Jack was going to kiss her but now that seemed ludicrous. *It's all in my head*, she told herself. She was just silly and giddy on sun and afternoon beer and she needed to get over herself. Jack would never do anything like that. He was playful, for sure, perhaps a bit flirty from time to time, but he was harmless. And she would never do anything like that to Alan anyway. So why was she feeling so guilty all of a sudden?

She felt the rush of cold air as she let herself into the air-conditioned villa and saw the kids still playing cards and making their way through a family-sized bag of crisps. She watched them for a while and then she heard the front door open and Alan and Angie returned with bags of supplies. She went over to help them unpack and a few minutes later Jack came inside, still in his swimming trunks, and put his arms around Angie.

'Get off, you're soaking wet,' she said with a half-laugh, pulling away from him.

'I can't resist,' Jack said.

'I mean it, Jack, this dress is dry-clean only!'

'Take it off then.' He started pulling the strap of Angie's dress down.

Sophie and Alan caught each other's eye.

But Angie just pushed him off and sent him back outside. 'You've met Holiday Jack then,' she said.

'Holiday Jack?' Sophie asked.

'Yes, Holiday Jack forgets who he is and acts like he's on some sort of eighteen to thirties holiday in Kavos. He often makes guest appearances on our summer jaunts. Ignore him, he's harmless.'

Angie sounded flippant but Sophie's cheeks burned. It was as though Angie was talking directly to her and she felt another rush of guilt about what had happened in the pool. Was Angie giving her a warning or was she simply trying to justify Jack's behaviour in the kitchen? And while she sounded light-hearted, was there something more serious behind her tone?

She didn't know but she wanted to find out. 'Angie, do you fancy going for a sunset walk?' she asked.

'Sounds romantic,' Angie replied.

'Well you're dressed for it. Alan, are you and Jack okay to hold the fort for an hour or so?'

'Of course,' he said. 'I've already promised to referee a game of water polo.'

'Come on then,' Sophie said. Angie nodded, wiped her hands on a tea towel and started following Sophie towards the front door. As they were about to open it, Indie barged through it from the outside, her face like thunder.

'Indie what's the matter?' Angie asked.

Indie scowled in response and marched up the stairs, slamming the door.

Angie looked at Sophie apologetically. 'I'd better see what that's all about. Most likely she's been on the phone with her boyfriend and they've had a row. Rain check on that walk?'

'Of course,' Sophie said, although she was disappointed. She watched Angie make her way up the stairs and considered what to do with herself. From outside she could hear the children splashing and shrieking in delight and occasional shouts from Jack and Alan, who were supervising. *Sod it*, she thought, *I'm going out anyway.*

She pulled on her trainers and let herself out of the house, making her way down the track and starting her ascent of the hill. As she navigated the rough terrain, climbing higher and higher and sweating under the glare of the late afternoon sun, she felt a rush of pleasure from the exertion and remembered how much she used to love swimming and the sheer physical effort of pushing herself to the limit. She tried to remember now why she'd stopped. It had all got a bit too much, the early morning starts, the constant training, and when she'd left home to go to journalism school, that part of her life had faded into her past like a distant memory.

She perched on a large, flat rock for a while, watching the sun dip down into the sea, and saw things with a clarity that she hadn't felt in a long time. How long had she just been gliding through life, in her comfort zone, stuck in the mundanity of the day-to-day? When had she last challenged herself? *When I get back from this holiday things are going to change*, she told herself. No more plodding along, waiting for life to happen. It was time to seize it with both hands. She wasn't sure what that meant yet, but she was going to find out. With a renewed purpose, she jumped off the rock and made her way back to the villa.

She knew from the minute she got back that something wasn't right. The room's atmosphere was thick and everyone seemed subdued, even the children.

She sidled up to Alan. 'What's going on?' she asked him quietly.

'Indie and Angie have had some sort of blazing row,' he replied.

'So why is everyone else looking like Christmas has been cancelled?'

'Apparently this is the effect that Indie has when she's in one of her moods.'

'Oh dear, I'd better go and find Angie,' Sophie said, leaving her husband to hide out in the kitchen and making her way outside to look for her. She quickly spotted her sitting by the side of the pool, her long, slim legs dangling in the water.

'I hear World War Three has broken out,' she said, sitting down next to Angie, but she didn't reply. 'Everything okay, Ange?'

'Yes, fine.' Angie's stock response to everything.

'Was it a row with the boyfriend?' Sophie asked.

'Something like that.'

Sophie imagined that Indie's temper tantrums could be incredibly wearing on her mother and tried to think of something reassuring to say. 'Don't take it personally. She's going through puberty. She's confused and angry, but she'll grow out of it.'

Angie stared forlornly at the water. 'Well she's ruined the last night of the holiday.'

'Don't be daft,' Sophie said, surprised by Angie's melancholy. 'If Indie wants to sulk, that's her prerogative. But the rest of us are going to have fun. I'll light the barbecue; you get the wine.'

As she stood up to leave, Angie reached out and grabbed her hand. 'I adore you, Sophie, you know that, don't you?'

'Yes of course,' Sophie said, smiling down at her. 'As I adore you.'

'Was everything okay with you and Jack? While Alan and I were at the supermarket?'

Sophie felt uneasy again. 'Yes of course, absolutely fine.'

'What did you do?'

'We sunbathed, had a swim, nothing special. Why do you ask?'

'No reason,' Angie said, turning away. 'Forget it.'

Sophie went back inside to get the matches, Angie's words echoing around her head. What was going on? Was Angie really suspicious of her and Jack or was Sophie just reading too much into it? She looked over at Jack, who was in the kitchen marinating some meat, a cocktail on the counter next to him, humming away to himself. He must have sensed her gaze because he looked up and gave her a wink. She smiled back at him, perplexed. She had a strange feeling that she was getting involved in something she hadn't planned.

'Want me to fix you a cocktail, Brennan?' Jack asked her.

'Of course she does,' came a voice from behind her, 'and while you're at it, one for me too please.' Angie appeared at Sophie's side and put an arm around her. 'Sophie and I are going outside to take our drinks on the patio. You and Alan are in charge of dinner.'

And with that, she gently guided Sophie out of the villa, chatting away easily about the incredible olives she'd found in the supermarket, as though the entire conversation they'd had by the pool hadn't happened. And Sophie, relieved to see Angie back to her old self again, relaxed. They sat down on rattan chairs, sampling olives, sipping cocktails and watching the children play hide and seek in the garden, and she tried to push all thoughts of Angie and Jack's behaviour and her own mixed feelings to the back of her mind and enjoy their last night together.

By the following morning, Indie had emerged and was sunbathing by the pool, reading a magazine and eating a cheese sandwich, as if she didn't have a care in the world.

'Glad to see Indie's feeling better,' Sophie whispered.

'Yes, she's calmed down now, thank goodness,' Angie said. She gave Sophie a tight hug. 'I can't believe you're going home today. I'll miss you.'

'I'll miss you too,' Sophie said. 'But you'll be back home

before you know it, so just enjoy the rest of your holiday and think of us bored at home in Finchley.'

She heard their taxi pull up and they all piled in and waved out of the window as it drove away from the villa. In the distance she could see the Taylors standing side by side, waving back. She watched them until the car turned a corner and they all disappeared. Tom and Katie, distraught about being parted from their friends, both started sobbing simultaneously and Sophie, who was sitting between them in the back seat, put a comforting arm around them both.

'It's okay,' she told them. 'It was a wonderful holiday and it's natural to feel sad that it's over but you'll feel much better once you get home to your own rooms and your toys.'

'Can we go on holiday with them again next summer?' Tom asked.

'Well it's a bit early to plan that, love, but I'll speak to Angie about it,' Sophie assured him.

After a few minutes the children's tears began to subside. Tom reached for his iPad and headphones, while Katie snuggled up to Sophie and closed her eyes. She glanced at Alan, who was in the front seat attempting to speak Greek with the taxi driver. The man was delighted by the stilted attempts of his English passenger to communicate in his language and was enthusiastically encouraging him, exclaiming 'bravo!' every so often. Alan, looking tanned and healthier than she'd seen him in a long time, was concentrating so hard on remembering the Greek words he'd been practising that he was oblivious to her gaze. As she watched him, she realised that they'd never had that night out together.

She turned her head to look out of the window, watching the horizon and the little boats dotted around the ocean as the car sped along the coastal road towards the airport. She felt a bit like the children, she realised, as though she'd been ripped from paradise and dumped back into real life against her will. They'd get home, Alan would sink down on the sofa and put the TV on, the kids would go off to their rooms to play and she'd start the mammoth task of working her way through the laundry. It was all so predictable.

She remembered what she'd told the children just minutes earlier, how they would feel much better once they got home, but at that moment all she felt was loss. Loss that the holiday was over. Loss that Angie got to continue her adventure with Jack while she had to go home, back to real life. She remembered her promise to herself the previous day. Things were going to be different when they got home. They had to be. Because she needed some excitement in her life.

13

Angie locked the front door and followed her children down the steps and onto the street. She quickly kissed Indie and Benji before they had time to object and then she stood and waved as they disappeared down the road on their bikes. Once she could no longer see them, she turned and started making her way in the opposite direction with Ellie and Freddy. They'd got about halfway down the road when she heard Sophie calling out behind her. She waited for them to catch up, Tom and Katie hurtling down the road on their scooters.

'Hello, stranger, long time no see!' Sophie said when she caught up, catching her breath and linking her arm through Angie's. 'What are you doing on the school run?!'

Although they had been back from Greece for over a fortnight, Angie had been lying low. Normally after a holiday she returned home feeling fully charged and ready to rejoin the rat race. But this time she had felt horribly deflated and she couldn't shake the feeling off.

She hadn't expected the holiday to be such an emotional roller coaster. She'd convinced herself that a couple of weeks in the sun was just what she needed to shake off her low mood and for the first few days it had been the perfect antidote. She had sunbathed alongside Sophie, played games in the pool with the children, swam in the crystal-clear ocean and spent evenings under a starry sky, drinking exceptional Greek wine and putting the world to rights. She and Jack had been their usual power pair, the ultimate hosts and the life and soul of the party, and she had enjoyed slotting back into the role that they'd been famous for in their old south London life.

Okay, so Jack might have embarrassed her once or twice – like when he'd told her to strip off in front of Sophie and Alan, or suggested they all go skinny dipping together one evening, or tried to persuade Alan to go out clubbing with him – but she'd laughed it off as she always had done in the past. She had even been contemplating how silly she was to worry she was having some sort of breakdown when all she had needed was a holiday. But then the row with Indie had completely shattered her illusion that a bit of sun, sea and sand could solve all her problems.

When Indie had marched into the villa, it had been obvious that she was in one of her famous dark and stormy moods. Usually Angie preferred to leave her to it until she had calmed down and they could have a more rational conversation, but in her foolishly blissful holiday mode, she decided to go up straight away. It had been like walking into the lion's den.

'Darling, what's wrong?' she asked, discovering Indie lying face down on the bed, her long dark hair falling all around her. She reached out to stroke it but Indie batted her away.

'I don't want to talk about it.'

'I understand, but maybe I can help?'

Indie looked up and Angie could see her tear-stained face. She glared angrily at Angie, as though she desperately needed to direct her rage somewhere and had decided that Angie was as good a person as anyone. 'Since when have you ever helped me?'

Angie tried to stay calm. 'You're upset but I'm not sure that's fair.'

'Of course you're not.'

'What's that supposed to mean?'

Indie sat up straight now and Angie could see her daughter preparing for battle.

'You don't care about anyone but yourself and your work. You're never at home and when you are, you're on your laptop or phone the whole time anyway. When I try to talk to you, you treat me like I'm one of your stupid clients. You pretend to care about me but you don't.'

Angie was caught completely off guard by her daughter's explosion. 'Indie, where has this come from? I don't understand what I've done wrong here.'

'No of course you don't! This is what I'm talking about,' Indie stormed. 'Nothing is ever your fault, is it!'

Angie took a deep breath, feeling her holiday glow quickly evaporating. 'Okay, let's start again,' she began. 'What happened?'

'I told you, I don't want to talk about it.'

They were going round in circles, so Angie stood up and sighed. 'Okay, Indie, I'll leave you to it but I'll be downstairs if you need me and if you want to talk, I'm always here.'

'But that's *it*,' Indie said. She seemed disappointed that her enemy was leaving when she was in the fighting mood. 'You're not here for me. You're not here for anyone but yourself. Have you even asked me how things are at school? Do you even care? Everyone acts like you're this amazing person, this Super-woman, and you play up to it. You think you're better than everyone else. The way you talk to us, the way you talk to *Dad...*'

Angie pounced immediately. 'What do you mean, the way I talk to Dad?'

'Forget it.' Indie recoiled slightly, realising perhaps that she'd pressed the wrong button.

'No, Indie, I won't forget it. What do you mean?'

Indie looked her mother. 'You talk to him like he's a child. You belittle him. It's no wonder he needs a break from you sometimes.'

Her words hit Angie like a train. Indie had been accusing before but she had never gone this far. She was torn between outrage that her daughter was talking to her in this manner and terror at the words she was saying. Because if her teenager thought it, then did it mean that everyone else thought it too? And, worse still, did Indie know something that she didn't about Jack?

'What are you implying?' Angie could feel herself standing taller and squaring up to Indie now, a lioness showing her dominance over a cub. Indie was old enough to remember when she'd thrown Jack out for a few days: was she talking about that? Or was there something else? She moved a step closer to Indie.

Her daughter immediately backed down. 'Forget about it, Mum, just leave me alone.'

'No, you started this so you can finish it. What do you mean?'

'Let's just say that he looks like he's been having far more fun with Sophie on this holiday than with you, that's all I'm saying.'

It was a low blow but it hit the spot. Angie glared at Indie before turning around and storming out of her room, as though she were the petulant teenager. In her own room she sat down on the side of the bed and realised that she was shaking. What the hell had just happened? All she had wanted to do was comfort her distressed daughter, assuming she'd be soothing her over a silly row with a friend or boyfriend. Instead, Indie had all but told her that she was a terrible, selfish mother and an even worse wife whose husband preferred the company of her best friend. And worse still, instead of brushing it off as the untrue and impulsive words of an angry teenager, she had let them get to her, to infect her with their venom.

Her feelings of doubt and insecurity came flooding back, as though they'd been waiting in the sidelines the whole time for their opportunity to return. And they came thick and fast now as she tried to process her daughter's words. Was her whole life a lie? Did everyone pretend they adored her when they actually hated her? Were they talking about her behind her back?

She thought of Jack and Sophie. Surely nothing was going on. Jack would never do that to her, *Sophie* would never do that to her – would she? She shook her head, trying to physically remove the idea from her mind. No, it wasn't possible.

'Angie, are you up there?' Jack was calling her now. She'd better go down before they realised something was wrong. She stood up shakily and looked at herself in the mirror. She looked pale, despite her tan. *She's just a teenage girl, lashing out at the closest person*, she told herself. *You always hurt the ones you love. She doesn't know what she's talking about.* Trying to force the row out of her mind, she put some lipstick and bronzer on and made her way down the stairs.

'All okay?' Jack asked, glancing up at her.

'Indie's in a mood,' she told him. 'She won't tell me why.'

Jack stood up from the sofa. 'I'll have a word.'

'She won't talk to you,' Angie called out to his retreating back but he simply turned, gave her a wink and carried on walking.

He emerged half an hour later with the full story. Indie's boyfriend, Noah, had been caught snogging another girl and the photo was all over social media. Everyone was talking about it and a few hours ago, Noah had sent her a brief text:

we're ovr.

'She feels humiliated and she thinks that everyone is

laughing at her behind her back, which to be fair, they probably are,' Jack explained. 'It turns out that the group of girls she hangs out with have been fairly bitchy of late and she's feeling excluded.'

'I had no idea.' Angie felt awful at the idea of Indie being upset at school or being the victim of mean behaviour by other teenage girls. How had she missed this? But she knew the answer already. Indie was right, she had been too busy and too self-absorbed to notice.

'I wouldn't worry too much,' Jack said, as calm as he always was, like he was a bloody parenting expert. 'They'll all be best friends again tomorrow. Indie's a popular girl, if anything I think the other girls are a bit jealous of her. And a fiver says she'll have a new boyfriend by the time term starts and Noah will be kicking himself for having messed up.'

'Did she say anything else?' Angie couldn't help asking.

'About what?'

'About me?'

'What's this got to do with you?'

'Oh never mind, Jack, forget it.' She felt irritated with him and wasn't sure why, until she released her relief that Indie hadn't brought up their row had been replaced by disappointment that her daughter had confided in Jack but lashed out at her.

'Am I a good mother?' she asked him suddenly.

Jack frowned. 'Of course you are.'

'I just don't understand why she couldn't have talked to me.'

Jack came up to her and she let him put his arms around her, closing her eyes and breathing in his familiar smell. 'She's a teenage girl, Angie, there's no point trying to reason with her. Just let her be. She loves you and she knows you're there for her.'

But despite his reassurances, she couldn't escape the thoughts that were now consuming her. Her holiday glow was well and truly gone, a sticking plaster to hide the truth. She watched Jack all evening, scrutinising the way he was with Sophie, but there was nothing to see. They chatted and laughed like the two friends that they were and she tried to shake the paranoia from her mind, knowing that it would get her nowhere.

The next morning she woke up to find Jack lying on his side, looking down at her. 'Morning, gorgeous,' he said.

'Morning,' she said, wiping her eyes. 'Jack, can I ask you something?'

'Always.'

'Are you happy?'

'Christ, Ange, isn't this a bit serious for first thing in the morning?'

'Please, Jack, I need to know.'

'Is this to do with Indie? I told you, you shouldn't take it to heart...'

'It's not just that.'

He looked down at her, concerned. 'Are you okay?'

'I'm fine,' she insisted. 'Please just answer the question.'

'Of course I'm happy.'

She wanted to talk more, to probe him, but Freddy barged in brandishing a book and hurled himself onto the bed. 'Mummy, Daddy, can you read me a story?'

Jack lifted him up and settled him into bed between them. He began to read and the little boy snuggled up to him, desperate to be as close to his father as possible. Angie watched them for a while and then got out of bed and went downstairs to make coffee. As she was reaching for the mugs Indie emerged and approached her, eyes lowered.

'Sorry, Mum.'

Angie put the mugs down and looked at her daughter. 'Me too.'

They smiled tentatively at each other. It was a ceasefire, for now. At least Angie was reassured by the fact that Indie had apologised. To her it confirmed that not only did Indie regret her outburst but that her daughter's words hadn't been meant, that they had purely been said in the heat of the moment. It wasn't until a couple of days later that she learned the truth. Jack, seeing how upset Angie was after the row and putting two and two together, had ordered Indie to apologise upon pain of having her phone confiscated for the rest of the holiday.

On the ferry, as they made their way to the next island, she stood on the deck, closed her eyes, breathed in the warm salty air and tried to relax. She felt a presence beside her and looked over to see Jack standing next to her. He put his hand in hers.

'I am happy, Angie. Very happy,' he had said.

She had smiled. At least one of them was.

Angie had returned from holiday determined to make a change. She couldn't go on like this any longer. She'd arranged a meeting with her superior at work and told him that she wanted to work more flexibly. From September, she said, she would be coming in later and working from home a couple of days a week if she wasn't in court. She could see the surprise on his face but he agreed, realising that, as with all things Angie, it was a statement not a request. As she left the meeting, she suspected that she had just blown her chance of becoming partner, but it was the sacrifice she had to make. She needed her career, but she needed her family to need her too.

For how could she blame the children for loving Jack more than her when he was the one who was always there for them, mopping up their tears, making their dinner, sharing laughs with them? And how could she blame Jack for feeling neglected when she was never around for him? She was going to make herself indispensable to her family again, she vowed. Once her mind was made up, she was certain that this was finally the solution to all her problems.

But Jack had seemed put out when she first told him of her plans and she realised how much he enjoyed being a part-time stay-at-home dad, and how much pleasure he took in being the one that the children turned to. She had, perhaps naively, assumed he'd be delighted by her change of priorities, but it quickly became evident that she'd misjudged him.

'I'm not trying to oust you, Jack,' she said. 'But you and the children are what matter the most to me and I feel like I'm missing out.'

'So, do I have to up my hours at work again?' Jack was petulant.

'I'll still be working full-time; my income won't change. So really, it's entirely up to you, Jack, do whatever you like, whatever makes you happy.'

To him, this had all come out of the blue. The only Angie he had ever known was a workaholic who ran her life and her family with military precision. But she would show him, she'd show them all, that she really could find the perfect balance between the two – that she did deserve the title of Superwoman after all.

When she told the children she was planning on being around more, Indie and Benji barely responded. Ellie and Freddy, still wonderfully sweet and optimistic, jumped up and down with excitement at the prospect of their mum taking them to school. She hugged her younger two children tightly to her and prayed that they didn't grow up too quickly.

In any event, a week later the company that Jack worked for had landed a contract to produce a major new documentary and they asked him to be on the team, which meant he'd be busy, so it had all worked out rather well. She put the prospect of Jack working and socialising away from home again to the back of her mind. *He adores me, he adores our children, I have nothing to worry about, it's all in my head*, she told herself over and over again until she believed it.

Sophie was surprised when she saw Angie leaving the house with the kids. In the two years since they'd lived next door to each other she'd never seen her do a morning school run. But it was quickly replaced with delight at the prospect of seeing her. They had barely talked since the holiday and Sophie had been absolutely bursting to tell her the exciting news.

'It's so lovely to see you!' she said to Angie when she finally caught up with her.

'It's my new school year's resolution,' Angie explained. 'I've decided to work a bit more flexibly so that I can be more involved with the childcare.'

'Good for you,' Sophie said. 'I've made a new school year's resolution too!'

'Oh yes, what's that?'

'I'm going to train as a swimming instructor.'

The seed had been planted in Greece. All the way home, Sophie had thought about how much she had enjoyed being back in the pool and the pleasure of doing something physical again. She had loved teaching Tom and Katie to swim and wondered, for the first time, whether she could make a living out of it. She'd competed at a high level when she was younger and had won a number of competitions which she knew would look good on applications. She had tentatively broached the idea with Alan, interested to see how it felt when she said it out loud, and in typical Alan style he had been great about it.

'It sounds like an excellent idea, love,' he said. 'You'd be a brilliant teacher.'

'Are you sure it's all right, though?' Sophie asked. 'The training itself isn't that expensive but I'll probably have to work evenings and weekends and I doubt I'll earn my fortune.'

'Nothing ventured, nothing gained,' Alan said. 'I think you should go for it.'

Alan's reaction had spurred her on and the next person she'd been desperate to tell was Angie. She waited in anticipation now for her reaction.

'Well! That's quite a change of career,' Angie finally said.

'I know, but I've been thinking about it non-stop since Greece and I'm really excited about it. I'm going to look for training courses this week and take it from there.'

'What about your writing?'

Sophie felt like a teenager again, trying to persuade her parents that she was making the right decision. Was it her or was Angie sounding disapproving? 'I fell out of love with that a long time ago,' she said. 'There's no point in trying to flog a dead horse. It's time for a new challenge, a new career start. I know it's not going to win me a Pulitzer Prize, Ange, but I'm really excited about it, okay?'

Why was she getting defensive? What was it about Angie that made her feel like she had to impress her?

But then Angie turned to her and beamed. 'I think it's wonderful,' she said. 'If you need any practise, you can always borrow Freddy. He's a really nervous swimmer and he's not enjoying the group lessons at all.'

'I'd love that,' Sophie said, relaxing again. 'Any time, you just let me know. Anyway, everything okay your end? I haven't even heard about the rest of your holiday.'

'It was lovely thanks, not as fun as our glorious week in the villa but we had a nice time.'

'Did Indie cheer up in the end?'

Angie winced at the memory. 'In the end.'

'I take it it's all off with the boyfriend?'

'Oh yes, there's a new one on the scene now.'

'Young love, eh?'

'Indeed.'

They walked to school side by side, watching the children nattering away happily, thrilled to be in each other's company again and Sophie had an idea. 'I was thinking, Ange,' she said, 'we've never been out, just the two of us. How about we get dressed up and hit the town on Friday evening, you and me? We can celebrate our new school year's resolutions!'

'That sounds lovely.'

'Fabulous, shall I book somewhere hip and cool where we'll feel terribly old?'

'Perfect.'

When she got home, Sophie turned the radio on and started researching Friday night dinner options, settling on a restaurant in Kings Cross that had good reviews but wasn't new or trendy enough to be full. Booking a table for 8pm she sent Angie a quick text to confirm the details and smiled with satisfaction. This was exactly what they needed, a girls' night. She couldn't remember the last time she'd been out in town – it would be just the ticket. She imagined her and Angie drinking cocktails and having a giggle, and she felt a frisson of anticipation. She couldn't wait.

Singing along to the songs on the radio, she made a cup of tea and turned her attention to googling local swimming courses. By the time she left to pick up Tom and Katie, she'd enrolled on a course starting next month and was feeling productive. As Mondays went, this one was going pretty well, she thought, dashing out of the door. By the time she arrived at the gates, out of breath, the kids were waiting for her and looking at her accusingly.

'You're late, Mum,' Katie said, scowling.

'By two minutes!' Sophie protested.

'But Ellie and Freddy have already gone home.'

'How about I make it up to you with a chocolate muffin from the café?'

The children's frowns immediately turned upside down and they each grabbed their mum's hand and began pulling her towards the parade of shops, talking over each other in their eagerness to tell her all about their day. As she listened to their chatter about who they played with in the playground and what they had for lunch, she felt gloriously light and for the first time in months, she realised that she hadn't thought about babies all day.

Perhaps it was finally time to close the book on that chapter and start a new one. She'd had enough disappointment over the last year to last a lifetime. Looking down at her two amazing children, she squeezed their hands. Things were on the up, she could feel it.

The rest of the week crawled along as she looked forward to her night out with Angie. When Friday finally arrived, she headed straight to the hairdresser after dropping the children off for a blow dry. As she was paying, she caught a glimpse of herself in the mirror and felt a glow of pride. She'd been going swimming at the local leisure centre almost every day since getting back from holiday, partly so she'd be prepared for the course and partly because she'd remembered how much swimming boosted her mood, and she was already starting to see the effects on her body. She was healthier, a little more toned. She might not be Rebecca Adlington, but she was looking and feeling better than she had done in years and that was good enough for her.

At school pick-up she chatted with the other parents but she couldn't wait for the day to be over so she could finally get ready to go out. She made the kids fish and chips and was out of her chair and running up the stairs for a shower the minute Alan got home at six. As she got dressed and put her make-up on she hummed along to the Disney song that was blasting out from the TV downstairs, where Alan and the kids were watching a film. Finally, with a panicked glance at her watch, she dashed down the stairs, shouting 'I'm off!' in the general direction of the living room, before making her way out of the back door and through the garden gate.

She hurried down Angie and Jack's garden, opened the back door and let herself into the house. Jack was in the kitchen and he gave a low whistle when he saw her.

'Looking good, Brennan! Off anywhere nice?'

'Dinner with your good lady wife,' Sophie replied.

Jack looked confused. 'Angie's not here.'

'Oh, perhaps I'm supposed to be meeting her there. I'll call her,' Sophie said cheerfully, pulling out her phone and calling Angie, who answered after a few rings, sounding flustered.

'Hey, Ange, I think we might have got our wires crossed, I'm at your house. Are we meeting at the restaurant?'

There was a long silence at the other end of the phone. 'Angie, are you there?'

'Oh my gosh, Sophie, I'm sorry,' Angie said. 'I completely forgot and I'm out with some clients. They're extremely important to the firm so I don't think I can get away.'

Sophie's heart sank. 'Oh, okay,' she said, unable to hide her disappointment.

'I feel awful, Sophie, I really am sorry, I'll make it up to you I promise.'

'No worries.' Sophie rang off and Jack looked at her sympathetically, having overheard enough to work out what had happened.

'I take it she's not coming?' he asked.

'No, she forgot,' Sophie said. She could feel tears pricking her eyes and was embarrassed. She knew it was pathetic to be upset but she had been so looking forward to the night out and now she was all dressed up with nowhere to go. Plus she'd had to pay a hefty deposit to secure the table which she was going to lose now. But most of all she was hurt that Angie could forget her so easily. Clearly their friendship was more important to Sophie than it was to Angie and the realisation of that stung. She felt like an idiot.

'Tell you what,' Jack said. 'Why don't you send the kids round here, grab that husband of yours and take him out for a slap-up meal instead?'

Sophie's spirits lifted a bit. She looked at her watch. If they got a wriggle on they could still make it in time for the reservation.

'Are you sure?' she asked Jack.

'Absolutely, go get him.'

With renewed enthusiasm, Sophie dashed back through the garden gate to find Alan. She hurried into the front room, ready to demand that he get up and put his best shirt on right now but stopped in her tracks. Tom and Katie were lying top to tail on one sofa in their pyjamas, their duvets wrapped around them like cocoons, while Alan was stretched out on the other under a woollen blanket. All three of them were snoring quietly.

What the hell? It was only 7.15pm! But Alan had previous for falling asleep in front of the telly and the kids were exhausted after their first week back at school. She gave Alan a little poke, but he didn't even stir. There was no way he would be able to rally in time to make an 8pm reservation in central London, even with the best will in the world. Feeling another wave of disappointment, she returned to the Taylor house to break the news to Jack.

'He's fast asleep and not going anywhere,' she told him, now utterly deflated. Jack regarded her for a moment and then said brightly, 'Wait there!'

He dashed off up the stairs leaving Sophie alone in the kitchen, miserable and wondering how long she should hang around for before going home and making some beans on toast. Five minutes later he emerged, wearing a dinner shirt and tie over his grey jogging bottoms.

'Jack, why are you half dressed for a formal?'

'If you can't go to the restaurant, I'm bringing the restaurant to you,' Jack said. He opened a kitchen drawer and riffled through some takeaway menus.

'We've got Indian, Chinese or pizza, take your pick.'

'Jack, you don't have to do this.'

'I know, but I want to. Now sit down and I'll fix you a cocktail.'

He turned some music on and started mixing ingredients. Ellie drifted in wearing her pyjamas, in search of a hot chocolate.

'You look nice, Sophie,' she said, giving her a cuddle. Sophie squeezed her tightly back. She had a soft spot for Ellie. 'Thank you, darling,' she replied.

She ordered a couple of pizzas and watched Jack expertly mix cocktails while simultaneously making two hot chocolates with marshmallows for Ellie and Freddy without even breaking a sweat. He headed upstairs to read them a bedtime story and then returned to the kitchen and rummaged around for some olives and crisps.

'Where are Benji and Indie?' Sophie asked.

'Indie's at a sleepover and Benji's at some drama weekend camp thing.'

'This is really sweet of you, Jack,' she said. 'I feel a bit embarrassed.'

'Don't be silly, it's nice to have some company. I had a date with some cheese on toast and a computer game. This is far more fun.'

They clinked glasses and Sophie took a sip of her cocktail. It was delicious but utterly potent. 'You're going to get me sozzled,' she warned him.

'Good,' he replied, drinking his with alarming speed. He put his glass back down and said, 'Don't be upset about Angie. It's not about you, she just has a habit of losing herself in work sometimes and everything else goes out of the window.'

'I thought she was supposed to be addressing that,' Sophie said a little snarkily, and felt bad straight away. 'Sorry, Jack, I didn't mean that, I'm just a bit grumpy about being stood up.'

'I know, I've been in your shoes myself.'

'You have?'

'Absolutely, like I said, when Angie is working on a big case, she's very single-minded. It's why she's so good at her job. But sometimes the rest of us can be collateral damage. I don't think she even realises that she's doing it.'

'That must be hard.'

'It is,' Jack said. 'You can't help but feel second to her career sometimes.'

This was the first time that she and Jack had talked about Angie like this and Sophie knew that she was being disloyal, as was he. But the effect of the cocktail, combined with her disappointment over their aborted night out, was making her careless.

'Has it always been like that?' she asked him.

'Yes, right from the start. When we decided to start trying for children, I thought things might be different and at first, they were. Angie adored being a mum and seemed so happy when Benji was a baby. But when Indie came along, she really struggled and ended up going back to work full-time six months later. It was the same with Ellie and Freddy. We had nanny after nanny until they were old enough to go to after-school and holiday clubs.'

Sophie watched Jack, sensing a disapproval that she had never seen in him before. She had always thought that he was proud of Angie's success, that he thrived on her Superwoman status, but now she wondered if she was only seeing part of the picture. Perhaps their relationship wasn't as perfect as she had always thought. Perhaps *Angie* wasn't as perfect as she had always thought. She was on dangerous territory now, she realised, and she was relieved when the doorbell rang, signalling the arrival of dinner. By the time Jack returned with the pizzas and made some fresh cocktails, Sophie was ready to change the subject.

'I bet you were a bit of a cad when you were younger, weren't you,' she said, taking a bite of pepperoni pizza and quickly wiping away the tomato sauce from her chin.

Jack grinned. 'I can't deny it,' he said. 'I had fun. Okay, a *lot* of fun. I miss it sometimes.'

'What do you mean?'

'I just mean, well, being an adult's hard, isn't it.' It was a statement, not a question. 'It's so relentless. I miss being care-free, that's all. Sometimes I just want to do something reckless.'

'Are you having a midlife crisis, Jack?'

He laughed. 'Maybe, but don't you ever feel that urge? To do something mad?'

Sophie thought for a minute. 'I mean, I've fantasised about abandoning my kids in the middle of Asda when they're being little sods, if that's what you mean?'

Jack studied her. 'You're a good girl, aren't you, Sophie.'

She stopped chewing and looked at him and he looked back. For a brief moment the world stopped. Then she heard a thump followed by wailing from above and they both jumped up and raced up the stairs. They found Freddy on the floor.

'Oh, Fred, did you fall out of bed?' Jack asked, scooping him up and giving him a cuddle. Ellie, who had come in to see what all the commotion was about, was now bouncing around excitedly, thrilled to see Sophie and insisting that she read her a story. It took half an hour to calm them both down and get them off to sleep and by the time they came back downstairs, the pizza was cold and Sophie was ready to go home.

'I'm going to head off, Jack,' she said. 'Thanks for a lovely evening.'

'Stay,' he said. 'It's still early, let's have another drink.'

'I'm okay, two of your cocktails is quite enough for me.' She gave him a kiss on the cheek. 'Thanks, Jack, I really appreciate it.'

'Good night, Brennan,' he said, looking crestfallen.

He really didn't want her to go, Sophie realised. She'd thought he just felt sorry for her but she understood now that getting dressed up and making a night of it had been as much for his benefit. She looked at him again, indecisive. *Should I stay or should I go?*

14

Indie kept her head down low as she hurried down Pemberton Road. It was only 2pm and she was supposed to be at school, but she'd had a big row with her best friend, Daisy, and she didn't want to stick around anymore. That dive was bad enough at the best of times but with all her friends taking Daisy's side and giving her the cold shoulder, it was unbearable. If only she hadn't dumped her new boyfriend last week, she could have hung out with him but he was still pissed off with her so she was giving him a wide berth.

Fortunately her teacher hadn't batted an eyelid when she presented him with a forged letter from her mum, explaining that she had to leave early for a dentist appointment, and she had rushed out of the school gates with relief, like a prisoner escaping their block. But once she was outside, she realised that she had nowhere to go. It was a cold, blustery, winter's day and she didn't fancy hanging around in the park all afternoon. She could go to a café but she might raise suspicion in her school uniform and she only had about 50p on her.

Then she remembered her parents telling her that Ellie and Freddy were going to football club after school and that they wouldn't be home until 5pm, and she started heading home, already planning to raid the chocolate cupboard and play on her iPad undisturbed for a couple of hours. Benji would probably guess that she'd bunked off when he found her at home already, but he'd cover for her; he was all right like that.

There were only a few weeks to go until Christmas and many houses in Pemberton Road had their decorations up already. Some of them had tacky light-up penguins and Santas outside and Indie always pretended to cringe when she saw them, but secretly she loved them. Christmas was one of her favourite times of the year. It made her feel excited like a little girl again, although she'd never admit that to anyone. But seriously, what was there not to like? She got loads of cool presents, pigged out on chocolate and hung out with her older cousins, who were a right laugh. Plus no school – which meant no Daisy – for two weeks as well. Result.

As she walked past the Brennan's house she glanced at the illuminated reindeers in the front garden. As neighbours went, the Brennans weren't too bad. Their kids seemed to live at her house but they kept Ellie and Freddy busy which, in turn, meant that they didn't pester her. Sophie was a bit mumsy but she'd always been good to Indie. She'd bought her an awesome present for her thirteenth birthday, a coveted bag that was sold out in most shops and had been the envy of all her friends. She had no idea how Sophie had managed to get hold of it: perhaps she was cooler than Indie had given her credit for. But as nice as she was, she doubted that Sophie would keep quiet about her bunking off school.

Indie pulled her hood down over her head self-consciously, lowered her eyes and picked up the pace, walking past the Brennan's house as quickly as she could and quietly letting herself in through the front door of her own home.

The house was warm and comforting and she took off her

shoes and coat, sighing with the relief of being safely inside. A noise from upstairs made her stop. Was someone home? She listened again but heard nothing. Perhaps it was just her imagination, or a noise coming from next door? She crept up the stairs as quiet as a mouse and peered through the open doors of her siblings' bedrooms and the bathroom but there was no one there. She relaxed and was just about to go back downstairs when she heard the noise again. It was coming from her parents' room in the loft. She panicked and froze on the spot, trying to decide whether to do a runner or face the problem head-on. If she left the house, where would she go? It was freezing outside. And what if Sophie *had* seen her come in and told her mum, then she'd be in huge trouble.

She had a brainwave. She'd pop upstairs, tell her mum or dad, whoever it was, that she had awful period pains. Then hopefully they'd give her a hot water bottle and leave her to it. Feeling calmer now that she had hatched a good plan, she made her way up the stairs, ready to announce her arrival, but stopped dead when she reached the doorway. Inside were two adults, completely naked, writhing around on the bed, clearly having sex.

And only one of them was her parent.

She stared in silent horror at the sight in front of her and then backed away slowly before they saw her. She crept back down the stairs, tugged on her shoes and let herself silently out of the house, rushing back down Pemberton Road as fast as she could. She shivered in the cold and cursed herself for not picking up her coat on the way out, but she'd been desperate to leave.

What the actual fuck? She felt sick to the bone. It was literally the most disgusting, horrifying thing she had ever seen in her life. How could they do this? They were vile, horrible, selfish bastards and she hated them. They had ruined everything. And they were meant to be the *parents,* the role models to their children. What an absolute joke. Now here she was, out in the cold all alone with no coat and nowhere to go. They'd done that to her.

Tears were falling down her cheeks and she wiped them away angrily. She crossed her arms tightly in front of herself to keep warm against the December chill and marched towards the park. Once she was inside the park gates, she stopped and looked around, trying to decide where to go. She glanced at the children's playground, saw that it was empty and made a beeline for it, sitting down on a swing and pushing herself up, up, up into the air.

She had loved the swings when she was a little girl. She used to beg her parents to keep pushing her, wailing so hard whenever they stopped that they would immediately start up again just to avoid the drama. She could have stayed on them for hours, soaring through the sky, feeling weightless and free. But her childhood was over now, she realised. She could never take her life back to the way it was after seeing what she had just seen.

The soothing to and fro movement of the swing calmed her down a bit and she considered her options. She could send a text now, revealing what she had just seen, and it would all be out in the open. But something was stopping her. It was too easy; they'd be let off too lightly. She was apoplectic with rage and she would never, ever, ever forgive them for this. She wanted revenge. But the question was, what was she going to do? She wasn't sure yet, but she knew one thing for sure. They were going to pay for what they'd done. She would make damn sure of it.

~

The problem was, once she'd opened the can of worms it was impossible to close it again. After years of blindly trusting that Jack would never cheat on her, an idea had come to Angie and planted itself in her mind. Perhaps she'd got it wrong this whole time. And once she'd allowed that single, solitary thought to become a possibility, it opened the floodgates for more.

Was this paranoia or realisation? She didn't know anymore.

She suspected everyone – a pretty girl from Jack's work, who had never been anything but lovely to Angie, suddenly became enemy number one when she called the house asking to speak to him. The waitress in the coffee shop where they went for brunch on weekends, whose face always lit up whenever she saw Jack ('It's because I'm a good tipper,' he said), Angie now saw in a different light. All the mums who asked where Jack was when she took Ellie and Freddy to school were now suspects in a crime of passion. At least she'd cleared Sophie of any wrongdoing: that was one step too far, even for Angie.

Still, she had never felt so out of control in her life. It was like she was going mad. One minute she was unravelling, imagining implausible scenarios in her head, the next she was talking herself off the ledge, reminding herself that she had no proof of any of this, that it might all be in her head. She considered confronting Jack, having it all out with him once and for all, but she was worried he would think she was crazy. She had always been so cool, so measured, she couldn't let Jack see what was happening to her: it was shameful.

No, she decided, she couldn't talk to Jack until she had some evidence. She had started covertly checking his phone and emails whenever she could, but she hadn't found anything suspicious yet. Each time she checked and found nothing, she felt a wave of relief but it never lasted longer than a few hours before she was working herself up into a state again. Day by day she was oscillating between suspicion and disbelief and she was exhausted.

Jack had been asking her what was wrong. She tried to behave as though everything was fine, but it was becoming harder to hide her feelings. Sometimes she found herself staring at him with fury or flinching from his touch and he would look at her, hurt.

'Have I done something to upset you?' he would ask.

'No it's not you, I'm just tired,' she always said.

'I'm worried about you, Angie. I don't think this new working pattern is helping. You're trying to squeeze the same amount of work into less hours and it's stressing you out. Perhaps you should consider going back to the old routine?'

'I can't do that, it's not fair on the children. They've just got used to having me around. And anyway, I'm enjoying the school runs. And you're busy on the new documentary.'

'Look, I know you want to do everything, Angie, to please everyone, but sometimes you have to let things go. You're not superhuman. None of us are.'

'I do know that, Jack.'

'But do you really? It's very easy to spread yourself too thinly, you know.'

'Jack, I'm fine.' She could tell he wasn't convinced but he didn't challenge her further. And on top of that her work, her haven, was causing her problems too. Despite supporting her request for flexible working it was now becoming clear what they really thought about it. She was getting fewer of the juicy cases, being invited to fewer meetings, as though she was slowly being frozen out. Her dreams of becoming partner were rapidly falling by the wayside. Her new school year's resolution to get a better work-life balance was working in theory but in practice it was benefitting neither part of her life. Everything was falling apart.

But she had to keep it together, she just had to. People relied on her. Her mum had just moved into sheltered accommodation and was having a difficult time settling in, so Angie was trying her best to make the place look homely and familiar. Christmas was around the corner and the children were counting on her to make it special as always. She had presents to buy and wrap, visits to arrange with family, panto tickets to order and, in a moment of sheer madness, she had offered to help out at the school's winter fair too. And that was on top of her usual heavy workload. She would just have to brush everything under the carpet for now and get through the rest of the year. She'd deal with it all in the New Year.

At least Indie was on good form. She was being uncharacteristically nice to Angie, loving even. It was a relief not to be constantly treading on eggshells around her. They had gone shopping together a few days ago, just the two of them, and had a marvellous time. Angie guessed it was because her efforts to be around more over the last few months had paid off, allowing them to bond again. After two years of sulking, Indie was emerging from her cocoon and blossoming into a beautiful, thoughtful young lady. She was so proud of her, as she was of all her children. Whatever happened, they had to come first. And if that meant plastering on a smile and getting on with life for now, then so be it.

15

Sophie admired her reflection in the wardrobe mirror and smoothed down a non-existent crease on her dress. It was the same one she'd worn for the night out that never happened with Angie a few months ago and after months of training and teaching in the pool it looked even better on her now. She had got her hair cut just before Christmas and it skimmed her shoulder blades in glossy waves. On her hairdresser's advice she had splashed out on balayage and a smoothing treatment too, an impulse decision she had made with the thrill of knowing that she was earning her own money again, even if it was a pittance compared to someone like Angie. *Angie.* She tried not to think about her and returned to looking at herself in the mirror again.

She had started the year feeling stuck in a rut. Her career had dwindled to a near halt, her children were growing up and becoming more independent, and their plans to have a baby were going nowhere. But look at her now! She had embarked on an exciting new career and was feeling better and healthier than she had in years. She was practically glowing. What a way to bring in the new year. The only thorn in her side was that she hadn't been able to share her joy with Angie. She tried to ignore the butterflies in her stomach at the idea of seeing her again.

There had been no row, no huge blowout which would explain the shift in their relationship, just a subtle pulling away from each other. One day they were the closest of friends, going on holiday together and spending their weekends in each other's homes, and the next they were barely communicating at all. They both had their reasons, perhaps one more than the other.

Now she couldn't remember the last time she had seen Angie, other than the occasional glimpse. She didn't even bump into them on the school run anymore as she had taken to driving instead on Angie's days, so as to avoid her. Tom and Katie, oblivious to the shift, continued to play next door but instead of going round to collect them herself, Sophie had started shouting over the fence for them to come home. She couldn't reconcile her feelings about it all.

She had enough going on in her life to distract her though. She had passed her swimming instructor training in October and had immediately signed up to a more advanced course. She had got a new job teaching at the local leisure centre and was thoroughly enjoying it. Although she was about twenty years older than most of the other teachers, they had welcomed her warmly and she had already earned a reputation for having a gift with nervous swimmers. They'd all gone out for a meal together just before Christmas and she had loved feeling part of a team again. When she wasn't teaching, she was often swimming herself, powering up and down the pool until her mind finally shut out the messiness of life and focused singularly on the job at hand. It was addictive, that feeling of clarity in a world of chaos.

A few weeks ago, she had gone to the doctor and asked for a prescription for the pill, closing the chapter on her baby-making days for good. Her life had changed over the past few months and so had she. Having a baby with Alan no longer felt like the right thing to do. She didn't know what the next year held for her yet but she knew that it was going to be very different.

When Jack had invited her over for a New Year's Eve party, as they were walking home from school together one day, she had been surprised. Her initial reaction was to say no.

'I'm not sure about that,' she told him.

'Why?'

'You know why, Jack.'

'You mean Angie?'

'Yes of course I mean Angie.'

Jack looked pained. They rarely talked about Angie, ignoring the elephant in the room whenever they saw each other.

'I think this party is what we all need actually,' he told her. 'A chance to clear the air.'

Sophie was still unconvinced, but Jack looked at her pleadingly. 'Come on, Soph, it's been such a strange time. I think Angie's having some sort of burn out but she refuses to talk to me about it, and life at home is not the most fun at the moment. I've not been out in weeks; I'm knackered and I need to have a laugh. And I really want to spend New Year's Eve with you.'

'And Alan?' Sophie reminded him.

'The whole Brennan brood if it means you'll come.'

Sophie thought about it. Her instincts were still screaming at her to turn down the invitation but Jack was looking at her like an adorable little puppy, making it impossible for her to refuse. And there was a small part of her that still hoped she and Angie could find a way back, no matter how unlikely that seemed. She looked at Jack and relented. 'Oh, go on then, you sod.'

The party had been weeks away then, so she could put it to the back of her mind and forget all about it. But after a whirlwind Christmas, New Year's Eve had arrived before she knew it and now she couldn't put it off any longer. It was time to face the music, or Angie at least, and she was feeling horribly nervous. She gave her hair one last smooth over, took a deep breath and made her way downstairs, where Alan and the kids were waiting for her.

'What do you think?' she said to Alan, giving him a little twirl.

'Beautiful, Soph, as always,' he said. Tom and Katie were hovering by the back door already, eager to get going. They both remembered how fun the party had been last year and were looking forward to staying up late and having a sleepover.

'Come on, let's go,' Tom said impatiently, tapping his foot, as Sophie scrabbled around for the food and drinks she had bought to take with them. With a final glance in the mirror, she nodded to Tom and he was out of the door and racing up the garden, with Katie on his heels, before she'd even put her shoes on. By the time she and Alan arrived, the children had already made themselves at home with the easy confidence of guests who knew they were welcome. Sophie shrugged her coat off and saw Jack making up drinks in the kitchen, while wearing a headband with sparkly balls bouncing around on top. She couldn't stop a grin from escaping. Somehow, he managed to pull it off. He turned around and his face lit up when he saw her.

'Brilliant, you're here! Let's get this party started!' He handed mocktails to Tom and Katie and proffered martini glasses at Sophie and Alan.

'What do we have here?' Sophie asked, peering suspiciously into the glass.

'A Jack Special,' he declared proudly as Sophie took a hesitant sip. She winced. It was tasty but potent as usual. She'd have to make sure she didn't get too plastered tonight.

'Where's Angie?' she asked, remembering how last year she

had gone upstairs to find her. She realised that she no longer felt entitled to do so.

'Upstairs beautifying herself with Indie. They've been at it most of the afternoon. Facials, hair, nails, you name it. I'm sure they'll be down in a minute but feel free to go on up if you want to?'

Sophie considered it and said, 'No thanks, I'll wait here.'

Angie admired herself in the mirror. She and Indie had spent the day pampering themselves and she'd even let her daughter curl her hair into loose waves. She'd done an excellent job, Angie thought, turning from left to right and enjoying how her hair bounced around lightly as she moved. She had treated herself to a new dress for Christmas and she loved the way it fit her – smart and subtly sexy. After a fun afternoon with Indie and two G&Ts, she was in a good mood.

It was time to put this disaster of a year behind her and start afresh. She would talk to Jack – properly talk to him – about how she was feeling. She would start making more of an effort with her friends again. And she would stop beating herself up when she couldn't successfully juggle the many balls in her life, focusing more on the ones that really mattered.

'You look beautiful, Mum,' Indie said.

'So do you, Indie.'

She really did. Indie had always been striking and now she was growing into a beautiful young woman. Some people had said she had model potential and Angie had to agree. How lucky, she thought, to be that young and attractive, with your whole life ahead of you. She smiled proudly at her daughter, grateful that she had wanted to spend New Year with her family.

'I can hear them downstairs, Mum. We'd better go down.'

With one last look at herself in the mirror, Angie turned around and replied, 'Let's go.'

As Indie made her way down the stairs, clutching her mother's hand protectively, she smiled in anticipation. Angie looked stunning, just as Indie had wanted her to. She had spent hours pampering her and perfecting her hair and she hoped that her father would notice. She felt a fresh surge of anger at the memory etched in her mind. Ever since that vile afternoon when her entire life had come crashing down around her, she had been planning her revenge. And when Jack had told her that they were having a New Year's Eve party, the idea had come to her immediately. There was nothing like an audience for the show she was planning to put on.

Of course, if she went ahead with it there would be some collateral damage and she did feel really bad about that, but that was life. People always got hurt. She knew that more than anyone. She felt like a coiled spring. Tonight was the night when the shit was going to hit the fan. Big time. And she was ready for it.

Angie and Indie entered the kitchen looking like some sort of supermodel dream team. Sophie felt instantly inferior, despite her earlier confidence. They were both wearing little black dresses, which showed off their long legs, their hair loose and curled, and long gold chains around their necks. Sophie braced herself as Angie came over and hugged her.

'Sophie, it's good to see you. I'm *so* sorry I've been useless recently. I've just been absolutely snowed under; I don't know where the days go. But it's inexcusable.'

Sophie hugged Angie back. 'No worries,' she replied, 'I completely understand.'

She felt like they were both lying to each other.

Angie stood back and looked her up and down. 'You look absolutely gorgeous, Sophie! Have you changed your hair?'

'Yes, a few weeks ago.' Sophie couldn't help feeling delighted that Angie had noticed.

'It really suits you, and that dress is beautiful!' Angie smiled at her again before moving away to greet Alan and then picking up the champagne that Jack had poured for her.

'Cheers,' she said brightly, raising her glass and they all clinked glasses, including Indie who was clutching a champagne flute filled with lemonade. Sophie caught her eye and the teenager stared back at her. Was it just her or was Indie looking at her a little strangely? Feeling uncomfortable, Sophie looked away. When she glanced back, Indie was smiling sweetly.

'Mummy says I can stay up until midnight,' she announced.

'Of course, darling, you're thirteen now,' Angie said, putting her arm around her daughter.

'Old enough for some champagne?' Indie asked hopefully.

'Nice try,' Jack replied. 'But you know the answer's no.'

Indie sighed theatrically and drifted off to see what her older brother was up to.

Sophie looked at Angie. 'How are things?' she asked.

'Oh fine, nothing to report,' Angie said. 'But never mind me, tell me about you. I'm dying to hear about your swimming course.'

Sophie started filling Angie in on her training and her new job, hesitantly at first and then more enthusiastically as she relaxed. Despite what had happened over the last few months, she remembered how lovely it was to be in Angie's company and how much she'd missed it. *I might as well make the most of tonight,* she thought. *I doubt it will happen again.*

Within a couple of hours, they were both in fits of laughter at Alan and Jack's attempts to dance to 'Gangnam Style'. Ellie,

Freddy, Tom and Katie, who had been determined to stay up late, had completely exhausted themselves by nine thirty. They took a child each, carrying them up the stairs like they were babies and settling them into their beds before heading back downstairs to continue their party.

'Who's for shots?' Jack asked.

'Christ, Jack, we're not twenty-one,' Angie replied.

'Oh, come on, Ange, it's New Year's Eve! One little shot won't hurt.'

'Not for me,' Angie said.

Jack looked at Alan. 'Al, mate?'

'Not a chance.'

Finally, he looked at Sophie. 'Come on, Brennan, don't let me down.'

Why not? she thought. *The children are asleep. After a momentous year, why shouldn't I go out with a bang?* She looked at Jack conspiratorially and grinned. 'Go on then!'

Jack beamed and dashed off to get the tequila. Sophie watched him as he diligently prepared lemons and salt before ferrying everything over to the table and passing a shot glass to her.

'One, two, three, *cheers!*' he said as they both lifted a glass to their lips. Sophie swallowed it in one go and winced, almost gagging. 'Jeez,' she said, wiping her eyes. 'There's a reason why I don't do this anymore.'

'I'll get us another one,' Jack announced, heading back to the kitchen.

Before she could protest, Sophie got the sensation of being watched again and saw Indie staring at her from the corner of the room. She looked around at the others, but they were chatting away and didn't seem to have noticed. When she glanced back at Indie, she was looking down at her phone. Had she imagined it? The tequila sloshed around her stomach and she felt queasy, but then Jack hijacked the stereo and put 'Gangnam Style' on for the third time that evening and everyone got up to dance. She joined in and tried to forget about Indie.

By midnight, she was half-cut and declaring to anyone who would listen that she hadn't had this much fun in ages. As the amount of alcohol she consumed increased, her anxiety about being around Angie decreased. They made their way unsteadily to the den so that they could watch the countdown and fireworks on television. Benji and Indie, who had disappeared to text their friends, rejoined them.

Sophie smiled, enjoying her drunken buzz. Change lay ahead but everything was going to be okay. More than okay. She couldn't wait. She started counting down.

'Ten, nine, eight, seven... Happy New Year!'

She turned to Angie and hugged her first before moving on to Alan.

'Happy New Year, Al!' she said, giving him a quick peck on the lips.

'You too, Soph,' he replied.

She looked for Jack who grabbed her and picked her up, spinning her around. 'Happy New Year, Brennan,' he said.

She laughed with delight and pulled away from him to wish Benji and Indie a Happy New Year. But just as she was about to move towards them, Indie stepped forward.

'I'd like to propose a toast,' she said, looking around the room at each adult, one by one. When her eyes fixed on Sophie, her hairs stood on end as she realised what no one else had yet. Indie was about to do something bad. Very bad.

'Lovely!' Angie exclaimed, beaming.

'I'd like to toast to the new lovebirds.'

Everyone looked confused. Sophie glanced at Jack, who was looking at Angie, who was watching Indie. The atmosphere shifted and their smiles started to falter.

'Indie...' Jack began, but Indie simply looked at him and shook her head.

'I'm sorry, Dad,' she said.

'Indie, what's going on?' Angie asked urgently.

Indie looked at her mother and raised her champagne glass of lemonade.

'To Mum and Alan – who have been having it off behind everyone's backs.' Indie announced with a flourish. 'I hope you'll be very happy together.'

16

Angie stood frozen with terror. This had not just happened. Surely this had not just happened.

How did Indie find out?

How much does she know?

The silence was deafening. Angie looked at her daughter and she stared defiantly back. She looked positively triumphant. Angie realised with alarm that Indie's warmth towards her over the past few weeks had been entirely false. She felt like she'd been slapped in the face.

Someone turned the TV off.

'What the fuck is going on?' Jack asked, looking at Angie.

'Mum?' Benji asked, looking between his sister, mother and father in confusion.

'Kids, out,' Jack said. Benji obediently turned to leave but Indie hesitated.

'*Out,*' Jack roared.

'I'm sorry, Dad,' Indie said again, before turning to Sophie. 'I'm sorry, Sophie. You're a nice person. You don't deserve this.'

Angie observed her daughter as she walked past. The look of

contempt on her face was something that she knew she'd never forget.

'I'll ask again. What the fuck is going on?' Jack's confusion had turned to fury.

Angie risked a glance at Alan who had sunk down onto the sofa with his head in his hands. *There's no getting out of this*, she thought. *There's nothing I could possibly say to make this go away.* She looked away. Alan was going to be no good to her at all; the man could barely hold it together. It was, as usual, down to her to take control of the situation.

The first few minutes of the new year ticked on by. It was meant to be the new start that Angie had been waiting for. A chance to sort her life out and put everything behind her. But the past had come back to haunt her and now all that was left to do was to find the words to explain why she had betrayed all of the people she loved in one fell swoop.

With a final glance at Alan she said, 'Look, can we all just sit down and I'll explain.'

'No, we can't sit down and you'll explain everything right now.'

Angie closed her eyes and tried to imagine herself at work, attempting to summon the calm control she felt when she was representing a client. *This is not my life. This is someone else's life. I'm just telling their story.* She opened them again and said steadily, 'Well I'm going to sit down.'

She perched on the sofa, all eyes on her. And she began to talk.

It was never meant to happen. And when it did, it was only ever meant to happen once.

Jack was working away all week and Angie had come home

early so that she could pick the children up later. She was working on a case about a woman who had been accused of assaulting her fiancé. Her mitigation was that she had found him on top of their kitchen table, having sex with one of the bridesmaids-to-be. Angie knew that the case was going to attract media interest and she felt sorry for the woman. She had reacted in a moment of humiliation and anger and as a result was going to have her name splashed across the papers. In her experience, women like that went one of two ways. They either hid away, avoiding attention and refusing to speak to anyone, or they sold the whole sordid story to the highest bidder. She wondered which way her client was going to go.

Yet the case had set her mind whirring. This woman had been convinced that her fiancé adored her but he was sleeping with her friend behind her back the whole time. He was even going to *marry* her, despite his affair. What kind of person does that, she wondered?

The same type of person as Jack?

He fit the profile after all. A previous track record of sleeping with plenty of women. Unpredictable behaviour. Disappearing for hours on end without telling her where he was going.

And then it hit her. She was just like the fiancée.

It was like a bolt from the blue. Suddenly she saw her past in a completely different light. Snippets of memories, small things she'd dismissed at the time, came back to her, loaded with new meaning.

When one of his female colleagues had started acting strangely around her for no reason, as though she felt awkward in her company, Jack had said it was because she was having personal problems. Was Jack the cause of those problems?

When a Sunday League football buddy of Jack's made a comment about him being a love-rat, then quickly backtracked and claimed he was referring to his university era, even though he hadn't gone to the same one as Angie and Jack. Jack had told her it was because they'd shared stories of their student days.

And then of course there was the pink thong. How quick she'd been to believe his story.

Had Jack been sleeping around behind her back? Were these late nights out really a front for his hook-ups with various women? Could he have been doing it, and getting away with it, for years? Did everyone know about it apart from her?

She had always told herself that she could trust Jack, that he'd never hurt her, not seriously. Yes, he'd been a bit of a party animal in his younger years but she thought she'd tamed him when they got together. Now she realised how naïve and stupid that sounded. You couldn't tame someone. A leopard never really changes its spots. Jack had never changed, not really.

She didn't have any proof. She hadn't walked in on her partner shagging someone on her kitchen table. Yet in her mind she had already convicted him. It was like a moment of revelation. She sat there, staring at the case notes, as the words blurred in front of her eyes, and considered the prospect that her entire marriage had been a lie.

And that's how Alan had found her, when he appeared at her back door asking to borrow some milk. 'Sorry to trouble you, Angie, I'm doing the invoicing and I'm gasping for a cuppa.'

'No problem,' she said, forcing a smile and beckoning him inside as she went to the fridge to grab a bottle. At the time, all she could think about was how quickly she could get rid of him.

'How are you?'

They were three simple words, a question that she answered every day without a second thought. Yet suddenly they were loaded with meaning and something gave way inside her until, before she knew it, she was crying. And then she was sobbing – partly for that poor woman whose bridesmaid-shagging fiancé had ruined her life but mostly for herself.

She couldn't remember the last time she had cried but once she started, she couldn't stop. Years of anxiety, frustration, anguish and guilt poured out of her until she was shaking with the violence of her tears. Poor Alan hadn't known what on earth to do with her. Really, he'd just been in the wrong place at the wrong time. Perhaps if he'd popped by another day, another time, things might have turned out completely different.

He walked carefully up to her, like she was a wild, unpredictable horse, and prised the milk bottle from her tightly clenched hand, placing it gently on the kitchen surface. Then he put the kettle on, made her a cup of tea and waited until she had calmed down.

'Oh, Alan, I'm so sorry,' she said when she was finally able to speak again, frantically wiping away her tears in embarrassment.

'You've nothing to be sorry about. Do you want to talk about it?'

'No, honestly, I'm fine.'

'Are you sure? A problem shared is a problem halved, you know.'

She looked at him then, really looked at him. He was such a nice man. Jack was funny, charming, charismatic, but was he a nice man? She wasn't sure anymore.

'I think I'm going mad, Alan,' she told him.

'Tell me,' he urged.

And so she did. She told him everything – about Jack, her suspicions, the pink thong. And then about how she felt like a failure, how her children loved their father more than her and she hated it but didn't know how to make it better. And, finally, how she hated herself. As she talked, he sat beside her and listened, and when she was finished, he put his arm around her and held her close to him for a long time. She leaned into him and a feeling crept over her, one that she hadn't felt in years. She realised what it was. She felt safe.

After a few minutes she had come back to her senses. She handed him the milk bottle.

'You'd better be getting on with your invoicing,' she told him.

'Are you sure? I don't like to leave you like this.'

'I'm feeling much better, honestly.'

He hesitated but nodded. Giving her arm a squeeze, he walked towards the back door.

'Alan?'

He turned and looked at her.

'Thank you. And please, don't tell anyone about today?'

'I won't say anything,' he replied. 'But you need to talk to Jack. You won't feel better until this is all out in the open.'

She nodded. 'I know. I will. Thank you.'

She really had intended on talking to Jack that evening, but then something or other had happened to distract her. Then the next day Freddy had a temperature and had to stay home from school and before she knew it, the opportunity had passed.

Looking back now, it was painfully obvious that she shouldn't have bottled it all up inside. She should have dealt with it straight away. If she had, it probably wouldn't have manifested itself in the way that it did. But she'd always been terrible at talking about her feelings and the longer it went unsaid, the harder it became to say it at all. So instead she tried to bury it.

But there was something else too, something niggling at her. She had enjoyed the intimate moment with Alan. He had listened so attentively to her as though, in that moment, she was the only thing that mattered in the whole world. She had always thought of Alan as a steady, perhaps even boring man, but now she saw him differently. She found herself thinking about him and wondering how different her life would have been if she'd married an Alan rather than a Jack.

Afterwards Jack would accuse her of wanting revenge against him for crimes that he hadn't even committed, but she knew it wasn't tit-for-tat that had prompted what happened next. It wasn't a case of the grass being greener on the other side of the garden fence either. No, it had been far more basic than that. By chance, Alan had become her knight in shining armour when she needed help and, like all fairy-tale damsels in distress, she had fallen for her rescuer.

He came round to see her again, a couple of days later. She had just got back from court and was opening up her laptop when he appeared at the back door and she rushed to open it and ushered him inside. 'Come in, it's freezing out there!'

'I hope you don't mind me coming by,' he said as he took off his dirty shoes and rubbed his arms up and down his jumper to warm up. 'I saw that you'd come home early again, and I've been waiting for an opportunity to catch you on your own and see how you are.'

'Not at all, it's lovely to see you,' she said. 'I'm still horribly embarrassed about what happened the other week though.'

'You have nothing to be embarrassed about, don't give it another thought.'

She smiled at him and a warm sensation crept over her body. He had checked up on her. He cared about her. Suddenly she didn't want him to leave and she was relieved when he accepted her offer of a coffee. He sat down on one of the bar stools and watched her as she made the drinks. She felt his eyes on her and subconsciously smoothed down her hair.

'Have you spoken to Jack?' he asked.

'No,' she admitted, handing him his coffee and sitting on the stool next to him.

'Why not?'

'Well that's the million-pound question, isn't it?'

Alan regarded her, waiting for a better response, until she

was compelled to say more. 'I've never been good at talking about my feelings, I have no idea why I blurted it all out to you. You're wasted on property, Alan; you should be a therapist. Anyway, I've always been more of a stiff upper lip type of person and until recently I thought it was working rather well for me.'

'But it's not.'

'Well clearly not. But every time I think I should say something to Jack, I convince myself that it's all in my head, and that if I tell him then at best, he'll think I'm a paranoid, jealous wife and at worst that I've actually lost my mind.'

'No man should ever make you feel any of those things.'

'Are you saying I deserve more?' The words were out of her mouth before she'd even processed them in her head. As soon as she said it, she realised it sounded like an innuendo.

But Alan didn't seem fazed. 'You definitely deserve more.'

'Do you think I'm losing my mind?'

'No, I don't. And I think that anyone who makes you feel like that isn't good enough for you.'

'So you don't think Jack is good enough for me?' She was challenging him now, and perversely enjoying herself, but he still seemed unruffled. She was quite impressed actually.

'Not if he makes you feel like this, no. From what you've told me, he's acted like a bit of an arsehole in the past, so it's understandable that you feel anxious. He's done that to you. But you're not being fair to him either, if you don't tell him how you feel. You're assuming that you know how he's going to react but you don't.'

She knew he was right but why was he so much easier to talk to than her own husband?

'I just feel so guilty,' she admitted. 'I feel like it's all my fault. I put my own needs before those of my husband and my children and now I'm being punished.'

'I don't like to hear you talking like this, Angie,' Alan said.

'None of this is your fault. You're an incredible person, come on now, you know that. You've achieved so much. Most women worship you and the men... Well, you know the effect that you have on men.'

They were embarking on dangerous territory now but she was not inclined to stop it. How long had it been since she'd had a conversation like this with a man? Since someone had admired her the way that Alan was doing? Oh God, she'd missed this feeling of power. She knew, in that moment, she could have him if she wanted him. Did she want him? She reached out and took his hand, stroking it with her own. He looked at it, and then at her, in surprise.

'Do I have an effect on you, Alan?'

He looked terrified at first. He was so easy to read and she could see that he was torn between desire and loyalty. She was the type of woman that someone like Alan would consider way out of his league. Most men saw her like that. Jack was one of the only ones she'd ever met who was confident enough to think otherwise. All Alan needed was one small, gentle push in the right direction and he would be hers. She was finally in control again and it felt good.

She leaned forward and kissed him. Time stood still as she waited for his reaction. And then he put one of his hands behind her head, grabbed some of her hair and kissed her back. He lifted her up like she was as light as a feather and put her on the kitchen surface, spreading her legs and pushing himself in between them. He was more passionate than she'd been expecting. She had underestimated Alan Brennan. She closed her legs around him and kissed him back.

Afterwards, they dressed silently and sat side by side on the kitchen surface, next to their tepid coffees. The spark between them that had been so electric minutes before had gone and they were Angie and Alan again, two neighbours who had committed an unspeakable act.

'Angie...' he began, and then paused, not knowing what to say.

'It's my fault,' she said. 'I kissed you, I shouldn't have done that. I'm sorry.'

'Can we just pretend it never happened?'

'I think that's the best we can do.'

He left soon afterwards. How could he stick around and make polite conversation after something like that? The aftermath was a total anti-climax. She was just alone, again, cleaning the kitchen surface and wondering what in God's name she had just done.

But somehow, she managed to convince herself that it was okay. She and Jack were even now, she told herself. He no longer had one up on her. She was no longer the victim. And as for Sophie, of course she felt bad but it was a one-off and it hadn't meant anything to either of them. It would never happen again and telling her would only cause a whole lot of unnecessary pain. Sophie was the best friend she'd ever had and nothing would change that, not even this. In truth, no matter how selfish it was, she didn't want to lose her.

She tried to act normally. On the other side of the fence, she suspected that Alan was doing much the same. There was too much for them to lose to blow their cover, she knew it and he knew it. As time went on it became easier. Months went by, life went on. No one suspected a thing and she even began to convince herself that it never really happened at all.

But then that damn summer holiday had thrown everything up in the air again.

She had sensed Alan's eyes on her all week. She had splashed out on some sexy bikinis and as she paraded around the villa or climbed out of the pool, she knew she looked good.

She enjoyed knowing that he was admiring her but she didn't feel guilty. She liked it when any man admired her and she wasn't sorry for it. All women liked to know they were attractive. It was just a bit of harmless fun, she told herself, it didn't mean anything at all. And anyway, Sophie and Jack were so busy having a laugh together that they barely even noticed.

So when Indie took it upon herself to inform her that she was a terrible mother and that her husband preferred the company of other women, bringing her fears and anxieties flooding back again, who could she possibly turn to but her knight in shining armour? The man who had never been anything but kind to her. The man who she knew was attracted to her.

She started thinking about him more and more. She remembered how he had made her feel last time. It had faded as soon as it was over but for a few moments it had been bliss, like a long dead spark inside her had been reignited. She had felt alive and invigorated again for the first time in so long. She knew it wasn't real, it was a temporary high just like a hit from drugs, but she wanted to feel it again. She needed to feel it. She tried not to think about Sophie.

By the time she got home from holiday, her yearning to see him was so strong that all she could think of was how to engineer a meeting between them. In the end it was easy. Jack was out working on a new TV series and Sophie had rediscovered swimming and, creature of habit that she was, went to the leisure centre at the same time every day. She knew that Alan was working on a house renovation up the road in Barnet. So when she sent him a text asking him to come round as a matter of urgency, he was at her door in twenty minutes.

'Everything okay, Ange?' he asked, as she let him in.

'Yes, it's fine. Coffee?'

He looked confused. 'You said it was an emergency?'

'It is an emergency. I need to talk to you.'

'What about?'

'What happened between us.'

Alan sat down on one of the kitchen chairs with a heavy sigh. 'I thought we'd agreed to pretend that it never happened. It was months ago. Why are you bringing it up now?'

'Because I've been thinking about you. A lot.'

Alan looked up at her in alarm.

She started walking slowly towards him, unbuttoning the top of her dress.

'Angie...' he began, holding up a hand to stop her. But already she could see he was conflicted. He wanted her. He was thinking about her in that bikini on holiday. Perhaps he thought about her at night too, when he was lying in bed. She'd always had power over men. Well, all men apart from Jack. She shook the thought of her husband from her mind.

'I want you. And I think you want me.'

'Angie, please,' he said. He was almost begging her.

She finished unbuttoning her dress. Underneath it she had put on the bikini she'd worn on holiday as a final touch. She looked at him and he looked at her, and she knew she'd won.

Over the next three months they met up a few more times. She would text him and he would come. Afterwards it was always the same; they knew it was wrong but they both knew they'd be back for more. And then a couple of weeks before Christmas, Alan finally ended it for good.

'This has to stop, Angie,' he said, as he buttoned up his shirt. 'I'm serious. I'm done.'

She considered trying to persuade him otherwise but she knew he was right. It had already gone too far, way too far. The worst of it, she realised afterwards, was that she didn't even care. Alan was not the answer to all of her problems. If anything, he'd made them so much worse.

She nodded. 'What do we do now?'

'I don't know. I've never been in this situation before.'

'Look, no one knows about it. Perhaps no one needs to. Why don't we just put it behind us and move on. Too much is at stake otherwise.'

She could see the relief on his face and knew that she had given him the get-out clause he'd been desperately hoping for. Men were all the same, even the nice ones.

'I think that's a good idea,' he said.

'Okay, so we're agreed.' She stood up and started getting dressed too. They turned away from each other, both conscious of their naked bodies now they had agreed to stop.

As he pulled his jumper on, he said, 'I want you to know, I've never done anything like this before in my life.'

'I know.'

'I love Sophie.'

'I know that too.'

He nodded. When he was finished dressing, they went back down to the kitchen. He opened the back door to leave, and then turned to look at her sadly.

'Bye, Angie.'

'Bye, Alan.'

She watched him disappear through the gate into his own back garden. And it was then that the crushing realisation of what she'd done finally hit her. She'd been living in a fantasy. Alan was not her knight in shining armour. They were not going to run off into the sunset together. He was the husband of her neighbour, her friend, and she had done a terrible thing.

But she had things to do so she poured herself a glass of water, opened up her emails and got on with her work, just like she had always done, all her life, no matter what it threw at her.

But she found she could no longer concentrate. It was different this time and she was unable to brush everything under the carpet. The guilt had started eating away at her and Jack had noticed and kept asking her what was wrong. She had no idea what to say to him. She could hardly accuse him of having affairs when the only proof she had of any indiscretion was that of her own. And as for Sophie, she could barely look the woman in the eye. So she started avoiding her, finding excuses as to why she couldn't stop for a chat whenever she popped round. Seeing the disappointment on her friend's face, which was later replaced with hurt when Sophie realised she was getting the brush-off, Angie felt even more wretched. The fact that they were neighbours was a fitting punishment for her crime, a relentless reminder of what a terrible person she was.

For a while she worried that Alan would crack under the pressure and confess everything to Sophie. She waited for her to appear at her back door, hammering it down and launching herself at Angie like a feral animal. Sometimes she woke up in the night in a cold sweat thinking that Sophie was in her room, watching her. But as the days, then weeks, went by and nothing happened, she began to breathe. If he was going to do it, he'd have done it by now. Their secret was safe. They had got away with it without hurting anyone but themselves.

At least that's what she'd thought.

But then her daughter, her flesh and blood, the girl she had conceived, carried, birthed, loved and nurtured for thirteen years, had somehow found out about it and had set out to destroy her. And by the time she realised what she was up to, it was too late.

17

At first, Sophie had laughed. She had actually laughed. When Indie had made her New Year's toast, she had assumed that it was some sort of outlandish joke and had instinctively chuckled in response because that's what you do with jokes. *I don't get it, though*, she thought.

Perhaps Indie was trying to cause a rift between her mother and father? She looked at Angie and Jack who were gaping at each other. *Well she's certainly done that.* Sophie was momentarily cross that the girl had dragged poor Alan into it. She glanced at him for reassurance, but he wouldn't meet her eye. And that's when it hit her. This wasn't a joke at all.

'What the fuck is going on?' Jack asked. She couldn't have put it better herself.

She continued staring at Alan in disbelief but he had his head buried in his hands and refused to look up, to look at her. Apparently, he had lost his voice as well as his fucking mind. She turned to Angie who had sat down on the edge of a sofa.

'I can explain,' she began.

After that, it was a blur of words.

It was a mistake.

It only happened a few times.

It didn't mean anything.

We both regretted it.

Then silence. Evidently Angie was done with her confession.

'When did it start?' Jack asked. 'How long has it been going on?'

She saw Angie glance at Alan, but he was still sitting like a useless lump of coal on the sofa, refusing to look at anyone. The cowardly bastard.

'Not long. It was over before it began,' Angie replied.

'That's not an answer,' Jack said.

Sophie's gaze was flitting between Angie and Alan. She didn't know where to look. She didn't know what to do. She wanted to do something, anything, yet she couldn't move.

'Tell them, Angie.' It was Alan. Finally the man spoke. 'Tell them the truth.'

Angie looked momentarily irritated, like Alan was a wayward client ignoring her advice and ruining her well-laid plans. Then she sighed with apparent resignation. 'The first time it happened was in January.'

'Jesus Christ, Angie!' Jack exploded.

Sophie's mind was racing. She couldn't process it. Alan was supposed to be kind and loyal. How could he do this? And Angie was supposed to be one of her closest friends. This was the kind of mad, crazy stuff she used to write about for magazines and now it was happening to her.

'I'm so sorry,' Angie said to Jack. Then she turned to Sophie. 'I'm so sorry.'

Sophie still didn't know what to do with herself. Should she leave? Should she stay? Should she slap Angie? Should she punch Alan? *This is the worst moment of my life*, she thought.

Then something clicked into place. 'When you thought you were pregnant, you were in a right state,' she said.

Angie looked at her with wide eyes. 'Sophie...' she began.

'I couldn't work it out at the time. I mean I knew you were done having children and didn't want any more, I got that, but it seemed like more than that. Like you were terrified.'

'What's she talking about, Angie?' Jack demanded.

'And then you were funny with me for a while afterwards,' Sophie continued. 'Nothing major, I could just tell something was off. I remember asking you at the Easter party but you wouldn't talk to me.' She paused. 'You didn't know who the father was, did you? Before you realised it was a false alarm, you didn't know whether it was Alan's or Jack's.'

Angie lowered her eyes.

'Angie?' Jack was staring at her in horror. So was Alan.

Angie looked like she was in hell. *Now she knows how it feels*, Sophie thought.

'Angie?' Jack shouted.

Slowly, Angie shook her head. 'No,' she replied.

Jack moved towards Alan. 'I think you'd better leave.'

Sophie still hadn't moved.

'You too, Sophie,' Jack said. He looked at her apologetically. 'I need to talk to Angie.'

'What about the kids?' Sophie said, suddenly. 'They're still upstairs.'

'I'll bring them round tomorrow,' Jack assured her.

'I don't want them in this house.' Sophie was starting to panic now. 'I don't want them sleeping under her roof.'

Jack put a hand on her arm. At least one of them was managing to stay calm. 'Let them sleep, Sophie. You'll only confuse and upset them if you wake them up now, in the middle of the night, especially in the state that you're in. They'll be fine here; I'll look after them. I'll bring them round myself as soon as they wake up.'

Sophie still didn't move.

'I promise,' Jack said. 'Trust me.'

She nodded and went to follow Alan out of the room. Just before she left, she turned to Angie. But although she had a million things that she wanted to say to her, she was momentarily speechless. She turned away again in disgust and left.

They walked back round to their own house in silence. Alan put the kettle on while Sophie sat down at the kitchen table and flicked absent-mindedly through some pictures that Tom and Katie had drawn earlier that day. She had been pottering about in the kitchen while they did them, listening to the radio and singing along while she did chores. When they had proudly presented their artwork to her, she had exclaimed in delight, grabbing them both and pulling them to her for a hug. Just a few hours ago, her life had been so blissfully normal and uncomplicated. Now she was struggling to process a seismic shift.

It all made sense now, why Angie had been so funny with her. She had been keeping her distance because she'd been sleeping with her husband. And there was Sophie thinking, fretting, that she had done something to upset her. At least Angie had acted like she'd done something wrong though. Alan, on the other hand, had behaved so normally that she hadn't had the slightest inkling that anything was up. The man she thought she knew better than anyone in the world had lied and cheated like he'd been doing it all his life. How could he do it?

She clutched tightly onto a picture that Katie had drawn of the four of them, Alan, Sophie, Tom and Katie, holding hands and smiling underneath a rainbow. Their perfect family of four. Her hands were shaking. She looked up at Alan, who was putting teabags in mugs.

'I don't want a cup of tea, Alan,' she said.

He paused, not sure what to do.

'Get me a whisky.'

Alan obediently went to the drinks cabinet to dig out the

stash of single malt that Sophie wouldn't normally touch. He poured them both a dram and carried the tumblers over to the kitchen table, sitting down opposite her and waiting for her to make the first move.

'Why?'

'I don't know.'

'Come on, Alan, you can do better than that.'

'Honestly, Sophie, I don't know why it happened. I didn't plan it and I've regretted it ever since. It was a moment of complete madness.'

'More than one moment,' she corrected him.

He looked pained. 'Yes, you're right. You mean the world to me, I never imagined in a million years that I would ever do anything like this. I still can't believe it myself.'

'Do you fancy her? Have you been lusting after her the whole time?'

'No,' he said. 'I don't want you thinking like that.'

'What do you expect me to think? You cheated on me, and if that wasn't enough, you cheated on me with my friend, with our neighbour.'

He lowered his head. 'I know.'

'There must be a reason. You don't just sleep with someone else for no reason.'

He rubbed his hand along the top of his head. 'We've been married a long time, Soph. I guess the spark had gone a bit, especially after all the baby-making business. And this thing, it felt exciting. And I just got carried away and let it get the better of me. I'll never forgive myself.'

'That's your excuse? You got carried away? What are you, a teenage boy?'

'I know it sounds pathetic. I just feel that perhaps we were stuck in a bit of a rut. What with constantly talking about having children and not actually enjoying ourselves anymore.

And then you got your new job and you've been so busy, so distracted.'

'So it's my fault?'

'No!' he protested. 'No, it's not your fault. It's all my fault – but you're asking for a reason and that's the only one I can give you. It doesn't justify what I did, but there it is. I'm so sorry.'

'So you keep saying.'

They sat in silence. Sophie took a sip of the whisky, winced and then forced herself to take a larger gulp. It wasn't going to save her marriage but it might numb the pain.

'I may have been a bit preoccupied with making babies, and the kids, and becoming a swimming instructor but this is hardly a fair punishment. I mean, yes we should have made more of an effort to spend time alone, the two of us, but it's hard with young children.'

'I know.'

'And you didn't even talk to me about it. You didn't even give me a chance to understand how you were feeling and try to make it better. I thought we could always talk to each other.'

'We can, Sophie.'

'I think what actually happened is that Angie is an incredibly attractive, sexy woman that pretty much all men drool over and when the opportunity presented itself, you thought with your dick rather than your head. It's really that simple.'

'Possibly, yes.'

'And I thought you were better than that.'

'Me too.'

He didn't even try to defend himself. Alan had never been any good at arguments. He always did whatever he could to avoid confrontation. She couldn't remember a single time in their entire relationship that they'd ever had a proper barney, where he'd raised his voice in any way.

'I don't know if I can get past this,' she said. 'Even if I could forgive you, which right now I can't even imagine doing, I don't think I can ever trust you again.'

'I will never do it again. Never.'

'But how do I know that?'

'You have to believe me, Sophie.'

She laughed in his face. 'Do you know why I married you? Even though you were so different to all the men I had been out with in the past? Because I thought that you would never hurt me. That I'd be safe with you.'

He looked crestfallen, but he said nothing. He tried to take her hand but she moved it away. 'I don't know where we go from here,' she said.

'I don't know either. But I'll do whatever it takes, Sophie. Whatever it takes.'

They looked at each other from across the table, tired, upset and afraid, and knew that whatever the future held for them, it wasn't going to be decided then and there. Eventually Sophie took herself to bed and Alan went to sleep in Tom's room. She lay there for the rest of the night, staring up at the ceiling, too shocked to cry, and wondered how she would ever get over the fact that the two people she thought would always have her back were the ones who had let her down in the worst possible way. For the first time since she had married Alan, since she had thought she had a partner for life, she had never felt more alone.

Jack brought the kids round first thing when Sophie was downstairs in her dressing gown putting the kettle on. She had been awake all night and was absolutely shattered. Tom and Katie had faces like thunder because they hadn't been allowed to stay at the Taylors' for breakfast.

'I don't understand why we had to come home so early,' Tom said in his sulky voice.

'Go upstairs and get dressed,' Sophie instructed the children firmly. When they were gone, she turned to Jack who looked like he hadn't slept either.

'Are you okay?' she asked.

'Not really, how about you?'

'Not really.'

'Did you have any idea at all?'

'No,' Sophie said. 'Now I know why Angie's been giving me the cold shoulder. But Alan? I can't believe he acted so normally all this time, as if nothing was wrong. That's what gets me.'

'I knew something was up with Angie but I thought it was burn out from taking too much on, trying to do too much. When she's stressed, she turns in on herself and withdraws from everyone else. I just assumed it was that.'

'Do you know, I actually though that Angie was upset with me? I was trying to work out what I'd done wrong. I even got paranoid that she suspected you and me of something, which I know is ludicrous.'

'She did.'

'What?'

'She did suspect us. Not just you though. Everyone. It seems she suspected me of cheating with everyone.'

'Blimey. And have you?'

'Have I what?'

'Cheated on her.'

'Never.'

'I'm so sorry, Jack.'

'Me too.'

Alan appeared then, stopping abruptly in the doorway when he saw Jack. Sophie wondered if there was going to be a show-down and panicked about the children walking in on them, but Jack ignored him.

He hugged Sophie and made to leave. 'Call me, any time,' he said.

She nodded. 'You too.'

She watched him go, considering what he had just told her. There was no doubt that Jack was a flirt and she could understand why it may have upset Angie in the past. Was he telling the truth about never having cheated on her? She thought back to the holiday when they'd been messing around in the pool. She couldn't be the only woman he'd turned the charm on with like that. But when she imagined him as a serial adulterer it just didn't feel right. Jack was like a harmless kid, thoughtless sometimes but not manipulative. Despite his fooling around – and he undoubtably sailed too close to the wind sometimes – Jack was loyal. His wife and children came first. Unlike her own husband, and Jack's wife for that matter.

'Sophie, we haven't got much time,' Alan said urgently. 'The kids will be down soon. What do you want me to do? Shall I leave? Shall I stay? Just tell me and I'll do it.'

She didn't even look at him. 'You'll stay, for now,' she said. 'Tom and Katie mustn't know anything is wrong, do you understand?'

'Okay. But what about us?'

'I don't know.' It was all she could give him.

When the children emerged a few minutes later, she planted a smile on her face and set about making them breakfast. Inside she was miserable, not helped by the throbbing headache brought on by tequila, whisky and lack of sleep. She felt so wretched that she didn't even know how she was going to make it through the day, let alone the next few weeks.

She knew that some women in her position would have kicked Alan out immediately. Others would have gone round and had it out with Angie. She didn't want to do either. She just wanted to go back to bed, curl up into a ball and hide away from the world. *Why aren't I raging?* Maybe it was because Alan had surrendered so quickly. Or maybe she was still in shock. When

Alan came down from having a shower, she told him that she wasn't feeling well and was going back to bed.

'No problem, I'll take the kids to the park for a kickabout,' he said.

She kissed the tops of Tom and Katie's heads and wearily walked up the stairs. As she climbed into bed, she heard them moving around, gathering coats, hats and gloves, the chattering in the hall followed by the front door slamming and then, finally, silence.

Should she call someone? Her mum, Eve maybe? But she didn't feel like it. She wasn't ready to talk to anyone about what had happened. She started googling pointless things on her phone, typing in *Should I forgive my cheating husband?* and *Why do people cheat?* None of the results brought any comfort or answers. Only she could decide what happened next and the truth was she didn't know. She loved Alan. She hated Alan. She couldn't imagine ever forgiving him. She couldn't imagine ever being without him. She thought of Tom and Katie and the effect it would have on them if they split up. It was just too much to process.

For the first few days, she operated on autopilot. Every morning she woke up and for a few blissful seconds she had no memory of what had happened. But then it all came flooding back and the feeling of dread would engulf her again. At night she and Alan lay side by side like strangers. They rarely spoke to each other when they were alone and she knew Alan was waiting for her to be ready before they talked, but she still hadn't found the right words to say to him. He had cheated on her; he had betrayed her; he said he wouldn't do it again. What was there left to say? She continued to wait for her anger to come, assuming that once it had sunk in, she would be furious and would lash out at him. But she remained numb.

She was too afraid to leave the house in case she bumped into Angie. She became a hermit, hiding away at home while Alan took the kids out on his own. Tom and Katie, used to the freedom of letting themselves through the garden gate to play with Ellie and Freddy whenever they wanted to, were moody when Sophie told them that they couldn't go round.

'But why?' Tom asked.

'It's Angie,' Sophie said, 'she's not well. Anyway, you'll see them at school.'

The new term started three days later. She hadn't heard from either Angie or Jack and she couldn't face either of them. As she got out of bed that morning, forcing herself to stand up despite every bone in her body wanting to stay under the covers, she turned to Alan.

'You're taking the children to school this morning.'

'Soph, I've got to be on site at 8.30am.'

She looked at him. 'You're taking them.'

He looked like he was about to protest but he nodded instead. The minute he left with the children she sank down onto the sofa. She wanted to go swimming but she didn't have the energy and she wasn't due at work for another two days. She literally had nothing to do.

She had been waiting for Tom and Katie to go back to school so that she'd have the space she needed to process what had happened and decide what to do. But now that she was here, she was just as confused as ever. They couldn't go on living like strangers forever, it wasn't sustainable. She had to make a decision sooner or later: could she forgive Alan or was their marriage over? *If only it hadn't been Angie. If it had been someone else perhaps I could have moved past it.*

It was only half true, adultery was adultery, but the humiliation of it being with Angie was excruciating. *Why her?* At last, the anger started to bubble up inside her and she thumped the pillow. Then she did it again, and again, until before she knew it, she was battering it with both arms, screaming, shouting and eventually crying. She cried and cried until she had no tears left and then she sat and stared at a family photo on the wall for a while. Alan had his arm around Sophie and they were both pulling a silly face. Tom and Katie were laughing. They'd taken it on holiday in Greece last summer, when they went away with the Taylors. Angie and Alan had already slept together by then. Come to think of it, Angie had taken the photo.

Eventually she stood up and went to make herself a cup of tea. As the kettle boiled, an image of Alan and Angie kissing appeared without warning in her head and she felt another wave of anger. She picked up Alan's favourite mug, the one that declared he was the *World's Best Husband,* and hurled it across the kitchen. It hit the wall and fell to the floor, smashing into pieces.

The doorbell ringing made her jump. *What if it's Angie?* She didn't want to see her but she knew it had to happen eventually. She couldn't remain prisoner in her own home forever. But was she ready for it yet? And what if it wasn't Angie after all? It could be Jack, wanting to talk, or even the postman just delivering a parcel. She considered ignoring it but then the bell rang again and curiosity got the better of her. Taking a deep breath and steeling herself, she opened it and looked at the person on the other side in surprise.

It was Indie.

18

It had all gone according to plan. Mission accomplished. Yet Indie hadn't felt the euphoria that she had been expecting. Actually, she'd felt pretty rubbish. She had looked at the devastation on her dad's face and the horror on Sophie's and realised that she was responsible for that. The hurt and resentment that she had been harbouring for weeks, that had manifested itself into an intense desire for retribution, seemed to be deserting her. She felt afraid.

Still her mum deserved it, she persuaded herself. She had got what was coming to her. Alan too. But it wasn't enough anymore, it wasn't enough to justify the fact that she had just thrown a massive hand grenade into the middle of this situation. The fall out was going to be huge. When she had been plotting and planning, she hadn't cared whether her mum would be angry with her but she did care now. Now that she actually had to face the music. And what if her parents divorced now because of it? Because of her? What if her dad never spoke to her again?

She curled up on her bed in the dark and hoped that someone would come to her – her dad, Benji, even her mum, so that she didn't have to be alone. She heard hushed voices down-stairs. But no one came. She finally cried herself to sleep in the early hours but she was awake again at dawn. Her first thought was that something terrible had happened but she couldn't quite put her finger on what it was. And then it all came back to her and she felt horror, guilt and fear all wrapped into one. She thought about running away but she didn't know where to go and she didn't have any money. In the end, she lay under her duvet and waited.

Finally at 8am there was a gentle knock on the door and Jack opened it, holding a mug of hot chocolate, which he gently placed on her bedside table. As he perched on the edge of her bed and looked down at her, she pretended that she had just woken up. Rubbing her eyes, she sat up and took the hot drink but refused to look at him. She desperately wanted to find out what had happened last night, but she couldn't bring herself to ask, so she scowled instead.

'Are you okay?' he asked, putting his hand on top of hers.

She looked at him in surprise. 'Aren't you angry with me?'

He smiled sadly. 'No, Indie. You shouldn't have done what you did, in the way that you did, but you should never have been involved in the first place. You're a child. I'm so very sorry that you got dragged into this mess, I really am. It must have been absolutely horrible for you.'

Her dad's kindness, his understanding despite what she'd done, set her off again and she was sobbing, spilling hot choco-late all over the duvet until Jack gently removed the mug from her hands and put his arms around her.

'I'm sorry, Dad, I'm so sorry.'

'I know,' he said, hugging her even tighter.

When she had recovered, he handed her the drink back and she took it gratefully, craving the comfort of a childhood favourite. When they were younger Angie used to make hot chocolate for them every Friday before their baths. A little treat to celebrate the weekend, she would say.

'I've messed up,' she said.

'Well, maybe a bit, but it's not your fault.'

'What's going to happen now?'

'I'm going to be moving out for a while.'

Indie looked at him in horror. 'Dad, no! You can't leave. She should go, she's the one who caused all of this.'

'I know it's hard for you to understand, Indie, but Mum needs to be here, with you.'

'No she doesn't! Make her move out! You stay here and look after us.'

'I'll be round to see you all the time, don't worry.'

'No!' Indie was getting desperate now. 'Dad, you can't leave me here with her.'

'It's just temporary, Indie, until we work out a long-term solution. You must remember that your mother loves you very, very much.'

'Please take me with you, Dad. I'm begging you!'

He looked briefly torn, but then his expression hardened. 'I'm sorry, Indie, but you need to stay here. You need to be able to get to school every day and anyway, your brothers and sister need you. And you've got to make it right with Mum.'

'I'll never make it right with *her*.'

Jack looked thoughtful and Indie prayed that he was about to change his mind about making her stay, but then he said, 'Mum hasn't been well, Indie. She's not been well for a while. But we brushed it under the carpet. We shouldn't have done that. I'm not justifying her behaviour but I'm saying that she deserves your understanding. She loves you so very much.'

'So you keep saying.'

'That's because it's true.'

'Are you going to get a divorce?'

As soon as she'd said it, the question brought back memories from the past, hazy memories of having asked it before. Had they been here before? A vague recollection of Jack going to stay with Uncle Sam came slowly back to her. Yes, she remembered now. It was a few years back, not long before they put the house on the market and moved up here.

'I don't know, darling. It's too early to talk about things like that.'

'If you don't take me with you, I'll run away.'

'Indie, I need you here. I need you to look after your brothers and sister, to keep an eye on Mum and make sure she's okay. It's an important job and I'm trusting you to do it. Please.'

She looked at her father's pleading face and knew that she probably owed him one now. 'Fine,' she agreed huffily. 'But if anything kicks off, I'm out of here.'

'Okay. Deal.'

She took a sip of her hot chocolate and then said, 'How's Benji?'

'Confused, upset. I've already been in to see him.'

'I'm sorry,' she said again.

'I know.'

'I don't want to come downstairs, to face Mum.'

'I understand but you can't live in your room forever.'

She smiled, despite herself. 'Why not?'

'Come on, Indie, you might as well rip the plaster off. I'll come with you if you like?'

'Or I could pack a bag and leave with you instead?' she asked hopefully, even though she already knew what his answer would be.

'Come on, Indie, I'll be with you the whole time.' He reached out a hand.

'Promise you won't leave me alone with her?'

'I promise.'

She climbed out of bed and walked reluctantly down the stairs, sick at the prospect of seeing her mother. She was angry with her and terrified of her, and she wasn't sure which emotion was going to win in a confrontation.

At the bottom of the stairs she almost bolted out of the front door in her pyjamas but Jack kept a firm hold of her hand and gently pulled her towards the kitchen. When they reached the doorway, she saw Angie sitting at the table. She heard the TV behind her and guessed that Ellie and Freddy were watching cartoons in the den. She wished she was with them.

Her mother looked up and fixed her gaze directly on her. She wanted to stare back, to prove that she wasn't afraid of her, but she couldn't stop herself from lowering her eyes. Her courage and self-righteousness from last night had gone. She braced herself for Angie to go at her full throttle. Instead the room was silent. *What is she waiting for?*

Finally she couldn't take it anymore and she looked up, locking eyes with Angie, but her mum's expression wasn't what she had been expecting at all. She looked tired, sad and defeated. There was no hint of anger on her face. Indie, who was used to seeing her mother perfectly made up, confident and in control at all times, found the transformation unnerving.

'Hi, Indie,' she said.

'Hi,' she replied, moving slowly towards the kitchen table.

'Can we talk?'

Indie glanced at her dad. He nodded reassuringly and sat down at the table, gesturing for her to sit beside him. After a moment's hesitation she did.

Her mother frowned. 'I think it would be better if we talked alone. Woman to woman?'

Indie shook her head. 'Dad stays.'

Angie nodded wearily. 'Okay.'

They regarded each other before Angie spoke. 'Indie, what you did last night hurt a lot of people. I only wish that you had come to talk to me about it first.'

Indie started to protest but Angie held up her hand. 'Let me finish. What you did was hurtful. But I can't begin to imagine what you've been going through, finding out what you did. I am so deeply, deeply sorry for that. It was unforgivable of me.'

Angie had tears in her eyes and Indie welled up too. She blinked furiously, determined to hide her emotion from her mother.

'I've behaved terribly,' Angie continued. 'I've hurt your father and I've hurt you and your siblings which is the last thing I'd ever want to do. I understand why you're angry with me and I'm not asking for your forgiveness, but I do want you to know that I love you very much. And if there's anything you want to ask me, I'll answer truthfully. No more secrets or lies between us.'

Indie thought for a moment and then asked, 'Do you love Alan?'

'No.'

'Why did you do it?'

Angie glanced at Jack before she answered. 'I've been trying to work that out myself,' she said carefully. 'I've been feeling worried and low for some time now and I didn't talk to anyone about it. Instead, I let myself do something very stupid.'

'Do you love Dad?'

'Yes, very much, but I was also angry with him.'

Indie was confused. 'Why?'

Angie looked pained. 'I got an idea in my head about him.'

'Which was?'

Angie looked reluctant to say.

'You said no lies, Mum.'

'I thought Daddy was having an affair. But he wasn't.'

She'd asked for the truth but now she had it, Indie was feeling even more uncomfortable. Her mother was being so frank, so honest. She'd never had a conversation with her like this before, like they were two grown-ups. She'd been telling her mum to stop treating her like a little child for ages and now that she had, Indie didn't know what to do with it.

'Why is Dad moving out when you're the one who made the mistake?'

'It was Dad's decision. He's offered to go and stay with Uncle Sam for a while, to give us a bit of space. I've decided to take some time off work. So, I'm going to be around a lot more and I want to use that time to make it up to you all, to be a better mother.'

This was all far too civilised, Indie thought, her temper flaring. Too damn civilised. Where was the anger, the hate, the recriminations? She looked at Jack, who seemed so calm.

'Why aren't you angry, Dad? Why are you both being so nice, so *polite* to each other?'

She heard a noise behind her and swung round to see Benji standing in the doorway. She had no idea how long he'd been listening to their conversation. She glanced at her brother and smiled in what she hoped was a conciliatory way but he didn't look at her.

'I am angry,' Jack replied. 'And I'm hurt. But right now you, and your siblings, are our number one priority. There's plenty of time for Mum and me to talk things through but first we need to make sure that you're okay.'

'Can I go and live with Dad?' Indie asked, directing the question at her mother.

'We've discussed it and we've decided that it's better if you all stay here, in your own home. Dad will be over all the time to see you.'

'But I want to be with Dad.'

'I understand but there's not enough room at Uncle Sam's and it's too far to go to school every day. It's just for now, Indie, until we work out something more permanent.'

'Like a divorce?'

She saw her parents looking at each other before Angie replied, 'I don't know.'

Indie opened her mouth to speak and then shut it again. What was there left to say? She wanted to shout and scream at her mother, to tell her that she was an absolute cow, but her calm, brutal honesty had taken the wind out of her sails. She had another thought. 'Have you spoken to Sophie?'

'No.'

'Are we going to have to move house again now?'

'I hope not.'

'Bit close to home, Mum, your lover living next door.'

Shouting erupted from the den and Jack stood up and dashed off to investigate. As he left the room, Benji sat down beside Indie in his empty seat. Angie looked at them both and then leaned forward and said urgently, 'Obviously Ellie and Freddy don't know anything about this and it has to stay that way, okay? They're too young to understand.'

'What are you going to tell them then? About Dad moving out.'

'Just that he's staying with Uncle Sam for a while.'

'What about Tom and Katie though? They're, like, best friends. Are they still going to be allowed to hang out?'

Angie looked crushed. 'I don't know, Indie.'

Jack returned to the kitchen with Ellie and Freddy in tow and Angie plastered a bright smile on her face and stood up to start making breakfast. Indie remained seated for a moment, watching as her mum cracked eggs into a bowl and Jack set the table, and it was so horribly fake and wrong that she couldn't bear it any longer.

'I'm going to have a shower. I don't want breakfast,' she said. No one stopped her. As she turned on the shower and waited for it to heat up, she grabbed her phone and sent a quick message to Daisy. *SOS. Can I come over? Family gone mad.*

The sooner she was out of this mad house, the better.

19

Sophie's first instinct when she saw Indie standing on her porch was to slam the door in her pretty little face. But then she took in the teenager's terrified expression and took pity on her.

'Come in,' she said.

Indie followed her into the living room and sat down on the sofa, fidgeting nervously with her hands. For a while nobody spoke, until Sophie said impatiently, 'Come on then, out with it.'

'I've come to say sorry,' Indie said, looking down at her nails.

'Did your mum send you round?'

'No?'

'Your dad?'

Indie looked guilty and Sophie nodded. 'How is he?'

'He's moved out.'

This was a development. Sophie wasn't particularly surprised to hear it but she wondered why Jack hadn't told her himself. She hadn't heard from him since New Year's Day.

'How's your mum?' Sophie couldn't help asking.

'Not great,' Indie said. 'In a bit of a state actually.'

Sophie nodded. She should be pleased to hear it but she wasn't particularly.

'How are you?' she asked Indie who, despite her heavy make-up, looked tired and gaunt. Although she had done something pretty shitty, she was still just a child.

'Fine,' she said, her shaking hands betraying her words.

'I'm not angry with you, Indie,' Sophie began, and then stopped. 'Okay, I'm a bit angry with you, but I don't blame you. It wasn't your fault.'

Indie finally looked at her then, for the first time since she'd arrived. 'Thank you,' she said.

Sophie nodded and began to stand up, assuming that the conversation was over, but Indie seemed reluctant to leave yet.

'Was there anything else?' Sophie asked.

'Is Alan still here?'

'Not right now no. If you mean, is he still living here then the answer is yes.'

'Are you going to get a divorce?'

It's none of your damn business, Sophie thought, but she bit her tongue. 'I don't know. That's between me and Alan.'

'I think Mum and Dad are going to get a divorce.'

Indie looked as though she wanted Sophie to disagree, to tell her that she was wrong, but she couldn't do it. She said nothing.

'I've been remembering things,' Indie continued, 'from the past. It's not the first time Dad's moved out. I think they've been having problems for years.'

Sophie's eyebrows shot up at this revelation. She had always thought Angie and Jack were the perfect couple. Affectionate, attractive, vivacious, they were basically cover stars for a magazine about successful marriage. Was it really possible that it had been an illusion? All the time she had spent with Angie over the last few years, drinking cups of tea or glasses of wine, she had never breathed a word about trouble in paradise. Nor had Jack for that matter.

But even if Angie had been unhappy, nothing could justify what she had done. And as for her own marriage, that had definitely been a happy one. Hadn't it? Another image of Alan and Angie together flashed across her mind and she winced.

'Anyway,' Indie said, breaking the silence. 'I'd better get to school. I'm super late.'

'Thanks for coming by,' Sophie said, walking her to the front door. 'Listen, Indie, if you need anything, or you want to talk to someone, I'm always here.'

Indie gave her a small wave and made her way down the road. Sophie stood and watched her until she disappeared around the corner and then she shut the door quietly, thinking about how interesting it was that the daughter had come to apologise but not the mother.

Angie opened the front door and let herself back into the house, closing it behind her with relief. She'd been feeling sick about the school run, terrified that she might run into Sophie, or that all of Sophie's friends would be huddled together in the playground staring at her, hating her. She deserved it but she didn't have to like it. However, with Jack not living at home for the time being, she had no choice but to get on with it. She'd made the children leave earlier than usual to reduce the chances of them bumping into the Brennans, much to their disappointment.

'But, Mum, can't we scoot to school with Tom and Katie today?' Ellie had pleaded.

'Not today, come on,' Angie had replied.

In the end, they got to school so early that they didn't see anyone they knew. But on her way home, she saw the Brennan children hurtling towards her in the opposite direction. Her stomach lurched in fear but then she spotted Alan, not Sophie, dashing after them. Their eyes met and they nodded at each other, but they didn't wave. They hadn't said a word to one another since the party and she wasn't sure that there was any point in them talking. They'd fucked up big time. There was never going to be any future for them, and now they both had to focus on fixing the damage they had caused in their own lives. It was each man for himself.

She felt wretched. How had she let this happen? She had known that sleeping with Alan was a mistake but for a short while she just hadn't cared. She had wanted to feel reckless, rebellious, desired. She never gave much thought to the aftermath until she was in it. Now her husband hated her, her daughter hated her, her best friend hated her and she hated herself. She'd thought she'd hit rock bottom before, but she'd been nowhere near. This, right here, was rock bottom.

Jack could barely look at her. He put on an incredible performance in front of the children, so much so that he had even fooled her once or twice. But when they were alone, he made sure that she was under no illusion as to what he really thought of her.

'You've humiliated me,' he said to her after Indie's big reveal. 'You've betrayed me. And with *him.* Our neighbour. Our friend. How could you have done it, Angie?'

She tried to explain it to him. The way his behaviour had made her feel, her growing mistrust of him, the stress of moving away from their old life, trying to be the best at everything, keeping things locked up inside for so long, and how it had all finally got too much for her. But when she said it out loud it sounded feeble, even to her.

Jack had been scathing. 'You should have talked to me, Angie. I asked you over and over again what was wrong. Why do you have to bottle everything up all the time, even with your own husband? It's not natural. And as for not trusting me, I've never cheated on you. That was you. You did that.'

'I know,' she said.

'You need some help.'

'I know that too.'

She didn't know if they were going to get past this. Deep down she wondered if she even wanted to. It was exhausting being married to Jack. He was the only man that she had ever really loved, the father of their four amazing children, but did he make her happy? Would she ever trust him or feel secure in their marriage? And would he ever trust her again, for that matter? Did she have the energy to fight for him, to fix the damage? She wasn't sure anymore.

And then there was Sophie, who was probably only a few metres away from her now, in her own house, although there was far more than a brick wall dividing them. Her neighbour, her friend, who had never been anything but warm, generous and kind to her. How could she face her after what she had done? She hadn't just destroyed her own marriage; she had destroyed Sophie's too. Perhaps she had been slightly envious of Sophie and Alan's happy marriage in the past but she felt no pleasure at being responsible for breaking it up.

She had to go and see Sophie, to get the inevitable confrontation out of the way, but every time she steeled herself, she found an excuse to delay it. They could never be friends again, that much was obvious, but could they survive living next door to each other? They had to find a way to make it work because Angie couldn't bring herself to move house again. She almost laughed at the irony of the situation. She had insisted that they move to Finchley to get away from the bad memories, for a new start. But what Jack had done paled in comparison to what she had done. And when word got out, as it inevitably would, how could she look anyone in the eye at the school gates? Would rumours spread around school? Would her children find out about it? It didn't bear thinking about, yet it was the reality that she knew she would probably have to face.

Bile rose in her throat and she rushed to the toilet in case she was sick. After retching a couple of times, she sat down on the cold, tiled floor of the bathroom. She contemplated making a gin and tonic even though it was only nine thirty in the morning. She almost did it but stopped herself at the last minute. Instead, she put the kettle on and gave herself a talking to.

Her life may have fallen apart, but she still had a family to look after. It was time to start putting herself back together, piece by piece. She had already called in sick at work and asked for a meeting with HR to discuss a sabbatical. She was going to look for counsellors today and make an appointment as soon as possible. She would give Jack a few days and then ask him to meet with her so they could start rummaging through the rubble of their marriage and see if there was anything worth salvaging. As for Benji and Indie, she'd make it up to them. She'd make it right.

As she made a coffee she glanced at the crystal fruit bowl, the one that had been a wedding present, and it brought back memories of that hot summer's day when they had first moved into the house. How long ago that seemed now. She had hoped that a fresh start would repair their marriage. Now look at what had happened. *I'll find a way through*, she told herself, feeling the familiar stirrings of the confident, capable Angie that she used to be so many moons ago. She had always been good in a crisis. *One step at a time*. But she had to do something important first and she couldn't put it off any longer.

20

Sophie was staring out of the kitchen window, watching the rain hammer down onto the patio, when Angie burst into the garden. She was rushing through the downpour and clutching onto her hood to keep it from blowing off her head.

How dare she use the garden gate, like we're still mates, after what she's done? Adrenaline started to course through Sophie, her body preparing itself for fight or flight. *Which one though?* She considered moving away into another room, not answering the knock on the back door, which was increasingly imminent. But she remained where she was. This conversation, showdown, confrontation, whatever you wanted to call it, had to happen sooner or later so she might as well get it over with. Rage, intermingled with nerves, fluttered around inside her, amplifying with every step Angie took towards the house. She peered in through the glass door and spotted Sophie in the kitchen before giving a tentative knock.

Sophie watched her, standing outside in the rain, for a few more seconds and then walked over to unlock the door, moving aside to let her in.

'Thanks,' Angie said as she brushed water from her coat before hesitating, perhaps unsure whether to take it off or not.

Sophie watched her silently. *She doesn't know if she'll be staying*, she thought.

Eventually Angie shrugged the coat off. 'Hi,' she said.

Sophie nodded back at her.

'Can we talk?'

Sophie nodded again. She inhaled and exhaled deeply a few times. She was too livid to speak.

Angie moved towards the kitchen table and sat down, waiting for Sophie to join her but she remained where she was and leaned back against the kitchen cupboards, arms folded. They regarded each other. Sophie took in Angie's dishevelled, unmade-up appearance and wondered how it was possible to vehemently despise someone you had previously adored.

'I'm so sorry,' Angie began. 'That's what I've come here to say. I know that those words probably mean nothing to you, but I still wanted you to hear them.'

'And now I have.'

'What I did was unforgivable,' Angie continued. 'There's no justification for it, so I'm not even going to try. I made a terrible, stupid decision and hurt people who didn't deserve it. I know you hate me, and I don't blame you, but I can assure you that I probably hate myself more.'

'I doubt that.'

'There we must agree to disagree.'

Passive aggressive cow. Sophie was almost vibrating with indignation. She looked at Angie, sitting so calmly at her kitchen table, and felt like she might explode. She wanted to run at her, pull her hair, rip it out in strands, scream at her. But she stayed where she was, pushing her folded arms tightly against her body, clenching and unclenching her fists. She used to think that Angie was so beautiful but now all she saw was a bitter, selfish woman and she loathed her for it.

'I don't think you're capable of hating yourself, Angie. You're too narcissistic. You always have been, I think, although I'm only really seeing it now.'

Angie was looking up at her, perhaps trying to decide whether to defend herself or just sit quietly and let Sophie say what she needed to say. Before she had a chance to make up her mind, Sophie continued. 'When I first met you, I thought you were a bit of a snob. But I decided to give you the benefit of the doubt. I invited you into my home, into my life. Our children *played* together. Our husbands drank beer together. As time went on, I began to think of you as the friend I'd never had. But this whole time, you really didn't give a shit about me, did you?'

'I did–' Angie began, but Sophie interrupted her.

'No, you didn't. The only person you care about is you. You even let me comfort you, support you, when you thought you were pregnant, even though you knew the baby could be Alan's. You knew I wanted a baby. How could you do that? How could you be so cruel?'

'I'm so sorry,' Angie said but Sophie was barely listening.

'Do you know how hurt I was when you started giving me the cold shoulder? I thought, *What have I done to upset my lovely friend?* I tormented myself trying to work it out. Even when Jack warned me about you, I still blamed myself.'

'What do you mean Jack warned you?'

Sophie felt a short, sharp satisfaction at how quickly Angie had pounced on that. 'He told me that you were obsessed with your work and that everything else took a back seat, even him and the children. But even then, I still defended you.' She laughed bitterly. 'Back then of course I thought the worst thing you'd done was avoid me a few times and forget about our dinner. It didn't occur to me that you were sleeping with my husband.'

'I do care about you, Sophie. A lot.'

'No you don't! You don't care about anyone. Did you even like Alan? Or did you just sleep with him because you could? To make yourself feel wanted. Was he the first person you came across or was it a calculated decision? I mean, he's hardly your type, is he?'

'It's hard to explain,' Angie said. 'Alan was very kind to me at a time when I needed kindness. I mistook my feelings of gratitude for something else. I didn't plan what happened and I certainly didn't set out to seduce your husband, believe me, but I take full responsibility for what happened. I just did something incredibly stupid to make myself feel better.'

'And you say you're not a narcissist?'

'Look, I know you don't want to hear this from me right now,' Angie continued. 'But Alan loves you very much. I've always thought it, ever since I first met you both and if I'm being honest, which I really want to be with you, I always felt a bit jealous. I would love to be adored.'

'But you are adored! Jack adores you.'

'It's complicated, Sophie. All I can say is that Alan is a genuinely nice man.'

'Well, I certainly used to think he was.'

'And he cares about you more than you know.'

'I don't really want to talk to you about how Alan feels about me, thanks.'

Angie fell silent.

Her whole demeanour is different, Sophie thought. *She looks defeated.*

'Jack's moved out,' Angie said. 'I don't know if he's coming home.'

'I can't say I blame him.'

'I know,' Angie said sadly. 'I've messed everything up.'

'Yes.'

'If I could take it all back, I would.'

'But you can't.'

'No.'

'So, I think you need to get the fuck out of my kitchen.'

Angie nodded and stood up. The conversation could never have ended any other way and they both knew it. 'Ellie and Freddy are asking to see Tom and Katie,' she said, tentatively. 'Perhaps we could sort something out, for the sake of the children?'

'I don't think so.'

'We don't have to see each other; I could send them round and you could send them back at an agreed time?'

Angie sounded desperate. Perhaps this was her attempt to fix what had happened. It would never be fixed between the adults but maybe she thought she'd feel better if she managed to stop the children from becoming collateral damage. The problem was that Sophie didn't want Angie's children playing in her house, like nothing had happened, no matter how innocent they were in all of this. And she certainly didn't want her children in Angie's house. There was no way that the kids could continue to hang out as normal, having sleepovers at each other's houses, as if the two families were still the best of friends. How could she even think that was possible right now?

'No, Angie.'

'Okay.' Angie nodded again. 'I understand. I'll leave you to it.' She put her coat on and began walking towards the back door.

Sophie considered asking her to use the front but knew that it would sound petty.

Just before she opened the door, Angie looked back at her. 'I know we'll never be friends again. I don't deserve your forgiveness. But for what it's worth, I think that Alan does.'

'That's none of your business.'

'You're right, it's not.' And with that, she was gone.

Afterwards Sophie sank down onto a chair, exhausted. Her marriage was in tatters and she had lost her close friend to boot. Where did she go from here? Perhaps in a different world, under different circumstances, she might have found herself walking across to Angie's house in search of a listening ear. But that was impossible now and would never happen again.

She thought of Jack, who had moved out, and wondered if she should do the same, but she knew that she couldn't do that to the children. They needed her and she needed them. She was stuck here, living next door to the woman who had seduced her husband. The question was, did she let Alan stay or did she kick him out? It was the hardest decision she had ever made in her life. And as she tried to work out what to do, she started sobbing. She cried for all the things she'd thought she had, just a few days ago, and everything she had lost since. Because whatever happened next, she knew one thing for sure; her life was never going to be the same again.

21

TEN YEARS LATER

Katie Brennan tapped her foot impatiently on the vinyl floor and peered round the long line of people in front of her waiting for their recommended student vaccinations. She was itching to leave so that she could go and explore but judging by the excruciatingly slow speed the queue was moving at, she suspected she was in for a long wait. The sports hall was packed with other freshers, all eager to get on with navigating their way around campus, making new friends and arranging nights out. She smiled self-consciously as she caught the eye of a boy in the queue next to her. He smiled back. They both shuffled forward a couple of steps.

'Looks like we're in for a long wait,' he said.

She nodded in agreement. She'd arrived at university two days ago. Her parents had dropped her off and lingered for too long, fussing around her as she unpacked, finding excuses to stay. She had eventually told them, kindly but firmly, that it was time for them to leave. Even then, they had been reluctant to prise themselves away, clinging on to her tightly as they hugged her goodbye. She was the baby of the family and she wasn't sure that they'd ever be ready to let her go.

'We're so proud of you, Kitty Kat,' her dad had said. 'Who'd have thought, a Brennan at Oxford University?'

She had wanted to go to Oxford ever since she had read and later watched *His Dark Materials*. She had been bewitched by the idea of the magical city so steeped in history, with its long list of extraordinary alumni who had changed the world in so many different ways. When she finally saw it in person, after begging her mum to take her for a day trip, she hadn't been disappointed. It was just as special as she'd built it up to be in her mind. She vowed there and then that she would earn her place at the prestigious university.

She had always been a good student. Her schoolmates called her a swot although never maliciously. She was popular enough not to attract the attention of bullies, and her brother, Tom, was a heart-throb so it was in the other girls' interests to be nice to her. But even so, she had known that getting into Oxford was a push. So, while her friends went to parties or spent hours on social media, she studied. She was only satisfied if she achieved the top marks in her class, which she usually did. She got the highest grades in the year in her GCSEs, much to her parents' pride, and she tackled her A-levels with the same determination. She threw herself into as many extracurricular activities as she could manage so that she'd have plenty to write about on her application. She spent hours preparing for her interview, practising her answers over and over again until she was even dreaming about it. She would wake up in a cold sweat, terrified that she'd blown it, before she came to and realised that it hadn't even happened yet.

In the end, she needn't have worried. She received an unconditional offer and just like that, her dream became a reality. Even now, she wasn't sure if it had quite sunk in yet.

Still, when the day came, she had been ready. It was time to fly the nest and begin the next chapter in her life. She knew the sacrifices that her parents were making to enable her to go to university. They did okay but they were hardly swimming in cash. Katie had offered to get a job so that she could pay her way but they would not hear of it. It was nothing, they insisted, they could manage just fine, she should concentrate on her studies.

Her big brother, Tom, had left for Manchester University two years before her and he'd had no qualms about taking their parents' money and spending most of it on booze. He came home in the holidays, regaling her with stories about crazy nights out, and she listened to it and wondered if he did any studying at all. She wanted to make new friends and have fun but more than anything, she wanted to immerse herself in university life, to smell the dusty books in the library, to gaze at the architecture of the university buildings, to be inspired and to learn.

Her phone pinged and she fished it out of her pocket. It was a message from her mum.

Just checking in to see you're okay. Have you had your jabs? xxx

She typed out a quick reply.

Just waiting now, call you later xx

Her mum called and texted her several times a day. They had always been close, the two of them, and Katie knew that she was struggling with empty nest syndrome, so she was trying to be patient with her. As she pocketed her phone and moved forward another inch in the queue, she spotted a girl from her college. She caught her eye and gave her a little wave and the girl waved back, mouthing, 'Coffee after this?' Katie nodded her agreement.

Everyone had been so friendly. Her dad had been worried that Oxford would feel like a private school club and that his beloved daughter would feel excluded from the clique but she hadn't experienced that so far. It seemed that they were all just a bunch of young people trying to make friends and settle into their new digs. She had been invited on a pub crawl with a few people from her college that evening and she was looking forward to it. She considered what to wear. Jeans and a smart top, she decided: she didn't want to overdo it.

Finally, after forty-five minutes, she reached the front of the queue and got her vaccinations. As she was pulling her sleeve down afterwards, she looked around for the girl whose name she had completely forgotten and saw her waiting by one of the exits. She smiled and walked up to her.

'Katie, right?' the girl said. 'I'm Freya.'

Katie grinned with relief, grateful to Freya for reminding her of her name, and they walked together towards a coffee shop that Freya knew. After ordering their drinks and finding a table, they sat down opposite each other and began the usual pattern of small talk; where they were from, what they were studying, whether they knew anyone else in Oxford.

As they talked, Katie suddenly got the feeling that she was being watched. She turned her head slightly and saw a boy, about her age, sitting a few tables away. He was studying her intently. She looked away and tried to switch her attention back to Freya, who was still chatting, oblivious to the interruption.

'So Mum was trying to persuade me to go to Exeter for ages so that I could live at home. I was like, "Erm, no thanks, Mum." I couldn't wait to get here.'

Katie smiled and nodded but she was distracted. She glanced quickly back over at the boy and saw that he was still looking at her. He was exceptionally good-looking, with olive skin, dark hair and an intense stare that was currently fixed directly on her.

'Do you know that boy?' Freya asked, following her gaze.

'I don't know,' Katie replied, confused. 'I don't think so.'

'He's really looking at you,' Freya confirmed. 'He's fit. Hang on, he's coming over!'

She felt a presence by her side and glanced up to find him standing over the table looking down at her. He was tall and quite broad. He looked like someone who did a lot of sport. A captain of the football team type. The type of boy who didn't normally talk to her.

'Do we know each other?' he asked.

'I'm not sure,' she replied. Now that she was looking at him properly, she felt a jolt of recognition, but she still couldn't place him. He definitely hadn't gone to her school. Was he from her hometown? Maybe a friend of a friend or someone she had seen out and about?

'Where are you from?' he asked.

'Cambridge,' she replied.

'That's not it,' he said, rubbing his face as he tried to work it out.

'Perhaps she just looks like someone you know?' Freya suggested.

'Maybe,' he agreed and then shrugged. 'Anyway, nice to meet you, I'm Freddy.'

'Katie,' she said, firmly shaking the hand that he had held out to her.

'Katie Brennan!' he suddenly exclaimed. 'That's it, you're Katie Brennan!'

Katie was perplexed. 'Have we met?' she asked.

'We used to be neighbours, in Pemberton Road,' he declared triumphantly. 'I never forget a name. You were in the same year as me at school. We played together all the time.'

'Oh my God!' Katie exclaimed, putting her hand to her mouth as the penny finally dropped. 'I remember! You've got a sister, haven't you? Emma?'

'Ellie,' Freddy said, pulling out a chair and sitting down without waiting for an invite.

'That's it, Ellie! Bloody hell, how are you? Do your parents still live in Pemberton Road?'

'Oh they've been divorced for years, after *you know what*, but Mum still lives there.'

Katie had no idea what he was talking about, so she just went for a sympathetic look. 'I'm really sorry to hear that.'

'It's fine, they get along pretty well actually. Dad remarried about five seconds after the divorce, some blonde ex-model. What about your folks? Are they still together?'

What an odd question. 'Erm, yes,' she replied.

'Well, props to them, for being able to get past it all,' Freddy said.

'I'm sorry, Freddy, I'm a bit confused, I've got no idea what you're talking about,' Katie said with a nervous laugh, starting to feel unsettled by the odd conversation with this blast from the past.

Freddy frowned at her and then his expression changed. 'You don't know,' he said.

'Don't know what?' Katie was getting exasperated now.

Freddy shifted in his seat, looking uncomfortable. 'Forget I mentioned anything.'

'Well I can't now,' she said. 'You've worried me. What are you talking about?'

Freddy glanced at his phone. 'Look, I can't talk now, I've got football practice in twenty minutes but give me your number and I'll call you later. Perhaps we can meet for a coffee?'

Katie nodded reluctantly and read out her number to him.

He typed it into his phone. 'It's good to see you, Brennan,' he said, and then he was gone.

'What on earth was that all about?' Freya asked her.

'I've got absolutely no idea.'

'Why was he asking all that stuff about your parents?'

'I don't know.'

Katie was starting to get a bad feeling. She tried to think back to when they lived in London but she remembered so little of her life before Cambridge. They had moved there when she was eight and it was the only place she had thought of as home in a very long time. It was only now, after seeing Freddy again, that she remembered long forgotten memories of life in London, of playing with the neighbours' kids.

They had a treehouse and a really cool den with a big TV and loads of toys, she thought. Yes, it was starting to come back to her now! *There were some older siblings too, a boy and a girl. Was there a gate? A gate between the gardens? Yes, there was!*

They had been such good friends, she remembered now. Her mum had been really close with their mum, whose name she couldn't recall. Why hadn't they kept in touch when they moved away? She'd have to call her mum and ask. But Freddy's words had freaked her out.

Across the table, Freya started talking about her course timetable and Katie nodded in all the right places, but her mind was racing as she tried to think back to the old house in Pemberton Road, clutching at the various straws in her memory to find the one that made Freddy's words fit. But she'd been so young and the only images she could conjure up were of happy days spent playing, splashing in the paddling pool, scooting to school together. She certainly didn't remember anything bad. None of what Freddy had said made any sense to her.

She drained the last of her drink, eager to get to the bottom of the mystery. 'Sorry, I've got to dash. See you tonight,' she said to Freya as she ran for the door.

As soon as she was outside, she called her mum's mobile but she didn't answer. She tried the landline next but it kept ringing on and on, and she was about to give up when she finally heard someone pick it up and then the breathless sound of her dad on the other end.

'Dad, it's me.'

'Oh hi, love, sorry, I've just got in.'

'Is Mum there?'

'No, she's at the pool, she's got coaching all afternoon. Anything I can help with?'

She loved her dad but it was probably wiser to wait and speak with her mum. But curiosity got the better of her and she couldn't resist bringing it up. 'Something weird just happened.'

'What happened? Are you okay?'

'I'm absolutely fine, Dad, don't worry. I just bumped into someone from the past and he said something a bit strange.'

'Who was it?'

'It was Freddy, you know the boy who used to live next door to us in Pemberton Road?'

There was silence on the other end of the phone.

'Dad, are you still there?' she asked.

'I'm here.'

'Anyway, he was asking if you and Mum were still together and talking about something that had happened and then when he realised I was confused, he kind of legged it.'

More silence.

'Dad?'

'You stay away from that boy, Katie, you hear me? He's bad news. His whole family is bad news.'

Katie was alarmed by her dad's reaction. She'd never heard him talk like that before. 'Dad, you're scaring me now, what's going on?'

She heard him sighing. 'I'm sorry, love, I didn't mean to scare you, I'm just shocked that's all. We haven't seen or spoken to that family in over ten years.'

'But we were friends with them, weren't we?'

'We were once, a long time ago. Not anymore.'

'What happened?'

'Perhaps you should speak to Mum.'

'Why can't you tell me, Dad?'

'I just think it's better if you speak to Mum. I'll get her to call you as soon as she gets back.'

Katie was even more worried now. 'Okay,' she said.

'Seriously though, Katie, stay away from him, okay? You're in Oxford to start your exciting new life, don't go digging up skeletons from the past. It will only cause trouble.'

'Except that I'm studying archaeology, Dad, so that's literally what I'm here to do.'

He didn't even laugh. Something was very wrong. 'You know what I mean.'

'Not really, no. You're talking in riddles.'

'I'm sorry, love, I'll get Mum to call you.' She heard the click as he rang off.

She stared at her phone, completely dumbfounded. What did she do now? On impulse she called her brother but, unsurprisingly, he didn't answer. He never did. She had no choice; she'd just have to get on with her afternoon and wait for her mum to call back. But as she started heading back towards her college, trying to focus on the thrill of her new surroundings, all she could think about was the boy who had appeared out of nowhere and opened up a rusty door to the past, which she had a nasty feeling she wouldn't be able to close again.

She was getting ready to go out for the evening when her mum finally called sounding flustered. 'Dad's just told me you saw Freddy Taylor?'

Taylor, that was it. The Taylor family. 'That's right.'

'What did he say?'

'He asked if you were still together and made some comment

about some drama from the past that seemed to involve us. What's going on, Mum?'

'Can I come up and see you? I can drive over tomorrow morning?'

Katie felt dread in the pit of her stomach. If her mum didn't want to have the conversation over the phone it must be bad. 'Can't you just tell me now, Mum? It's starting to stress me out.'

'I'd rather talk to you face to face. I'll head over first thing. What's an acceptable time for a fresher to meet their mother in the morning?'

'I've got a few induction things I have to go to actually, but I can meet for lunch? Midday?'

'Okay, text me the address of where you want to meet and I'll see you there.'

'Mum, is everything okay?'

'It's fine, love, it's fine. Please don't worry.'

Katie put the phone down and continued applying mascara to her eyelashes. Whatever this big secret was, it would have to wait until tomorrow but she didn't like the sound of it. Not one bit. She thought of her dad's bizarre warning to stay away from Freddy Taylor. She couldn't believe that he had actually tried to forbid her from seeing him, it was like something out of a soap opera and so unlike her father. He was one of the most easy-going people you could ever meet. In any event, she didn't think it mattered as she had no intention of seeing Freddy again.

She heard a knock on her door and Freya popped her head round. 'Ready to go?' she asked.

Katie gave herself a quick once-over in the mirror and grabbed her bag. 'Let's do it.'

The revelations would have to wait for now.

'Angie and Jack Taylor were our neighbours in Pemberton Road.'

Katie's mother was clutching her coffee nervously with both hands. Katie nodded for her to continue.

'They moved in when you were about five, Tom was seven. We became friends, close friends. They had four children and you and Tom used to play with the younger two, Ellie and Freddy, all the time. You were as thick as thieves.' She smiled at the memory. 'We even had a gate put in between the two gardens. Do you remember? We used to wander in and out of it all the time. It was one of the happiest times of my life.'

Her mum took a deep breath. 'Then one day it came out that Dad and Angie had been having an affair. It was a very brief thing, over before it started really.'

Katie stared at her mother, open-mouthed. Had she just heard correctly?

'As you can imagine I was furious when I found out. I was hurt and humiliated and I couldn't believe that Dad – or Angie – could have done that to me and Jack. You're old enough to hear the truth now so I'll give it to you straight. The reason your father and I stayed together at first was because of you and your brother. I didn't want to break our family up.'

Katie was numb with shock. 'Are you telling me that all this time, you and Dad have just been pretending to be happy for our sake?'

Sophie shook her head. 'Not at all. You're the reason why we stayed together at first. But we were both committed to fixing the damage and we worked hard to save our marriage. Eventually we found a way through it and found each other again, as cheesy as that sounds. I can honestly say, hand on heart, that we've been very happily married for the past ten years, Katie. It's important to me that you know that.'

Her dad, her lovely, reliable, trustworthy dad, had an affair with the neighbour? Katie tried to remember Angie. She had a hazy memory of a glamorous looking woman but it was the exotic scent of her perfume that she remembered the most. She could almost smell it now.

'Oh, Mum,' she said. 'I can't believe it. I had no idea that any of this had happened.'

'Well, you were too young. Dad and I tried our best to keep things as normal as possible. He stayed at home, with us. We stuck together. But living next door to Angie was too hard. I couldn't escape it; it was like torture. After a few months we decided to sell up and move to Cambridge for a new start. It was the right decision for us.'

'How could you forgive Dad though?' Katie genuinely couldn't understand how she could get past a betrayal like that.

'Marriage is hard, Katie. Real life isn't a fairy tale, you know, human beings are imperfect, we all make mistakes. But I had a choice, did I let your father's indiscretion destroy ten years of a happy marriage and break the home we'd created for you and Tom, or did I forgive him? I knew I had to at least try and so I did. I'm not saying it was easy but we got there in the end.'

'But how could you trust him?'

Her mother smiled at her. 'I don't know really. Of course I didn't at first, it takes a long time to rebuild trust once it's been broken like that but I knew deep down that he was still the wonderful, kind and thoughtful man that I loved. He just made a mistake.'

Katie couldn't decide if her mother was the saintliest person in the world or the stupidest. 'Does Tom know?'

'No, he doesn't.'

Katie thought back over her childhood, seeing it with a fresh pair of eyes. It had been a happy one, she thought. Surely that wasn't an illusion. There had never been any hint of animosity or resentment between her mum and dad. They had just been normal parents – happier than most normal parents, in fact. How had her mother hidden this secret for so long?

'Well, it seems Freddy knows all about it,' she told her.

'I don't know how he knows. He was the same age as you when it all happened. What's he like, anyway?'

'He's okay, I only met him for a couple of minutes,' Katie replied with a shrug. 'He's good-looking,' she added grudgingly.

'That doesn't surprise me one bit, knowing the gene pool that he came from.'

'What was his dad like?'

'Jack? Cocky, immature, a total flirt, but all talk and no trousers really.' Sophie chuckled to herself. 'Funny that he was the loyal one out of the two of them in the end.'

'Dad told me to stay away from Freddy.'

'Do you have plans *not* to stay away from him?'

'I don't know, Mum! I literally bumped into the boy in the coffee shop yesterday.'

'Dad's upset because it's opened up a whole can of worms after we put it all behind us. But he has no right to order you to stay away from anyone. Only you can make that decision.'

'I doubt I'll see him again anyway,' Katie said. 'I don't think he's in my college.'

'Listen, Dad's really upset about all of this. You know he loves you so much. Perhaps you could give him a call? Just to clear the air?'

Katie thought about it. 'Maybe, but not just yet. I need some time to get my head around it all. I feel like he's not the man I thought he was anymore.'

'Oh, but he is Katie, he *is*, trust me. He is exactly that man.'

'Not to me, Mum.' Tears pricked at her eyes and she tried to wipe them away.

'Oh, Katie.'

'Sorry, Mum, I'm just a bit shocked that's all.'

'I understand, love, but please remember what I said. Your father and I love each other very much and we love you even more. This all happened so very long ago. It's ancient history.'

Katie nodded through her tears. 'I will call him, Mum; I just need some time.'

'Take as much as you need.'

After her mum had left, Katie wandered around the city on her own for a while, watching all the other students around her, walking in groups or riding their bikes through the narrow side streets. Her brain was spinning at a thousand miles per hour as she digested everything she had just learned. She couldn't help but feel resentful that her blot-free memories of her childhood had been irrevocably spoiled. She was angry with her dad and also, probably unfairly, with Freddy and her mum too. They were all part of the deception to some degree. She had been left completely in the dark for all these years, unaware of this momentous thing that had happened.

She was desperate to talk to someone about it but she felt so far away from her friends, who were scattered all over the place, settling in at different universities, embarking on gap years, interning or starting new jobs. Apart from the few people she'd met over the last few days, she didn't know anyone in Oxford and she felt horribly alone. If it was any other type of problem she'd probably have got the first train back home to her parents for some comfort but given that they *were* the problem, that wasn't an option.

She found an empty bench and sat on it, lost in her thoughts, until a new one popped into her head. She did know someone in Oxford. Someone who might actually be the only person in the world who could understand what she was going through. She reached for her phone, pulling it out and going to her missed calls. There it was, at the top of the list, Freddy's number. He had called her, letting it ring once, so that she could save the number but she hadn't bothered. She had assumed at the time that she'd never see him again.

She looked at the number, knowing that if she went ahead with what she was considering, she would be going against her father's wishes and digging up things that were probably best left in the past. Was it really worth the trouble? Before she could stop herself, she pressed dial.

22

They met in a city centre pub. Freddy put his pint and her white wine spritzer on the table and sat opposite her. They smiled at each other and she wondered if he was as nervous as she was. He certainly didn't look like it. He had an easy confidence about him that suggested he would be comfortable in any situation, even the odd one that they found themselves in.

'Cheers,' he said, raising his glass and she lifted hers up to clink it. She wondered whether they should start with the usual small talk before deciding to cut straight to the chase.

'I've spoken to Mum now, so I know what you were talking about yesterday.'

His smile faltered. 'I'm really sorry, Katie, I just assumed you knew, which was stupid of me. I felt like such a douchebag afterwards.'

'How did you know?' Katie asked. 'We were so young.'

'Indie told me about it a few years ago,' he said. 'Of course she and Benji were old enough to remember the whole thing but they'd been under strict instructions not to drag me and Ellie into it. When I was about fourteen or fifteen I started asking questions about why Mum and Dad had split up and Indie was more than happy to fill in the gaps.'

'Your parents must have been furious with her.'

'Not really, by then I was old enough to know the ugly truth. I think Mum was relieved more than anything that it was all out in the open.'

'I don't remember anything about it at all. I can't believe I had no idea.'

'I think I always knew *something* was up,' Freddy said. He took a sip from his drink and continued. 'I had no idea it was that but even as a young child you can sense tensions in your parents' relationship. I think the affair was the straw that broke the camel's back.'

'So did you parents split up straight away?'

It felt strange asking someone she barely knew such intimate questions but Freddy didn't seem rattled. 'Pretty much. Dad moved out and we all stayed on with Mum at Pemberton Road. Dad got a flat up the road in Crouch End, although he often came to spend the weekend at Mum's. It sounds weird, I know, but they've always been friendly. They probably weren't when it all kicked off but I don't remember. Now I think they get on better as friends than husband and wife.'

'How very modern,' Katie said.

'I know. When Dad remarried a couple of years later, Mum even came to the wedding. Although she did have a few comments to make about the new bride's age.' He laughed at the memory.

He doesn't seem to harbour any anger or resentment, Katie thought. She couldn't get her head around it at all. 'Has your mum remarried?'

'No. There's been a bloke or two I think, but nothing serious.'

'It must have been so hard for you all, having your parents split up.'

'You know, it really wasn't that bad. Mum and Dad made sure it wasn't. They were very cool about it and they still are now. I think it probably hit Indie and Benji harder as they were that bit older. Indie and Mum had a difficult relationship for a while and she ended up leaving school and moving out when she was sixteen. She's a model now,' he added proudly.

'Wow,' Katie said, impressed. She vaguely remembered Freddy's sullen and slightly terrifying older sister. 'What about the rest of you?'

'Benji's an actor, he's currently in that BBC drama, *The Boys*? Have you seen it?'

When Katie shook her head, he shrugged. 'It's quite good. Ellie lives in New Zealand and works for a conservation charity. And here I am, the baby of the family.'

A model, an actor, a charity worker and an Oxford University student. *What a family of high achievers*. Katie braced herself for the inevitable question that she knew was coming.

'How about you?'

'Well, Mum and Dad stayed together,' she began. 'We moved to Cambridge, that's where Dad's family is from. Mum's a swimming teacher and she coaches the county youth team and Dad works in property. Tom's at uni in Manchester. A bit boring really.'

It all sounded horribly mundane compared to Freddy's jet-setting, successful family and Katie felt self-conscious. She took a gulp of her drink.

'And you're at Oxford,' Freddy said, raising his glass again.

'Yes.' She looked down at her drink and realised with disappointment that she'd finished it. She didn't want to leave. Given everything that had happened over the last twenty-four hours, he was probably the last person she should want to see but she was enjoying his company. There was something about him that made her feel at ease. 'Another round?' she asked, hesitantly.

He nodded and she stood up and made her way over to the bar.

When she returned, he was flicking through his phone. 'Here,' he said, showing her a photo. 'Here are Indie, Benji and Ellie. We took this photo a couple of months ago when Ellie came back for a holiday.'

Katie looked at the photo and felt another jolt of recognition. It may have been more than a decade since she'd seen the Taylors but looking at their faces brought back vivid memories.

'And here's Mum and Dad.' He showed her another photo of Angie and Jack, looking at each other and laughing. They definitely didn't look like divorcees.

'It's unusual I know,' Freddy said again, reading her mind.

'Fair play to them.'

'Anyway, how are you feeling?' Freddy asked. 'I've had years to get my head around all of this, but you've only just found out. It must have been a shock.'

'I'm not really sure how I feel,' Katie confessed. 'I'm upset, I'm angry. With Dad of course, but also with Mum for keeping it from me. And even a bit with her for standing by him after he betrayed her like that. I dunno, I feel like my whole life has been a complete lie.'

Freddy nodded sympathetically. 'I get that. But for your mum to forgive your dad for something like that, to be able to move past it, that takes strength not weakness.'

He has a point, she thought grudgingly. 'I know, it's just, well, it's a bit messed up.'

'Have your parents always seemed happy to you?'

'I've never really thought about it before,' Katie said, 'they were just normal parents. But yes, thinking about it now, they have always been happy as far as I know.'

'And have they been good parents to you?'

Katie thought back over the last few years, to her mum

spending hours each evening helping her prepare for her university interviews, making her endless cups of tea while she studied, comforting her when she was feeling sad, tired or over-whelmed. Supporting her one hundred per cent without ever putting any pressure on her. And to her dad, picking her up from parties at midnight without so much as a murmur of complaint about having to stay up so late for her. Ferrying her to and from friends' houses. Working extra hours to pay for her university tuition. Crying when she got the unconditional offer from Oxford.

'The best,' she said.

'So from where I'm sitting, you've had a happy upbringing with parents who adore you, and each other, and now you're at one of the best universities in the world, about to start the most exciting chapter of your life. Fuck the drama and move on.'

'You're not studying psychology by any chance, are you?'

'Medicine.'

'Oh excuse me, Dr Taylor.'

'Quite right. If you call me anything else, I simply won't respond.'

She looked across at him. 'Thanks for listening, I appreciate it.'

'Any time, Brennan.'

No one had called her Brennan before and she liked it. She smiled at him, feeling shy. He really was incredibly attractive. And easy to talk to. And not as cocky as she'd assumed. There was a connection between them, she felt, maybe because of their shared history. Or was it something else? She wondered if he had a girlfriend. *What am I thinking? I barely know the boy and whichever way you look at it he's bad news. And anyway, a boy like him would never go for a girl like me.*

She drained her spritzer and stood up. 'I'd better be off.'

'No worries,' he said. 'I'll walk you back to your college.'

'There's no need,' she protested, 'I'll be fine.'

'I insist, it's getting late.'

'Okay thanks.'

Just a walk home. Then I'll never see him again. He was a nice enough boy but no good could come of having anything to do with Freddy Taylor. Too many lives, and hearts, were at stake. Right there, as they made their way out of the pub and onto the pavement outside, she made a promise to herself that she would forget all about him and get on with her life.

Hi love, just me, how's it going? Did you get that paper finished in time? Mum xxx

Katie looked at the message and then put her phone down. She'd reply later. Her mum was still texting her all the time, even more so if that was possible. She was worried about her, Katie knew, but there was no need. She was absolutely fine. More than fine.

She had just completed her first university assignment and was feeling great about it. She'd worked all hours researching, writing and polishing the paper until she knew that it couldn't get any better. She'd almost felt a bit emotional when she submitted it earlier that afternoon.

The past few weeks had been a whirlwind. She had immersed herself in learning and had loved every second of it. This was what she was here to do, to study and to challenge herself. Nothing else mattered. She spent most of her time in lecture halls, the library or working in her room. But tonight she was going out with Freya and some of the other students from her college to celebrate handing in her paper and she was looking forward to letting her hair down.

She grabbed her things and made her way downstairs to the quad, where they were all gathering to go out. She spotted Freya and made a beeline for her. The two girls had become good friends, saving each other a seat at breakfast, meeting for coffee between lectures and generally looking out for each other. It felt lovely to have someone to talk to. She had even told her about the whole affair thing and Freya had listened to it all, wide-eyed with disbelief.

'So let me get this straight. The hot boy who we saw in the café is the son of the woman who had an affair with your dad?'

'Yes.'

'And you didn't know about any of this.'

'No.'

'Christ, Katie. And what about hot boy? Have you heard from him again?'

She had. Freddy Taylor had texted her twice asking if she wanted to meet up and she had ignored both messages. No good could come of seeing him. It would distract her from her studies, cause unnecessary distress to her parents and probably end in heartbreak when she fell madly in love with him and he just wanted to be friends. It was altogether just a bit icky.

But late at night, when she was alone in her new room, trying to get used to the unfamiliar surroundings, smells and sounds, she thought about him. She couldn't stop thinking about him.

Katie didn't believe in fate; she was too pragmatic. But even she had to admit it was pretty freaky that they had bumped into each other after all this time, that they were studying at the same university. Why was it that when she was finally leaving home to start her new life, the past had decided to catch up with her? It made no sense. She could only hope he had finally got the message that she wasn't interested in seeing him again and would leave her alone.

Once everyone had assembled, they slowly started making their way to a nearby pub to start their evening. As they walked, Katie chatted easily with Freya and a couple of the other girls. She was feeling light with the anticipation of a well-earned night out and her face lit up with the pure joy at being here, with these people, in this amazing city.

When they reached the bar, a few of them broke off to see if there was a table free and she headed to the bar to get the first round in. The queue was two people deep and she waited patiently for her turn. Finally she saw her opportunity and squeezed her way through to the front, propping her elbows on the bar and looking absentmindedly across to the other side. Her stomach flipped. There he was, Dr Bloody Taylor, pint in hand, chatting with a glossy-haired girl.

She couldn't not look as the girl threw her head back and laughed, putting one hand on Freddy's arm. As she stared at them, she could feel her good mood slipping away from her until she was left with nothing but misery. It was one thing ignoring his messages and pretending he didn't exist, but it was quite another seeing him in the flesh with his girlfriend.

She felt a sharp jab in her side and looked at her neighbour in indignation. He was pointing at the barman, who was waiting for her impatiently. 'Are you going to order?' he asked her.

'Sorry,' she said, leaning forward to give her order. As she paid and piled the drinks onto a tray, she risked one last glance across the bar but Freddy had gone. She took a deep breath and turned around, making her way through the crowd, drinks balanced precariously on the tray. She scanned the room, looking for her friends, trying to perk herself up again. *It can still be a good night*, she told herself. *Don't ruin it by getting into a funk.*

'Need some help with that?' She swung round to see Freddy, standing inches away from her, holding out his hands.

'No thanks,' she said, holding the tray protectively to her.

He rolled his eyes and gently took it from her. 'Come on, Brennan, where are we going?'

Finally spotting her mates in a far corner, she beckoned for him to follow her and they made their way over to the table. Freya raised an eyebrow when she clocked Freddy but Katie pretended that she hadn't seen. Freddy put the drinks down, passed her white wine spritzer to her and then studied her for a long time, until she was feeling thoroughly uncomfortable.

'Hello, Brennan.'

'Hello, Dr Taylor.'

'So, I'm starting to get a bit of a complex.'

'Why's that?'

'The unanswered messages?'

'I'm sorry, I've just been really busy, you know, what with the course starting and having lectures and so on.'

She knew he didn't buy it but he didn't push her either. 'Fair play, how's it all going?'

'Wonderful,' she said, grinning with pleasure. 'I love it here. How about you?'

'Yeah, it's great,' he said. They shuffled around a bit, unsure what to do next. She didn't want him to leave but she knew that she had to hold firm. She remained resolutely silent.

Eventually he said, 'It was nice to see you. I'll leave you to it.'

'Have fun with your girlfriend.' She cringed as soon as the words were out of her mouth.

He smiled at her, a frustratingly smug smile, as if he could see into her mind and knew exactly what she was really thinking. 'Not my girlfriend.'

'Well, if you play your cards right, she might be by the end of the evening.' Why on earth had she said that? What was wrong with her? She wanted the ground to swallow her up.

'Well, in the unlikely event that does happen, I'm pretty sure

I'll end up with a punch in the face. She's my friend Noah's girlfriend.'

'Oh.'

'Oh indeed.'

'I'm sorry,' she said, rubbing her face self-consciously.

'For what?'

'For not replying to your messages. For this horrific awkwardness.'

He grinned. 'I've had worse.'

'It's just a bit much really.'

'What is?'

'Seeing you again after all this time, hearing about what happened to our parents, not speaking to Dad, barely speaking to Mum.'

'Ah I see,' he said. 'So I bring back bad memories, right?'

'No, it's not that. Well, it is a bit, I guess.'

She glanced at her friends, who were all watching her curiously. Freya gave her a thumbs up and a wink. Freddy noticed it too and she groaned inwardly as he made an unsuccessful attempt to suppress a smile.

'Look,' he said. 'If you don't want to hang out, I totally get it. But I like you, Brennan. I enjoy spending time with you. So, I guess the ball is in your court.'

She looked at him, and she looked at her friends, and in that instant, she made her mind up. If she couldn't take a risk at university, when the hell could she?

'Do you want to get out of here?'

He grinned. 'I thought you'd never ask.'

23

'Brennan, wake up, you'll be late for lectures.'

She groaned and put a pillow over her head. 'Nooooo, it's too early.'

'Katie!' He was shaking her gently now. 'It's 8.45.'

'Shit!' She leapt out of bed and started rummaging around for her clothes. 'Why didn't you wake me before?'

'I've only just woken up myself.' He was brushing his teeth, wearing nothing but his boxers and her tummy gave a little flip, as it always did when she saw him. But there was no time for any of that, she was going to be late for class and she had never been late for anything in her life. Well not until recently anyway.

Freddy Taylor had floored her. He had broken down every one of her protective barriers, piece by piece, until she was completely helpless. She couldn't keep away from him even if she tried. She was completely in love with him. All of the teenage crushes and brief relationships she'd had in the past seemed silly and juvenile now, as though she'd been wearing learner plates, just practising for the real thing. This, here, was the real thing.

For the last six weeks they had been inseparable. When she

was with him nothing else mattered. When she wasn't with him, he was the only thing she could think of. Even when she was walking down the street, she was looking for him, searching the crowds for his face, hoping to bump into him even though it had only been a few hours since they had parted. Leaving him in the morning to go to lectures was torture. She had aced her first assignment but she knew that she had been distracted since, she was off her game when it came to her studies and it couldn't go on for much longer. But she was infatuated with Freddy and it thrilled and terrified her.

She had only just started speaking to her dad again and the ceasefire was delicate. She couldn't even imagine the fall out if he found out who she was sharing her bed with almost every night. She hadn't even told her mum and it was probably the first time she had kept a secret from her – if you didn't count the time when she stole a mascara from Boots and felt so wretched about it that she snuck it back into the shop. It didn't feel right, keeping something this important from her, yet she tried to reconcile herself with it by reminding herself that her mum had kept an even bigger secret.

It was always there, the elephant in the room between them. They were in the shouting from the rooftops stage of their love yet neither of them had told their families about the other. Sometimes it was easy to forget about it, as they strolled hand in hand through the streets of Oxford together or wrapped them-selves around each other in bed, listening to music and drinking cheap wine. But then one of their phones would ring and they'd look at it guiltily before tucking it away under a pillow and it was always obvious who had called. One of them would change the subject but by then it was too late, the mood in the room had changed.

Occasionally it was thrilling, this illicit affair between them. But the thrill was always replaced with dread in the end. The secret was fast becoming a burden that she was struggling to bear and what was even more frustrating was how annoyingly blasé Freddy was. They'd had a row the previous evening about it, their first ever, and it had left a bitter taste in her mouth even after they had cleared the air.

They had been discussing going home for Christmas and Katie had finally spoken the words that had been on her mind since they first got together.

'Are we going to tell our parents?' she asked, as they had a pint together after lectures.

'I don't see why we should.'

His dismissiveness irked her. *Does our relationship not mean enough to you to bother telling your parents? Is this just a bit of fun for you, while for me it is my whole, entire world?*

He saw her expression and looked confused. 'Have I said something wrong?'

'I just wonder why you don't think we should tell them?'

'I don't think it's any of their business.'

'Are you ashamed of me?'

'Of course I'm not ashamed of you. Where's this come from?'

She wanted to tell him the truth but she was twisting herself into knots, getting herself into a pickle for no reason. 'Well we spend all our time together but how often do we go out with your friends? And you won't even tell your parents about me?'

'How often do we go out with *your* friends?' he asked. 'Hardly ever. I thought you liked spending time just the two of us. I've got no problem taking you out with my mates if that's what you want, Katie.'

He had called her Katie, not Brennan, which meant that he was annoyed with her. She was furious with herself for causing conflict that didn't need to be there, but she was on a roll now.

'So you're just going to go home for Christmas, return to

your old life, act like nothing has happened, perhaps hook up with your old girlfriend from school and forget all about us?'

'For God's sake, Katie, stop being unreasonable. I never said that.'

'So what did you mean?'

Freddy was looking exasperated. 'I just mean that my family are a bunch of nosy arseholes and if I want to keep this to myself, why shouldn't I?'

'And it's not because you're worried about how they'll react?'

'Not particularly.'

'Oh yes, I forget, you have such a modern, accepting family, they'd probably slap you on the back and congratulate you on your conquest.'

'Jesus, Katie.'

They glowered at each other for a minute until finally his expression softened. 'Okay, so I get what this is about now.'

'What's that?' She sounded petulant but she didn't care.

'You want to tell your parents but you're scared about how they'll react and you're worried that I'm not going to tell mine because I don't think this is serious enough.'

He had her there. 'Are you sure you're not studying psychology, Dr Taylor?'

He smiled, relieved for the break in tension. 'Talk to me.'

Her anger slowly ebbed away. She looked down at her drink and then back up at him. He sat, patiently, waiting for her. 'You're right on both counts,' she said at last.

'Well firstly, if you want to tell your parents, you absolutely should. And secondly, if you think that I'm ashamed of you, or that I'm not serious about you, then you don't know me as well as you think you do. I love you, more than I've ever loved anyone.'

It was the first time that either of them had said those words out loud. She knew she should respond but she was momentarily floored and simply gaped at him, mouth open wide.

'Now I'm starting to think you're ashamed of *me*,' he joked, trying to lighten the mood.

'Oh God, Freddy, you know I'm not. I... I love you too.'

'Well I'm glad we've established that. So as far as I'm concerned, as long as we both know that, then does it matter who else knows?'

'It does to me,' Katie said. 'I'm close to my parents; I've always been open and honest with Mum. I hate keeping this from her.'

'So tell her.'

'But I'm terrified about how she'll react and Dad even more so.'

'Do you want me to come back with you so we can tell them together?'

'Noooooooooo.' She shook her head violently. 'Thanks, Freddy, but somehow I don't think that would help.'

'So why don't you play it by ear? Get home for Crimbo, see how the land lies and take it from there?'

'You do know me, right? You've seen the timetables on my wall and the daily to-do lists on my phone? I'm a lady who likes to plan.'

'You didn't plan this.'

She had to agree. 'You're right about that.'

'And look, if you want me to tell my parents, I absolutely will. I've got no problem with that at all, okay?'

She nodded, pleased that they had made up, but the conversation hadn't really helped her with her predicament. It just didn't seem to bother Freddy as much as it did her. After they'd gone to bed, he had fallen asleep almost instantly and she had watched him sleep for a while, staring at his ridiculously handsome face and wondering how it was possible that something so wonderfully right could also feel so horribly wrong. She knew that, as much as she loved him, she would never be at peace until it was all out in the open, for better or for worse.

As she hurriedly dressed and grabbed her coat now, she gave Freddy a quick kiss and made for the door. 'See you later,' she said and he nodded as he rooted around in the piles of papers on his desk for his phone. Once she was outside, she ran full pelt until she reached the university building. She dashed up the stairs, making it to the lecture theatre in the nick of time. Catching her breath, she spotted Freya and made her way over, grateful to her for saving a seat.

'Thanks,' she said, throwing herself down next to her.

'Fun night?' Freya asked, taking in her dishevelled appearance.

'Kind of,' Katie said. Freya was about to probe further but their lecturer began talking. Katie quickly turned her phone on to silent and tried to concentrate on the lesson.

On her way out of the lecture theatre her mum called her. 'Hey, love, just double-checking the arrangements for next week?'

Katie knew that her mother was already well aware of the arrangements and just wanted to chat but she said patiently, 'You're picking me up on Saturday, about midday.'

'And that works for you?'

'Yes, Mum.'

'Great, oh I'm so excited to have you and Tom back for the Christmas holidays. I've got your stockings out ready.'

Katie smiled to herself. 'Let me guess, the light-up reindeer is out the front too?'

'Of course.'

She thought of her parents, diligently putting up their Christmas decorations together, going shopping to get all of Tom and Katie's favourite foods, making up their beds with their childhood festive duvets and she suddenly yearned for home. 'I love you, Mum,' she blurted out.

'I love you too. Are you okay?'

'I'm fine, I'm just looking forward to coming home.'

'Me too, love.'

After they had hung up, Katie sat down on a bench to gather her thoughts. But she already knew what she had to do. She was going to come clean to her parents over the holidays. Freddy might be able to live with this secret but she couldn't do it anymore.

24

Indie propped her elbows on the balcony railings and looked out at the sun setting over the ocean. She reached for her packet of cigarettes and lit one, inhaling deeply and watching little boats in the distance, fishermen heading out to work now the afternoon heat had passed. She looked down at the pool area of the hotel below her. The crew had finally finished packing away the cameras and lights and were having a drink at the bar. She wondered if she should join them. One of them had been quite good-looking. She stubbed out her cigarette and was about to make her way back inside her room to change when her phone rang. She glanced at the screen to see who it was and then, smiling, answered it.

'Hey there, squirt.'

'Hey yourself, big sis,' Freddy said. 'And where are we at the moment?'

'Canary Islands,' Indie said. 'Shooting a summer collection. Good job it's still warm here in December otherwise they'd have to photoshop my nips out of all the photos.'

'Delightful, thanks for that image, sis.'

'Any time.' Indie was still looking down at the crew, hoping that they didn't leave before she had a chance to join them. Perhaps they could all go out for dinner this evening, she thought, she'd had enough of bland hotel food and would kill for some *patatas bravas*.

'Mum says you're not coming home for Christmas?'

'No,' Indie said. 'I'm going to Singapore, then Thailand for New Year.'

'Sounds awful.'

'It really will be.'

'Well I just wanted to bend your ear about something, if you don't mind.'

'Bend away.'

'I've met someone and I'm thinking of telling everyone about it at Christmas. I wasn't going to, but I think it's important to her that I do.'

'Okay, and why is this a big deal?' Indie was confused. None of them had ever had any issue bringing new boyfriends or girl-friends back to meet their parents. Even when Ellie had turned up with her first girlfriend when she was seventeen, despite not having told anyone she was gay yet, Angie and Jack hadn't batted an eyelid.

'It's a big deal because of who it is.'

'Oooh!' Indie was intrigued now. 'Are you shagging someone famous?'

'No, it's no one famous.'

'So who is it?' Indie saw one of the crew stand up and felt herself getting impatient.

'Katie Brennan.'

'Who?'

'Katie Brennan,' Freddy repeated. 'She used to live next door to us in Pemberton Road? Her mum was good friends with our mum? Her dad shagged our mum?'

Indie nearly dropped the phone in shock. She hadn't thought about that family in years. 'What the hell, Freddy?'

'I know, but it's not like I planned it. I bumped into her in Oxford – she goes here too – and it just happened. There's something between us. I can't explain it.'

'A shared history of fucked-up-ness?'

'No, something real, Indie. I love her. I'm in love with her.'

Indie had never heard her kid brother use the L-word before. 'Wow, Freddo, it sounds like it's serious.'

'It is, and that's why I want to tell everyone, but the more I think about it, the more stressed out I get about it. What if Mum goes ballistic? What if Dad gets upset?'

'It's your life though, and if you want to spend it with the most inappropriate person you could ever have possibly found then that's your decision.'

'Thanks for the reassurance.'

Indie thought for a moment. 'You really love this girl?'

'Yes.'

'And she really loves you?'

'Yes.'

It had been more than ten years since Indie, intent on punishing her mother, had made her New Year's Eve revelation. When she thought back to her thirteen-year-old self, she felt ashamed about how she had behaved. She had acted like the bratty little child that she was and, in turn, had hurt so many people. For years she had tried to justify it to herself – it was her mum's fault not hers; the truth would have come out eventually anyway – but after her parents had divorced and Sophie and Alan had moved away, she had wondered over and over again if she had done the right thing. She had destroyed one marriage and possibly a second.

'Are her parents still together?' she asked now, already dreading the answer.

'Apparently so.'

'Blimey.' She tried to sound nonchalant, but she felt a flood of relief. She had always liked Sophie. Even after Indie had done what she had done, she had been really nice to her. She hadn't deserved what had happened to her. After they had moved away and Indie could no longer glare at Alan whenever she saw him in the street, she had instead directed her anger squarely at her mother, blaming her for ruining everyone's lives, particularly hers. She had been too young then to understand the complexities of her parents' marriage, her mother's breakdown and all of the factors that led to the brief but destructive affair.

She had left home at the earliest opportunity, signing a modelling contract with her parents' consent, and staying with her dad, or with friends, until she was old enough to get her own place.

Maybe it was having her own space, or growing up, or simply a case of absence making the heart grow fonder but somewhere along the way her feelings towards her mother had thawed. Whatever crap Indie had thrown at her Angie had never reciprocated with anything but love and empathy. When Indie had demanded that she sign the modelling contract her mother had agreed without protest, even though Indie knew that she would have much preferred her to go to college first. She had called and texted Indie regularly, never giving her a hard time when she didn't respond for days on end. And when Indie, who got too big for her boots and started turning down modelling jobs she deemed beneath her, had run out of money and found herself back on her mother's doorstep, she had welcomed her with open arms.

It was then that they had started to repair their damaged relationship. These days they got on pretty well and although Indie spent much of her time on the road, she looked forward to checking in with her mum whenever she was back in London.

She thought about Freddy, her slightly nerdy and amazingly good-natured kid brother, and this girl who had been tiny when it had all kicked off. It was some weird fate that they had found each other again after all this time. Or was it karma? She wasn't sure but she knew one thing – the past had finally caught up with her and it was time to face her demons.

'Do you know what, Freddo? I'm not missing this showdown for love nor money. Change of plan, I'm coming home for Christmas.'

After she hung up, she looked down and saw that the crew had disappeared. They'd probably gone off to a bar already. She stood out on the balcony for a while, watching the sea instead. Her mother had made a big mistake all that time ago but so had she.

And it was time to make amends.

25

Katie looked out of her dorm room window and saw her parents hurrying across the quad towards her building. She reached for her bags and cast a glance around her room, feeling forlorn. It was only for a few weeks, she reminded herself, then she would be back again.

In the three months since she had moved to Oxford, her life had changed beyond recognition. She loved her parents and was looking forward to spending Christmas with them, but she was also being wrenched away from the place – and people – that she had quickly grown to love. And going home also meant telling her parents about Freddy, which she was dreading. She had to resist the urge to barricade herself inside and refuse to leave.

With one last glance around her room, she let herself out, locked the door and made her way down the stairs to meet her parents. Her phone beeped and she took it out of her pocket and read the message. It was from Freddy.

Just got on the train. Your parents arrived yet? xxx

She slipped it quickly back into her pocket as she caught sight of her parents. Her mum's face lit up when she saw her. 'Oh, Katie, look at you, you're so grown up!'

'Mum!' Katie protested, laughing. 'You only saw me two weeks ago.'

'I know but it feels like forever.'

Katie kissed her mum and then stood back and looked at her dad. He looked like he'd aged about ten years in three months. He stood awkwardly, unsure about whether he was allowed to hug her or not. They had spoken on the phone a few times – stilted conversations at first, which gradually eased into their normal patter as time progressed – but although her mum had visited several times, she hadn't seen him since she left home. Watching him now, looking so nervous and indecisive, broke her heart and she threw her arms around him.

'Hi, Dad.'

'Hi, Kitty Kat.'

'Come on, Alan, help Katie with her bags,' her mum said, fussing. He took them off her and threw them easily over his shoulders and they made their way to where the car was parked.

'Tom's getting in at five,' Sophie explained. 'He's already made plans to go out tonight but I've told him we're having a family dinner first whether he likes it or not. What about you? Any plans to see your old friends?'

Katie didn't want to admit that she'd barely spoken to any of her school friends, that she'd been too absorbed in her new life to even think about her old ones. 'Not tonight, but I'm sure I'll catch up with them at some point over the holidays.'

In the car on the way home, her mum chattered away constantly, trying to fill any awkward silences between father and daughter. Her dad, as always, said very little but chimed in every so often with an anecdote or two. Katie looked out of the window at the countryside rushing past and thought about

Freddy. She wondered if his train had arrived in London yet and who would be there to greet him. She pictured him returning to Pemberton Road, the street where she had spent the first eight years of her life, of him walking past her old house and thinking of her. She thought about the prospect of telling her parents about him and felt nauseous. And, more than anything, she thought about how soon she could be with him again.

Indie climbed out of the taxi in Pemberton Road and stood outside her mum's house. She glanced briefly at the house next door before quickly looking away, and then she took a deep breath, walked up the steps and let herself in through the front door.

'Hi, honey, I'm home!' she yelled, slamming the door closed with a satisfactory bang.

'Indie?' Her mum appeared from the kitchen, tea towel in hand. 'Indie! My goodness! What are you doing here? I thought you were going to Singapore?'

'Change of plan,' she said, shrugging off her coat and giving her mum an air kiss. 'Thought I'd spend Christmas with you lot of losers instead.'

'I haven't got your room ready–' her mum began but Indie stopped her.

'It's fine, Mum, don't worry.'

'Oh, I'm so delighted to see you. We'll have the whole family back together for the first time in... Golly, how long has it been?'

Ellie and her girlfriend, Chrissie, came down the stairs. Ellie's face lit up with delight when she saw her sister.

'Bloody hell, Indie, we didn't know you were coming!' Ellie looked behind her and shouted over her shoulder, 'Freddo, come down here, you'll never guess who's just rocked up!'

Freddy appeared a few seconds later, in his signature track-suit bottoms and jumper, the only one in the family who wasn't surprised to see her there. 'All right, sis,' he said.

'Where's Benji?' Indie asked, after she had hugged everyone.

'Oh you know Benji, he's busy, but he's coming over for dinner later,' Angie explained. 'He's got a new girlfriend, Bianca someone, he wants us to meet.'

'Not Bianca Friedman? The hot new actress Bianca Friedman?' Chrissie asked, eyes wide.

'God knows, I can't keep track of that boy,' Angie said, looking proud.

'And Dad?' Indie asked.

'Dad and What's-her-face are coming over too.'

Indie gave her mother a withering look. Jack had been remarried for eight years but Angie still referred to his wife as What's-her-face.

'Well, this calls for a celebration,' Angie said brightly. 'I'll get the champagne!'

Ellie and Chrissie started to follow her into the kitchen but Indie hung back and grabbed Freddy's arm. 'What's the plan?' she hissed. 'When are you gonna tell them about Katie?'

'Tonight,' he said. 'Get it out of the way.'

'I'm here for you, Freddo, I've got your back, okay?'

He smiled at her. 'I'm really glad you're here, Indie.'

'Tom, do you remember a boy called Freddy Taylor? He used to live next door to us when we lived in London?'

Katie's brother scrunched up his nose as he tried to remember. 'Vaguely,' he said. Then his face lit up with recognition. 'Oh yes I do! He had loads of brothers and sisters, didn't he? We used to play in their treehouse.'

'That's it,' she said, cautiously.

'Why?'

'I bumped into him, in Oxford.'

'Wow, small world.' Tom didn't seem that interested.

'We're kind of seeing each other.'

'Good for you.'

'The thing is... I'm going to tell Mum and Dad and I'm a bit worried about it.'

'Why?'

This was her opportunity to tell her brother the whole story. Up until now she had urged her mum not to burden him with the truth but she knew that if she and Freddy were for keeps there was no way they could keep it from him. In any case, it wasn't fair on him to be the only one in the dark. She looked at her brother, who was sprawled across the sofa, legs thrown over one of the arms, playing a game on his phone and she just couldn't bring herself to do it.

'Don't worry about it, I'm just being silly.'

'You know, I do remember him now. He used to wet his pants all the time. Fresh Pants Freddy, that's what we used to call him!'

Katie groaned. 'Thanks for that, Tom, I'll be sure to remind him.'

'Fresh Pants Freddy!' Tom was chuckling away to himself. Katie threw a cushion at him and went to make herself a cup of tea. He was still laughing when she came back.

'So, Mr Smarty Pants, how's university going?'

Eight pairs of eyes looked at Freddy expectantly from around the kitchen table. Indie watched her brother closely as he thought carefully about how to respond to Benji's question.

'Yeah, really good thanks,' he said. 'The course is really interesting; the digs are pretty tidy and I've met a good bunch of people. I'm in the university football team.'

'Good for you,' Jack said, 'I'm so proud of you.' He lifted his glass of champagne up towards Freddy and everyone followed suit.

'There's something else actually. Something I wanted to talk to you about.'

'Oh yes?' Jack was already distracted, tucking into the curry they'd ordered because Angie had said she couldn't be bothered to cook for so many people.

'I've actually met someone.'

'Ooooooh, Freddo's got a girlfriend,' Ellie said teasingly and Indie saw Freddy reddening.

'Good for you, lad. What's this mystery girl called?'

Freddy hesitated and looked at Indie. She gave him a reassuring nod.

'Her name's Katie. Katie Brennan.'

Jack continued chewing away contentedly, oblivious to the relevance of the name, but when Indie looked at her mother, she had completely frozen, fork still halfway to her mouth. She looked at Freddy, pale-faced.

'Katie Brennan?' she asked.

'Yes.'

'As in, *the* Katie Brennan? The one we used to know?'

'Yes.'

'Who's Katie Brennan?' Jack asked, sensing the change in mood. No one spoke for a moment.

'Dad, the Brennans.' Indie finally broke the silence. 'The family who used to live next door. Freddy is going out with the daughter.'

'*Christ!*' Jack said, as the penny dropped. Indie kept her eyes firmly fixed on Freddy. He had a determined look on his face but she imagined that he wanted to shrink down into his chair and disappear. She took his hand and squeezed it, and he smiled gratefully at her.

'I don't understand,' Angie was saying. 'How did this even happen?'

'It was a total coincidence,' Freddy explained. 'She's studying at Oxford too. I saw her in a café and recognised her. We swapped numbers and started meeting up. It just happened. There's something there, Mum, something special. We've been together for a few months now.'

'What's going on?' What's-her-face demanded. 'I don't understand.'

Everyone ignored her.

'Jesus, Freddo, you don't half pick them,' Benji commented. To his right, his new girlfriend was checking her phone, looking bored. She had turned out not to be the famous actress Bianca Friedman, thank God. That probably would have tipped this situation over the edge. Indie glanced at her mum, who still hadn't moved, and then at her dad, who was managing to look both perplexed and outraged.

'I'm sorry,' Freddy said. 'I'm sorry for blurting it out like this, and for any bad memories or hurt that it's bringing back, I really am. But I'm not sorry that I've met her. She's the best thing that has ever happened to me. I love her.'

You could have heard a pin drop. Indie glanced around the table. Most of her family were still staring at Freddy in shock. Chrissie and What's-her-face were looking confused and slightly pissed off about being in the dark about something so important. Bianca was still scrolling on her phone. Poor Freddy looked like a stubborn, petrified little boy. *How on earth do we get past this?*

But this was exactly why she had come back to her family now. To make up for what she did all those years ago, to have her brother's back when he needed her. She took a deep breath.

'Well, I for one can't wait for the wedding.'

Everyone's eyes turned to her and she looked defiantly back. She had achieved exactly what she wanted, to turn the attention away from Freddy onto her. *Trust Indie to say the most inappropriate thing possible, to make the situation worse*, they were thinking.

She waited for her mum to turn on her and start having a go, or for her dad to shake his head and say that he was disappointed in her. Then she heard a muffled snort and turned to see Ellie, desperately trying to suppress her giggles. Next came Benji, although he wasn't so subtle as he started guffawing loudly. Then Freddy joined in, a laughter that she suspected was more nerves than amusement.

Jack was staring at his children in bemusement. Then, as if powerless to stop himself, he started chuckling, quietly at first but getting louder and louder as he became infected by everyone else's laughter. Finally, Indie looked at Angie, who had found something very fascinating in her glass of champagne.

'Mum?' she asked, tentatively.

Angie looked up. She had tears running down her face, but her expression wasn't one of sorrow.

'Jesus Christ, Indie,' she said, between sobs of laughter.

Their mother's reaction was the cue they had all been waiting for and the table erupted. Benji was doubled over. Ellie was clutching onto Chrissie, trying to explain it all to her but unable to speak coherently. Jack was leaning back in his chair, eyes closed, howling. Then poor Freddy laughed so hard that he fell off his chair and it was game over. They all lost their marbles.

'So, love, how has the first term gone for you?'

Katie was sitting in the living room with her parents, nursing a cup of tea. Tom had disappeared out to the pub as soon as they'd finished eating.

'It's been amazing,' she said, smiling despite her nerves. 'It's such a special place and I'm loving my course.'

'That's wonderful,' Sophie said, beaming at her.

'Have you made friends?' Alan asked. Her happiness was always more important to him than her academic success.

'Yes,' she said. 'I've made some really good friends actually. We're already talking about renting a house together next year.'

'Good.' Alan nodded with satisfaction.

'There is something else,' she said tentatively.

'Go on.'

'I've met someone. A boy. It's quite serious.'

'Good for you,' Sophie said. 'That's lovely news.'

'The thing is, it's someone that you know. Or at least used to know.'

She could tell that her mum understood immediately. Her dad seemed confused.

'It's Freddy Taylor.'

They both stared at her. She watched as Sophie carefully put down her tea, as if worried that she might spill it otherwise. Alan paled.

'I'm sorry, Dad, I know you told me to stay away from him and I really did try I promise, but something happened between us. I can't explain it, but I just couldn't keep away.'

'How many students are there in Oxford?' he asked.

She was thrown by his question. 'Sorry?'

'How many students are there in Oxford?'

'I don't know, twenty thousand?'

'Twenty thousand kids and you choose to go out with this one?' He was incredulous.

'Alan,' Sophie said quietly, but he ignored her.

'Are you honestly telling me, Katie, that of all the boys in Oxford, this is the one you want?'

'Yes,' she said, not looking him in the eye.

'And you've got no problem with the effect this will have on your mother?'

'Alan...' Sophie said again, but he wasn't listening.

'You've known this boy what, a few weeks? Hardly long enough for it to be serious. You need to call it off right now, Katie, do you hear me?'

'But, Dad, I love him!'

'Don't be ridiculous, you hardly know him.'

He had never spoken to her like this before. 'I do know him, Dad, and he's a good person. A really good person. What happened in the past is not his fault and it's not mine either.'

'So, it's all my fault, is it?'

'Well, yes it is!' Katie's anger was rising to match her father's now.

'Oh I get it, three months at Oxford and you're a know-it-all now I see.'

'Alan!' Sophie stood up now. 'Enough.'

He was silenced immediately. He looked up at Sophie and Katie saw a flash of pain cross his face. 'I'm so sorry, love, I'm so sorry this has all come up again.'

'I know you are.' Sophie sat down next to him and took his hand. 'But this is not Katie's fault. And it's not the boy's either.'

'But I just don't understand it,' he said. 'There are so many people in the world. What on earth conspired to bring these two together?'

Sophie shrugged. 'Fate?'

Katie watched the exchange. It was as if they'd forgotten she was even in the room. Then Alan turned to her. 'I'm sorry, Katie, I didn't mean to have a go.'

'I know.'

'It was just such a shock. Your mum and I, we worked so hard to move on from that time and the thought of it coming back into our lives now is a lot to handle.'

'I know that too.'

'I'm not sure I can get my head around it all. What it means for you. What it means for us.'

'It doesn't have to mean anything, Dad.'

He looked at her sadly. 'Oh it does, Katie. It does.'

After he had left the room, on the pretence that he had some invoicing to finish, her mum went to the kitchen to get a couple of glasses of wine and handed one to Katie.

'I'm so sorry, Mum,' Katie was on the verge of crying now as she realised, probably for the first time, the hurt that her relationship might be causing her mother.

'You don't need to be sorry. You've done nothing wrong.'

'Except fall in love with public enemy number one.'

'Well yes, except that.'

'I did try to stay away from him at first, I honestly did. But there was just something there, Mum, and I couldn't get him out of my mind. I never meant to cause any upset.'

'I know that, love.'

'What do we do now?'

Sophie looked thoughtful. 'Leave your dad to me, he'll come round.'

'But what about you?'

'Don't you worry about me, Katie. Your happiness is all I care about and if Freddy Taylor makes you happy, then that's the most important thing.'

'Do you really mean it?' Katie sagged with relief.

'Of course I do.'

'But are you upset, Mum? Have I upset you?'

'I'm shocked, certainly. I'd be lying if I said it hadn't brought up some bad memories from the past. And there's no doubt that it's going to be a tricky path to navigate, Katie. I mean the usual meet the parents is going to be a bit different for us, isn't it? But we'll make it work.'

'Do you think Dad will ever forgive me?'

Sophie looked at her sadly. 'It's not about forgiving you, love; it's about forgiving himself.'

26

Sophie turned the car engine off and gazed out of the window at the house that had once been hers. It looked like it had been recently repainted and the old front door had been replaced with a contemporary one, blue with stained glass panels and a large chrome knocker. Outside, a 4x4 was parked in the driveway and she could see that their old curtains had been taken down and replaced with white shutters. The house, just like her, had moved on.

Next she looked at the house next door. In contrast, it wasn't that different to how she remembered it. The SUV had been replaced by something smaller, presumably now all the Taylor children had grown up and moved out, and there were some new flowers in the beds. But other than that, it seemed untouched, the last vestige of a former life.

It was eleven years since Sophie had last been in Pemberton Road and the prospect of returning to her past had haunted her. But this visit wasn't about the past, it was about the future. It was time to make things right, for the sake of the children. Katie and Freddy were coming up to the end of their first year of university and they were still madly in love. She had never seen her daughter like this before; she had been such a bookworm at school, never particularly interested in boys. At first, she had worried that it might distract her from her studies, that she would waste the opportunity she'd worked so hard for. But in typical Katie style she was still getting top marks in almost everything she did.

With the summer holidays approaching, she knew that Katie was keen to invite Freddy to stay with them, and Freddy had asked Katie to spend the weekend at Pemberton Road, but it didn't feel right to any of them when there was such animosity between the two families.

Sophie had made the suggestion a few weeks ago, when she was having lunch with them both in Oxford. She had met Freddy a few times since Katie had told her about their relationship and he was a lovely boy.

The first time she met him she had been so shocked by his likeness to Jack that she had stood there for a moment, speechless, staring at him. His physical appearance still unnerved her now but as she got to know him, she realised that he was nothing like his father, apart from their shared love of football. Jack was a joker and a flirt but Freddy was more thoughtful, more serious. And it was very clear to her that he was serious about Katie. As they tucked into their lunch, she had asked Freddy, for the first time, how his mother was.

'She's fine thanks, Sophie,' he answered politely.

'Is she still working flat out as a solicitor?'

'She works hard, definitely, but she's fairly chilled out about it all these days.'

'Do you think she'd like to meet up perhaps? For a cup of tea?'

Freddy looked shell-shocked. 'With you?'

'Yes, with me.'

'Mum, what's this about?' Katie was looking at her, concerned.

'I just think, with you two being together, perhaps it's time that me and Angie had a chat. Cleared the air. Made life a bit easier for you two.'

'Oh, Mum, you'd do that for us?' Katie looked like she was about to cry.

'Of course, Katie. If Freddy thinks it's a good idea.'

'I don't see why not,' Freddy agreed. 'Shall I talk to her?'

'Okay, why not,' Sophie said. 'I don't want her to feel cornered. Why don't you mention it to her and if she's up for it, you can let me know.'

Katie called her later that day. 'Freddy's spoken to Angie. She's agreed to talk to you.'

How noble of her was Sophie's first thought, but she quickly swallowed her pride. 'Great, text me her number and I'll get in touch.'

'I was thinking, Mum, why don't you meet up in Oxford? You know, neutral ground? Perhaps Freddy and I could even be there to make things a bit less intense?'

'It's a lovely idea, Katie, but I think this is something Angie and I have to do alone.'

As soon as Katie hung up, Sophie had typed out a quick message to Angie before she could change her mind.

It's Sophie. I think it's time we talked. For the children's sake. I can come to you?

Angie's reply had come twenty minutes later.

Ok. How about Sunday?

When she had told Alan what she was planning to do, he had nodded in weary resignation. 'I suspected it would need to happen eventually. I'll drive you.'

'Thanks, Alan, but I'm going by myself.'

'I don't like the idea of you putting yourself through this, Sophie, especially alone.'

'I'll be fine.'

Alan looked miserable. He still hadn't got his head around Katie and Freddy's relationship. They'd told Tom the whole story and it hadn't gone well. Even now, months later, Tom hadn't been back home to visit yet, and he always called Sophie on her mobile when he wanted to speak to her to avoid the risk of Alan answering the landline.

Sophie gained no pleasure from her son's animosity towards Alan. She had worked extremely hard to forgive him after his affair. The healing process had been long, and painful at times, but they had succeeded. The wounds had healed. The young children, the glue that had kept them together at first, had grown up and no longer bound them in the same way; yet they stayed together. Now she was with him because she wanted to be, because she loved him. Because he loved her. When she looked at him, she never saw the man who had broken her heart. She only saw her loving husband who had been by her side for twenty years.

But when it came to Angie, there had been no healing process, no cathartic marriage counselling. The wounds of her friend's betrayal had not been treated so the idea of seeing her again felt as raw as the day she'd left. With one last glance at her old house, Sophie took a deep breath and climbed out of the car. *I'm here now. Might as well get this over and done with.*

Nausea rose inside her as she made her way up the steps to the front door. With a shaking hand she knocked and waited for

Angie to answer it. When she did, a few seconds later, Sophie almost gasped out loud. Angie was still as beautiful as ever but she looked so pale, gaunt almost.

Before she could stop herself, she blurted out, 'My goodness, Angie, what's happened?'

Angie didn't say anything at first, she just stared at Sophie as though she'd seen a ghost. Finally, she sighed and said, 'You could always read me like a book. You'd better come in.'

Sophie followed Angie into the kitchen and took in the once familiar surroundings. It looked strikingly similar to how she remembered, with only a few small adjustments to suggest that a decade had passed. As Angie busied herself making tea, Sophie looked out of the bifold doors, straining to see if the gate between the gardens was still there.

'The people who bought the house from you insisted we get the gate taken out,' Angie explained, reading her mind. 'They thought it was a bit creepy.'

Sophie chuckled, despite herself. 'I guess it kind of was.'

Angie drew out the process of making tea until the silence was almost unbearable. Eventually she brought the drinks over to the kitchen table and gestured for Sophie to sit down.

'You look fantastic,' Angie said. 'You haven't aged a day in ten years.'

Sophie couldn't stop herself from glowing with pleasure at the compliment. She'd been swimming almost daily for years and was now a highly regarded coach in the region. She looked after herself well and she had gained confidence as she aged. Now she was fifty she was probably in better health, both physically and mentally, than she was in her twenties.

'Thanks,' she said. She knew she should say something nice in return but she couldn't bring herself to do it. The more she looked at Angie, the more she was certain that something wasn't quite right. According to Freddy she was on great form, working less, looking after herself more, but his description didn't match the woman sitting opposite her.

'Are you okay, Angie?'

'Shouldn't I be asking you that?'

'Maybe, but nothing about this is conventional, is it?'

'I'm okay,' Angie replied dismissively, 'I've just been a bit under the weather.'

'Okay.' Sophie shrugged. The silence returned.

'So, how are you?'

'I'm good,' Sophie replied. 'We live in Cambridge now, I'm still a swimming instructor. Alan still works in property. Tom's at uni in Manchester and, well, you know about Katie.'

Angie nodded. 'I hear she's a wonderful girl but I've not had the pleasure of meeting her yet.'

'How did you and Jack feel when you found out?' Sophie asked.

'We laughed hysterically for about half an hour and then got pissed as farts.'

Sophie looked at her in surprise. 'Really?'

'Really.'

'Are you and Jack, you know, still friends?'

Angie smiled. 'Yes, actually, we are. At first, we forced it for the sake of the children but over time it became easier. Now I can't believe we were ever married to be honest. He's remarried you know, I'm sure Katie told you, some woman half his age but she makes him happy.'

'And you?'

'Oh there were romances, here and there, nothing that stuck.'

'I'm sorry to hear that.'

'Don't be.'

She's still the same old Angie, Sophie thought, *as brusque as you like.* She sipped her tea.

'How did you and Alan feel? When Katie told you about Freddy?'

'We were shocked at first. Alan was quite upset. It just dredged up so much stuff from the past, you know? I tried to be supportive for Katie but it was far from ideal. We had to tell Tom, which was a disaster. After a while I got used to the idea. Freddy is a wonderful boy, such a credit to you and Jack. I'm very fond of him now. Alan's still not got his head around it yet.'

'It's quite the coincidence, them ending up at the same university and getting together.'

'Tell me about it.'

The two women smiled tentatively at each other. It was weird, Sophie thought, she didn't feel as angry as she had thought she would. It felt almost companionable, sitting here, talking to Angie. She hadn't been expecting that at all.

'Look, Sophie,' Angie began, 'for what it's worth, I really am so terribly sorry for everything that happened. I was the worst friend, the worst neighbour, the worst possible human being to you. I hate myself for what I did to you.'

'I appreciate you saying that,' Sophie replied.

'I know it's no excuse or consolation, but I was in a very dark place back then. It took me too long to get the help I needed and I'll always regret that. I don't ever expect you to forgive me but I want you to know that you coming here today means the world to me. You're an incredible woman, Sophie Brennan. I've always thought it and now I'm even more certain of it.'

Sophie was taken aback by Angie's show of emotion, something that she knew didn't come naturally to her, or at least not to the old Angie.

'I hated you,' she admitted. 'For months, I really hated you. I thought *how can a person do that to someone?* I never thought I would get past what you did. But it was all such a long time ago now and we're very different people. I don't hate you anymore, Angie, so don't waste time hating yourself. It's simply not worth it.'

To her surprise, Angie burst into tears. 'Oh, Sophie, I'm sorry, I'm so sorry.'

Sophie put her hand over Angie's, feeling an overwhelming urge to comfort her. This visit was turning out to be even stranger than she'd imagined.

'I've wanted to contact you so many times over the years,' Angie continued.

'I would have told you to piss off,' Sophie admitted.

Angie laughed through her tears. 'I'd have deserved it.'

'I was sorry to hear about you and Jack though, I really was. I always wondered, over the years, if you'd stayed together or not.'

'Our marriage was in trouble long before all this happened. The problem was that we never dealt with it, we just put our heads down and ploughed on. We didn't realise how bad it had got until it was too late. The affair toppled us but we'd been wobbly for years.'

'I had no idea.'

'We hid it well,' Angie said. 'Too well. That was the problem. I learned the hard way that keeping things in is always going to end badly.' She blew her nose and started shredding the tissue with her hands. 'After it all happened, I finally got some help. I went to the doctor, got a prescription for antidepressants, started seeing a counsellor. I got a job with a new firm which was more family friendly. Gradually I got my life back on track. But me and Jack, I think we were beyond saving. We married because we were madly in love but that alone is not always enough to keep you going forever.'

'Are you happy though, Angie? Have you been okay?'

'I've been fine,' Angie said. Then she looked up at Sophie. 'Well, I've been having a bit of a hard time recently.'

'Do you want to talk about it?'

'No. Yes.'

The words triggered a memory of a similar conversation they'd had together, many years back, sitting on a garden bench.

'You're not pregnant, are you?'

Angie laughed so hard that she started coughing. As Sophie watched her struggling to catch her breath, the nasty feeling that something was terribly wrong returned.

'Not pregnant no,' Angie said, once she had recovered. 'I've got cancer.'

'Oh, Angie, I'm so sorry.' Sophie gripped tightly onto her hand.

'I've started chemo and it's knocking me a bit for six to be honest.'

'What's the prognosis?'

'Not great.'

Sophie put her hand to her mouth, tears pricking her eyes. *The poor woman.* She tried to think of something positive to say, to urge her to stay strong, not to give up hope. People lived for years with cancer these days. Perhaps there was a clinical trial or a new treatment coming up. But the words kept getting stuck in her throat.

'I'm sorry, Sophie, you came here to talk about the kids and now I'm throwing all this drama on you. I promise I'm not trying to guilt trip you into liking me again.'

'You daft cow,' Sophie said, looking at her fondly. 'I could never like you.'

'Well that's a relief.'

'How are the kids coping with it all?'

'They don't know.'

'What? Why?'

'Because I haven't told them.'

'Well obviously, smart-arse, but why not?'

'I just can't do it,' Angie said, dabbing her eyes with her mangled tissue. 'I can't bear the thought of seeing their faces when I tell them.'

'Does Jack know?'

'No.'

'So who knows?'

'My doctor. And now you.'

Sophie's heart broke. No one should have to bear this kind of thing alone.

'You need to tell Jack,' she insisted. 'You need to talk to him now, and then he can help you tell the children. I'm serious, Angie, this is really important. You can't go through this alone and when the kids find out that you kept it from them, they'll be devastated.'

'I know,' Angie said.

'Have you been going to your treatments alone?'

'Yes.'

'Well that stops right now. You send me your list of appointments and I'll be there with you, each time. Do you understand?'

'Why are you being so nice to me, Sophie? I was such a bitch to you.'

'You really were. But you're my bitch and I'm not letting you go through this on your own.'

After she had said her goodbyes to Angie, threatening to call her the next day to check that she'd spoken to Jack, Sophie drove down the road until she was out of sight of the house and parked the car again. She put her head on the steering wheel and cried. She cried for everything that had happened ten years ago, for the life that she had left behind in Pemberton Road, the friend she had lost. But, more than any of that, she cried for Angie.

When she had calmed down, she sent Alan a text to tell him she was on the way, wiped her eyes and steeled herself to drive home. Life worked in mysterious ways but she knew now that there was a reason why she had ended up back in Angie's life again after all this time. Now was not the moment for revenge or recriminations. It wasn't even about the kids. Angie needed her, and even though everyone would think she'd lost the plot, Sophie was going to be there for her. She took a few deep breaths, turned the radio on and pulled out of Pemberton Road.

It was time to go home.

Angie's phone beeped from the bedside table and she shifted her weight gingerly so that she could reach for it. Her whole body ached with the effort. She looked down at her screen. It was from Sophie.

Just got back home. Call me later if you feel up to it.

Sophie had been with her to every chemo session for the past three months. Whenever Angie tried to tell her that it wasn't necessary or questioned whether it was interfering with her job, Sophie had simply waved her concerns away. They had spent hours together in a little cubicle, while the poisonous cocktail of chemicals was pumped into Angie's body. Sometimes they chatted, other times they watched TV. When it got too much for Angie and she closed her eyes, Sophie read to her or simply sat quietly by her side.

Angie had marvelled more than once at Sophie's ability to

forgive. She would never fully understand why Sophie was going so far out of her way to support her. After all, she had seduced her husband and almost ruined her life. But she also knew, after everything that she had been through, not to look a gift horse in the mouth. And Sophie was a bloody sparkly unicorn with a knight in shining armour on top. If it was all a ruse and she was going to turn around one day and stab her through the heart while she slept, it still would have been worth it, to have her by her side these past few months, to not feel alone anymore.

Her phone beeped again and she looked down at it. This one was from Jack.

I know you don't feel much like talking after a session but just want to say I'm thinking of you xx

A couple of minutes later, another one arrived, this time from Indie.

Greetings from Ibiza. How did the sesh go? Did you vom? Call me when you're up to it.

On Sophie's insistence, Angie had finally told Jack about her diagnosis and he had sat with her and held her hand while she broke the news to the children. With Freddy and Benji she had been able to do it face to face but poor Ellie, back in New Zealand, and Indie, who was on location in the States at the time, had found out via FaceTime. They had both wanted to come straight home but Angie had insisted that they didn't.

'I'm living vicariously through you now,' she had said. 'Don't let me down.'

Near or far though, they had all been incredible. She thought back to just a few months ago when she had first been diagnosed. She had never felt so scared, so hopeless and alone, yet she had considered it her punishment for crimes committed so long ago. She had driven away the people that she loved. She didn't deserve to be surrounded by anyone. She would face this on her own, she decided, and not drag others down with her. It was her penance.

Now of course she realised that, yet again, she had behaved like a total idiot.

Her phone beeped again. This time it was Freddy.

Hi Mum, how are you feeling? Katie and I will be over tomorrow lunchtime. Send me a list of what you want us to pick up on the way xx

Now that the tension between the two families had eased, Angie had met Katie a few times and had been enchanted by her. At first, she came across as a serious, quiet young thing, just like Angie remembered her as a little girl. But you only had to delve slightly beneath the surface to discover that she was wickedly funny, intelligent and kind. Just like her mother. She could understand why Freddy was crazy about her but they were so young and in all likelihood it wouldn't last forever. Did it matter though, in the grand scheme of things, she wondered? As long as they made each other happy now, who cared what happened in the future.

Perhaps it had served the purpose that it was designed to – it had brought the families back together. Ellie had told her that Tom was now following her on Instagram and they'd messaged each other a couple of times. She'd suggested meeting up when she was next in London and he'd seemed keen. It may happen, it may not, but the children being friends again was a possibility she had never imagined.

Her eyelids were getting heavy. She needed to sleep. She could almost feel the toxic drugs coursing through her body, killing off the bad cells but destroying the good ones too. For years she had thought that she was a bad cell, spreading unhappiness to the people around her. But for the first time, in the darkest of times, she felt something else. She felt hope. If Sophie could forgive her, then perhaps it was about time that she forgave herself.

She closed her eyes and drifted off.

EPILOGUE

Katie looked in the mirror, straightening her gown and cap self-consciously. A figure appeared in the background and she spun round to find her mum standing in the doorway to her bedroom, watching her. 'Crikey, Mum, you scared me, I didn't realise you were there.'

'You look beautiful, darling,' she said. Katie grinned and gave her a little twirl.

'Dad's packed up the car. Are you ready to go?'

'Just give me five minutes?'

'Of course, take your time.'

As she heard Sophie head back downstairs, instructing Alan to hold his horses, she grabbed her phone and typed out a quick message.

We're leaving shortly. See you at the hotel? Xx

He replied immediately.

See you in a couple of hours xx

Checking her holdall to make sure she had everything she needed, Katie shrugged off her gown, folded it up and pushed it into the bag, resting her cap on top. It was time to go. She picked up her bag and made her way downstairs to where her dad was standing by the front door, patiently waiting to drive her to her destination, just as he had been ever since she was a little girl on her way to ballet class or a teenager begging a lift to a house party.

'Where's the get-up, Kitty Kat? I wanted to get a photo.'

'I've packed it away, Dad, I'll put it on when we get there.'

'All right, love, let's go, you don't want to be late for your own graduation.'

How have I finished university already? she thought, as she climbed into her parents' car. It felt like five minutes ago that she was moving into her dorm room, unpacking her bags and trying to get rid of her parents. Now here she was, living with them again, albeit temporarily, having left the city that had been her home, and her heart, for three years. Her dad had come to pick her up at the end of her last semester and she had stood outside her student house, which she had shared with three of her closest friends, and felt a sorrow in the very pit of her stomach. *I'm not ready for it to be over yet*, she had thought, looking through the windows at the now empty rooms inside. It had been the best three years of her life.

And now they were all returning to Oxford for one last time so that she could officially graduate. Sophie had booked rooms at a hotel and they were going out for dinner and drinks afterwards. Freddy was staying at the same hotel with his family – not all of them because Benji was in the middle of filming a new rom com and it was too far for Ellie to travel, but Indie had surprised everyone by saying that she was coming. And of course, his dad would be there. But Katie knew there would be an absence that he would feel acutely, and she yearned to be with him now, to hold his hand and tell him that she was there for him.

As they sped down the dual carriageway, Katie looked out of the window, feeling emotional. She was looking forward to the ceremony and the party afterwards but it also marked the end of an important chapter in her life. Her mum had tried to reassure her that she had nothing to worry about, that she was simply closing the door to one adventure and opening the door to the next. 'You have the best years of your life still ahead of you,' she had told Katie confidently.

Katie knew that she was probably right but the thought of leaving her old life behind and no longer living in the same city as Freddy was horrible. They had been together since the beginning of university and now they were graduating together at the end.

They had both agreed to pursue their own paths. After getting his BA, Freddy had decided not to stay on for the clinical stage of his course and was returning to London to study for a master's degree in sports science. Katie was going to South America in September to work as an intern on an archaeology project. She hadn't wanted to apply when she had first seen the opportunity posted on the university noticeboard, but she hadn't been able to stop thinking about it. She had mentioned it to Freddy, trying unsuccessfully to sound blasé, but of course he'd seen straight through her and had urged her to go for it.

'It's too good an opportunity to turn down, Brennan. We've got the rest of our lives to spend together. What's a few months apart?'

'Okay,' she agreed. 'I'll do the application. I won't get it anyway.'

Except that she had. And now she was going to be away from Freddy for three months, perhaps longer if things went well, and she had no idea how she would cope. He had become so important to her that she now wondered how she had managed to live for so long without him. She thought back to when they were first reunited, how nervous she'd been of letting him back into her life, and was so thankful that she had taken the risk. It had been worth it and they had proven that by the fact that they were still together. And more than that, they had brought other people together too, like her mum and Angie. An unlikely friendship that had, despite all the odds, rediscovered itself again when Angie had needed it the most.

She couldn't say the same for her dad, who still stubbornly refused to visit Pemberton Road or socialise with the Taylors. But he was always extremely welcoming to Freddy when he came to stay and he had, she suspected, become fond of him over the years. Her dad was probably as nervous as she was about today because it would be the first time he had seen Jack. When her mum had told him the plan to stay in the same hotel and go out for dinner together afterwards, he had looked horrified. But Sophie had fixed her determined glare on him, the one she reserved for rare occasions, and said, 'This is for the children, Alan, and you're coming. And you're going to make an effort. And maybe even have fun, or at least pretend to.'

And he had sighed and nodded, knowing that there was no point in arguing with her. He would never really understand how his daughter had ended up falling in love with Angie's son. And he would never get why Sophie had rekindled her friendship with Angie and supported her so loyally during her illness. But Katie saw it for what it was, and it made her love and respect her mother even more. Her compassion, her ability to empathise and to forgive, was incredible. She no longer saw her as her boring old mum, but as one of the strongest women she knew.

'We're here,' Alan said, driving into a multistorey car park and looking for a space. Katie jumped out as soon as they had parked up and started grabbing bags, eager to see Freddy, who was waiting for them in the hotel bar. As they made their way towards the entrance, her dad hesitated and she gave him a reassuring smile. He nodded at her and together they made their way inside. The first person she saw was Freddy, who stood up and ran over to greet her, grabbing her bags. He led her over to the sofas where the others were sitting and she saw Indie giving her father the once over. She braced herself for what might happen next.

Please behave, Indie, she pleaded silently. She adored Freddy's big sister but she was unpredictable at the best of times. Sophie rushed forward to greet everyone, but Alan hung back, apprehensive. Katie briefly panicked, thinking that this had all been a terrible idea, but then she saw Indie saunter over and kiss her dad on the cheek.

'Nice to see you, Mr B,' she said.

Katie felt the breath that she didn't even know she'd been holding on to leave her body.

Next Jack shook his hand. 'Hi, Alan, fancy a beer before it all kicks off?'

She looked at Freddy and he grinned back. Perhaps it really would be okay after all.

She woke up the next morning, confused by being in an unfamiliar room before she remembered where she was and who she was with. She turned over to find Freddy sitting up in bed, checking his phone.

As she tried to get up, the hangover hit her. 'Ouch,' she said.

Freddy looked down and smiled. 'Ouch indeed,' he said. 'Someone had fun last night!'

'Oh God, was I terrible?' She racked her brains, trying to

think back over the previous day and whether she'd said or done anything silly.

'Nah, you were fine,' he said. 'I mean, as long as you don't count loudly informing my dad that he was incredibly generous for forgiving your dad – in front of your dad.'

'Ohhh,' Katie said, clutching her head. 'This is why I should never drink when I'm nervous.'

'Well, it was your graduation ceremony, so I think you're allowed. And no harm was done.'

The day had gone as well as it could, she thought, remembering it now. There had been a few awkward silences between the families, a sad moment when they had toasted to absent friends. And then, eventually, a gradual relaxation into the evening which had been made easier, sadly but truly, when her dad had gone up to bed early. After that they had all continued to get plastered in the hotel bar until the early hours and had a bit of a hoot.

'Question is, are you ready for round two?'

'Urgh,' came Katie's response as she put a pillow over her head.

'Let's go get a full English and you'll feel better. Dad and Indie are already down there.'

'Sounds horrendous.'

'Come on, Brennan, a nice greasy fried egg. Sausages dripping with fat...' he ducked for cover as she hurled her pillow at him.

They showered, dressed and made their way downstairs for breakfast. Katie picked delicately at some dry toast while Freddy tucked into a mountain of hot food, occasionally waving some bacon under her nose, much to her disgust. When they had finished, they checked out and made their way back to the car park.

'I'll see you soon,' Katie said, giving Freddy a kiss and waving at the other Taylors before getting into her parents' car.

As they pulled away, Sophie turned round in her seat and smiled at her. 'Have a good time, love?'

'Really good,' she said. 'A proper send off. Sorry if I got a bit tipsy.'

'Don't be silly, you were fine.'

'Sorry if I embarrassed you, Dad,' Katie said, her face reddening.

'You could never embarrass me, Kitty Kat. I'm very proud of you.'

It had been a pretty momentous thing for her dad to put himself through what he had yesterday, and Katie felt proud of him too.

'Are you sure you won't change your mind about this evening?' she asked him.

'No thanks, love, you go on ahead and have a good time.'

They dropped him off outside their house. Sophie jumped out of the car and climbed into the driver's seat and Katie clambered from the back into the passenger seat next to her. Together they waved until he had let himself back into the empty house and closed the door. Then they turned to each other.

'Can we grab a cheeky McDs on the way down, Mum? I've suddenly got my appetite back.'

'Oh go on then, I could probably sink a quarter pounder with cheese.'

Katie turned up the radio as they pulled out of their road and made their way back out of Cambridge again. She and her mum both started singing along at the same time, dancing in their seats. She laughed with a satisfyingly carefree abandon, and all of a sudden it hit her and she realised what her mum had been banging on about. Oxford had only been one part of her journey. She had her whole future in front of her and she was going to grasp it with both hands.

~

They pulled into Pemberton Road. Sophie took her seat belt off and got out of the car without so much as a glance at the house next door. It was someone else's house now, not hers. She had seen the people who lived there once, when she was visiting Angie. A young couple had come out. The woman was holding a baby while the man bumped the pram down the steps. Ahead of them a toddler had scooted off, nearly going straight into the road and the harassed looking man had abandoned the pram and ran after him, yelling at him to stop. Sophie had grabbed the runaway pram and held it until the woman could catch up and take it from her.

'Thanks,' the woman said gratefully, looking tired as she jiggled the wailing baby. She had a faint aroma of baby vomit about her. Sophie had smiled kindly at her, cooed briefly at the baby, and then moved on. Pemberton Road was housing the next generation of families now, making new memories for new people. Their babies would grow up, go to the local school that Tom and Katie had gone to. They would play on the same swings in the park. The parents would drink coffee in the same café. It was a constant cycle, forever changing, forever evolving.

Katie bounded ahead of her now, eager to get inside and Sophie marvelled at the speed at which young people could shake off hangovers. She was still feeling a little peaky after the late night, but she was determined to rally for the next stage of the celebrations. She followed her daughter up the steps and watched as the door opened and Freddy appeared.

'You made good time,' he said, giving Katie a kiss and stepping back to let her in. He hugged Sophie as she walked past. 'Can I get you a drink, Mrs B?'

'Cup of tea?' Sophie suggested.

'I don't bloody well think so,' came a voice from the living room. 'Champagne, Freddy.'

Sophie rolled her eyes and made her way into the living room. Angie was lying on the sofa, wrapped under a blanket. She sat up when she saw Sophie.

'Blimey, Angie, you could have made a bit of an effort,' she said, leaning down to kiss her.

'Oh bugger off,' Angie replied.

'How are you feeling?'

'Not too bad considering. Plus I'm up to date on *Neighbours* and *Doctors* now which is a bonus.'

'Bit lazy of you, Ange, to spend all day watching TV.'

'Very droll.'

Angie had been living with cancer for three years. She had outlived her doctor's prognosis and continued to find the strength from somewhere within to keep going. Apparently, she was a medical miracle which, knowing Angie as she did, did not surprise Sophie in the slightest.

But the cancer was just as determined, and after a much-needed respite, she was back on chemo again. When it had become clear that she wouldn't be well enough to go to the graduation ceremony, they had decided to bring the party to her instead. In the kitchen she could hear Freddy bickering good-naturedly with Indie as they got the champagne out of the fridge and gathered glasses to bring into the living room.

'Should you be drinking?' she asked Angie.

'Well, it's hardly the thing that's going to kill me now, is it?'

'Fair point. Where's Jack?'

'He had to pop home first and check in with What's-her-face. He's on his way round.'

As she heard the kids still chatting away in the kitchen, Sophie sat down on the floor next to Angie and took her hand. 'Are you really okay?'

'I am,' Angie said. 'Really, I am. I was disappointed that I couldn't make the graduation, I'd be lying if I said I wasn't, but at least I'm here. I don't take that for granted.'

'How are you feeling about having someone in the house again?'

Freddy was planning on living at home for a while. Everyone said it was because he wanted to save money while he studied for his master's, but everyone also knew it was because he wanted to spend time with his mum while he still could.

'I'm rather looking forward to it. This house was made for a crowd, for noise and chaos and laughter, not for one person rattling around in it. It needs a bit of energy in it again.'

'Is Freddy worried about Katie going away?'

'He says he's not but I'm sure he's secretly having visions of her dancing salsa under the stars with some Latino hunk.'

'I don't think you get many hunks around archaeological dig sites though.'

'Have you watched *Indiana Jones*, Sophie?'

'Well, I don't think he has anything to worry about. The only things my Katie gets excited about are fossils and Freddy.'

'They're young though. They've got so much to come. So much adventure but so much heartbreak too, probably.'

'Yes, true. And if that does happen, we'll be there to hold their hands.'

'Speak for yourself.'

'Oh stop feeling sorry for yourself, you old party pooper.'

Angie laughed and squeezed Sophie's hand. Sophie knew that she appreciated the humour, that the thing she hated most was pity. She'd always been too damn proud for her own good.

But at least she was finally letting people help her. She was letting them look after her for once.

The front door slammed and Jack appeared around the corner, with Benji behind him.

'Look at this reprobate who I've just bumped into trying unsuccessfully to park his flashy, oversized Range Rover into a massive parking space on the street,' Jack declared in delight. 'And it's even got parking assist on it!' He was roaring with laughter.

Benji scowled at him. 'I've only had the car a week, Dad, leave off.'

'Better learn to drive it, mate, before you start entertaining the ladies, that's all I'm saying.'

'Benji, you made it!' Angie said, her face lighting up.

'Yeah, we finished filming earlier than planned,' Benji said. 'Where are the others?'

'Kitchen.'

Benji wandered off and Jack leaned in to hug Sophie.

'Thanks for yesterday,' she whispered. 'For being so nice to Alan.'

He squeezed her. 'Anything for you, Brennan.'

The doorbell went again.

'Christ, it's like Piccadilly Circus around here,' Angie said.

'I'll get it,' Sophie replied, hoping it was who she thought it would be. She tentatively opened the door and shrieked with delight when she saw her son.

'Tom!' she said, ushering him in. 'I'm so pleased you made it.'

Tom worked as an accountant and lived with friends in Islington. He seemed to spend his time either working or partying and she rarely saw him these days, although she tried not to give him a hard time about it. Katie and Freddy had been to a couple of his house parties and said they were epic. She really didn't want to know the details. 'He's young and having fun,' she told Alan whenever he made a comment about their errant son. Every couple of months he would turn up at home for a Sunday roast or she and Alan would go to London and meet him for a drink. But he always called his dad religiously every weekend during football season to discuss the scores. It was their thing, just the two of them, and whenever Sophie saw Alan clutching onto his phone, waiting in anticipation for his call, she was glad that they had it.

Over time, she and Alan had got used to being alone again, just the two of them. For so long their lives, their whole existence, had been centred around the children. She hadn't known what to expect when they left home, fearing perhaps that she and Alan would have run out of things to say to each other. They had been through so much to stay together that she couldn't bear the thought of them falling at the final hurdle. She had been relieved to discover that they enjoyed each other's company more than ever. He still made her laugh, even after all this time.

They were trying to be more spontaneous, even if that just meant going to the cinema at the last minute or choosing dinner out rather than a takeaway. They'd booked a four-week trip to New Zealand over the winter. Sophie had always dreamed of going there and Ellie had been sending her tips and advice. They were going to stay with her and Chrissie for a few days in Auckland. She couldn't wait. And then after that it was straight back to intense coaching ahead of the British Swimming Trials, into which she was entering a couple of her junior swimmers. There was always something going on and that was just how she liked it.

'Where's this damn champagne?' Angie demanded. She raised her voice and called out, 'Stop gossiping in the kitchen, you lot, we're thirsty.'

They all appeared together, five out of the six kids, and started dishing out glasses to everyone. Angie, Jack and Sophie took their champagne and held it up.

'To Freddy and Katie,' they said in unison.

They all drank up and a second bottle appeared soon after. By the time the third one had come out, it was established that no one would be driving home that evening. By the fourth, someone had found a Latin music playlist and put it on at full blast so that Katie could prepare for her imminent departure to South America, and Jack was trying to teach Sophie salsa moves.

'How do you know how to do this?' Sophie asked as he spun her around, having a flashback to when they had gone to the barn dance and made a hash of the moves.

'Janine made me go to lessons for six months,' he said.

'Who's Janine?' Sophie was puzzled.

'What's-her-face,' Indie shouted over the music to her.

'Oh! I don't think I ever actually knew her real name.'

Jack glared at her. 'Nice, Sophie. Nice,' he said.

Laughing, she pulled him towards her. To her left she saw Freddy and Katie talking quietly in the corner. To her right Indie was dancing with Tom, thrusting her hips towards him while he stared down at her in stunned awe, like a man who had just won the lottery. All of his friends would know about this tomorrow, she suspected, as well as possibly all of the internet. Benji was on the phone talking to his latest girlfriend and trying to explain that he couldn't make it round to hers after all as he had got blotto with his mother and father.

Angie was sitting on the sofa with her champagne and soaking it all up, with a smile on her face. She had always loved entertaining. Sophie knew that she couldn't join in the way that she wanted and sometimes that was so upsetting and infuriating that it was hard to imagine ever making peace with it. But there were also moments of calm, moments of acceptance, and right now, for Angie, it was enough simply to be here. You could see it in her expression. She had got to see all four of her children grow up and become the people that they were meant to be.

Because they were grown up now, the children, they were finding their own paths and making lives of their own. They were ready to fly. And so was she. Sophie spun around in a circle, her arms stretched out wide, and closed her eyes.

THE END

ACKNOWLEDGEMENTS

Writing a book during lockdown was a challenge and I have a lot of people to thank for helping me to reach the finish line. My husband Jon, who held the fort at weekends when I disappeared upstairs for writing sessions and brought me cups of tea. And my children, Rose and Alice, who selflessly enjoyed extra iPad and TV time when the schools were closed so that I could get some work done. I know from your delight how hard it must have been for you...

Thanks to all the team at Bloodhound Books who saw the potential in *The Woman Next Door* and supported me throughout my publishing journey. Particular thanks to my editor Clare Law for the time you spent working through my manuscript and making it super shiny.

To my sister Zoe, who read my early draft and gave me some really useful feedback which, without a doubt, made the book much better.

To the real women next door, the magnificent Hannah and Sonia, the best neighbours a gal could ask for. And of course to Gill, the woman at the bottom of the garden. Our fence may not have blown down in a storm although the DIY 'chat flap' we sawed into it as good as destroyed it anyway. But I absolutely cherished our Friday night glasses of wine and putting the world to rights over the fence. Thank you for helping to keep me sane during this difficult eighteen months.

And finally, to every single one of you who has read, reviewed, shared or supported my books. Your encouragement has meant so much to me and inspired me to keep on writing, even when times got tough. Thank you.

A NOTE FROM THE PUBLISHER

Thank you for reading this book. If you enjoyed it please do consider leaving a review on Amazon to help others find it too.

We hate typos. All of our books have been rigorously edited and proofread, but sometimes mistakes do slip through. If you have spotted a typo, please do let us know and we can get it amended within hours.

info@bloodhoundbooks.com

Lightning Source UK Ltd.
Milton Keynes UK
UKHW010748121021
392079UK00003B/539

9 781914 614439